JOHN CREASEY
as
ANTHONY MORTON

CRY FOR THE BARON

D0885570

HODDER AND STOUGHTON

COPYRIGHT © 1950 BY JOHN CREASEY
FIRST PUBLISHED BY SAMPSON LOW 1950
REPRINTED 1958
HODDER PAPERBACK EDITION 1966

Printed and bound in Great Britain for
Hodder and Stoughton Ltd,
St. Paul's House, Warwick Lane, London, E.C.4, by
Hazell Watson & Viney Ltd,
Aylesbury, Bucks

CONTENTS

CHAPTER I

THE DIAMOND OF TEARS

JACOB BERNSTEIN blinked at the telephone and said: "Dear me, who ith that?" One thin pale hand, the delicate blue veins showing clearly beneath the powerful white light that shone above his head, covered the diamond which lay on the desk in front of him; and darkness fell upon the rest of the room. The bell kept ringing. "An invention of the Devil, that ith what it ith," lisped Bernstein. He stared at the telephone from his hooded eyes, with their wrinkled lids, as if willing it to stop. Beyond the radius of the light the small, untidy room was shadowy, the corners cluttered with old books and papers, boxes, jewel-cases—junk worth a fortune. But the light was bright on his hooked nose and thin, pale cheeks, his colourless lips and the black skull cap which he loved to wear.

Brrrr-brrrr; brrrr-brrrr; brrrr-brrrr.

Bernstein was alone in the house. Except for the harsh ringing there was quiet—inside as well as in the dark London street outside.

"Dear me, dear me," sighed Bernstein.

He leaned across the littered desk, making papers rustle as the loose sleeve of his old green velveteen jacket brushed over them, and rested the tips of his fingers on the telephone. The ringing affected his fingers like an electric shock. The instrument was the only new and modern thing here, an offence to the eye and to the ear of the old Jew, but one moved with the times, business was difficult. Bernstein was not greedy but content only when dwelling on the past or on such beauty as was covered by his right hand.

He lifted the receiver and the ringing stopped.

"Yeth, who ith it . . . ?"

"Thank you, yeth, I keep well, these old bones will last a long time yet, but pleath, who are you . . . ?"

"Tho!" Eagerness sounded in the word.

"Yeth . . . yeth, I quite understand, my friend. . . ."

"You haff not been mithled, I have the *Tear*. . . ."

"Dear me! Pleath, pleath, not on the telephone, we cannot dithcuth how much on the *telephone*. . . ."

"My friend, I am hurt, I am the dithcreet, no one shall know. . . . Yeth. If we agree on terms, yeth. . . ."

"I will be motht happy to see you here. . . .

"Yeth, to-night, if that ith your wish. . . . Yeth, I am alone. . . . I will open the door mythelf, thir. . . . In half an hour, yeth. . . . Goodbye."

The papers rustled again as he replaced the receiver on its cradle. He sat blinking into the shadows and at the heavy brown velvet curtains. In the street two people walked past briskly, nearby a car-horn broke the quiet. Bernstein slowly withdrew his hand, and scintillating beauty lay there. It was a diamond as large as the nail of his thumb, shaped like a tear, and at the rounded end tinged with red.

He sighed, straightened his back and stood up. His thin shoulders were bowed, and as he walked across the room he dragged his right foot across the threadbare carpet, a little, black-tufted crow of a man. He reached a corner which was almost in darkness, for the bright circle of light behind him shone on the desk. He stooped over a pile of books on a chair, and picked up a heavy, leather-bound volume tooled in gold. The uncut edges were dusty and he turned pages seared with age. He let them flutter through his fingers until he found two pages stuck together. Then he opened the thick book wide.

In the centre a square hole was cut out of the pages, and the hole was lined with cotton wool. He took the *Tear* between his thumb and forefinger, and tucked it into the cotton wool. He smoothed the leather cover, then laboriously picked up the other books and placed them on top of the hiding-place. He straightened up as if he were in pain and hobbled back to the desk.

Then he opened a large copy of the *Talmud* and began to read. Although his grey eyes were bleared and tired, he did not need glasses. Silence fell upon the room. The only movement was the quiver of his lips as he read, as if he were reciting to himself some much-loved sacred phrase.

Brrrr-brrrr; brrrr-brrrr; brrrr-brrrr!

He started—and stared at the telephone. "Again!" he cried, and shook his head angrily. "Again, why doth it go on, why doth it go on?" This time he stretched out for it more quickly, impatiently.

"Yeth . . . ?"

"Tho! My friend, again it ith good to hear from you. Even when you speak on this instrument of the Devil. . . . Yeth!" He chuckled and smiled, his expression much happier than when he had spoken before. "My dear Mithter Mannering, always, if I can help you. . . ."

"The *Tear*? Tho! It ith sad, but already I haff promised, if terms are agreed. . . . I mutht not do that, Mithter Mannering, you underthtand, it ith secret. . . . Not all wish the world to know they haff the *Tear,* so many are afraid of it. . . . My friend, you dithappoint me, yeth, it ith not nonsense. . . ."

"Mr. Mannering, it ith true, it ith a jewel of fate, but that doth not trouble such men as you. . . . It is so beautiful, Mithter Mannering. It ith worth more than the blood of man and the beauty of woman. . . . You want it for yourself . . . ? Tho! A client, a customer as you say, and also I haff the customer. . . . Tho . . . ! In one hour, one little hour if you will speak to me again. Yeth, if we do not come to terms, I can tell you hith name, why not? He remainth unknown only if he buyth the *Tear*. . . . Yeth, he ith rich, yeth. . . ."

"Good-bye, my friend."

He put the receiver back on its cradle, placed the tips of his fingers together and peered towards the books on the chair, nodding so that sometimes his face was in shadow, sometimes lit up. With a sigh he closed the *Talmud* and pushed it away.

Footsteps turned the corner and came towards the shop. They were a man's, hurried but firm. Bernstein did not move until a bell rang downstairs. Then he stood up, laboriously, and went to the window. He opened it and looked out.

"Who ith there?"

He saw a Homburg hat and a dark clad man, who moved back from the door so as to see him. The light from the window fell upon a familiar face.

"I told you I was coming, Bernstein."

"Yeth, yeth! One mutht be tho thure." He closed the window and hobbled to the door, out on to the landing, then down the narrow stairs to the street door. He hurried as best he could along the narrow passage, pulled back the two bolts, unfastened the chain, turned the key in the lock, and opened the door.

"You've been a hell of a time!" the visitor grumbled.

"My old bones, they will not move as I would like them to

move, but pleath, come in, come in. You are well?"

"I'm all right."

"Tho." Bernstein closed the door. "I will not be a moment." With painstaking care he bolted and locked the door again, while his visitor stood chafing. Then he turned and led the way upstairs. In the study he pointed to a chair by the desk. "Thit down, pleath."

"Where is it?" asked his visitor sharply.

"I will thow you, thoon. You are in a great hurry, my friend. Are you not well? You look——"

"I'm all right." The man breathed heavily, as if under some strain. Bernstein's wise old eyes narrowed, almost covered by the hooded lids. "Let's see it—or talk business first, whichever you like."

Bernstein sighed. "Tho. Bithness."

"What's your price?"

"It ith a beautiful jewel, my friend, never haff I theen a lovelier. Flawleth, quite flawleth, perfectly cut and the red— the blood on the stone. You know about the blood?"

"I know what I'm buying."

"You do not belief, perhaps, that it ith a stone of ill-fortune?"

"It's a diamond, the only one like it in the world. And I want it. What's your price?"

Bernstein placed the tips of his fingers together again, peered at the man. He was a student of men; rich and poor, good and bad. He knew, none better, that a man who loved precious stones might feel towards the *Tear* as a man felt towards his beloved; thought of the *Tear* could make nerves quiver and lips tremble, and sight of it bring ecstasy. But was his visitor affected by the jewel? Or was he torn by some baser emotion?

Bernstein looked everywhere except towards the corner where the diamond was hidden.

"For thuch a jewel the prithe ith high, very high."

"How much?"

"Now let me thee—yeth, let me thee. I do not think it would be too much to say one hundred thousand pounds. One— hundred—thousand—pounds."

"It's high."

"It ith not too high."

The man's lips seemed to writhe.

"I'll take it." He put his hand to his breast pocket and drew out a folded cheque-book. "I'll draw the cheque, you get the diamond." He pulled out a fountain pen—and the scared old eyes watched him and saw that he did not take off his gloves as he wrote. The man sensed that Bernstein was still looking at him, and stopped writing.

"What about getting the diamond?"

"In good time, my friend. You thee, there arc others who would buy that beautiful jewel. Two, perhaps t'ree, other. Yes. One ith to come, soon, to make the offer. Perhaps he will give more. Then——"

The man said: "You bloodsucking rogue, I'm paying you twice as much as it's worth!"

Bernstein said softly: "Are you?" He opened a drawer at his right hand and groped inside. "Perhaps that ith tho, indeed. Then I ask a question. Why do you pay twice as much ath it ith worth?"

"What do you mean?"

"I confeth I am worried by you," said Bernstein softly. "You are in tho great a hurry. There cannot be thuch a hurry." He looked pointedly at the gloves and the half-written cheque. "I will thee my other friends, and then——"

He drew his hand from the drawer—and into the eyes of his visitor there sprang fear. Bernstein pulled sharply, but the thing in his hand knocked against the drawer, which was only partly open. His visitor jumped up, knocking his chair to the floor. He struck savagely at the old man's face and sent him staggering sideways. Something dropped noisily back into the drawer. The visitor rounded the desk, while Bernstein thrust out his pale, trembling hands.

"No! No, you will not——"

The visitor thrust his hands aside, caught him round his scraggy throat, and squeezed. Bernstein's protest became a throaty gurgle. Holding more tightly, the man forced the small head back. The skull-cap fell off and the light shone on the pale, bald pate. Bernstein's eyes bulged. He struggled feebly, but that gradually ceased.

His body went limp.

The visitor maintained the pressure and held him, the body bent, arms hanging limply, knees sagging, until there was no sign of breathing. The killer took his hands away, and Bernstein fell limp, lifeless.

The man pulled open the drawer and saw the gun inside. He took the gun out and put it on the desk. He rummaged through the drawer and found a bunch of keys. He went to the door and switched on the other light, which fell on to Bernstein's face. The old eyes were half-closed and glazed, the mouth was slack and open.

The visitor began to search.

He found the safe and opened it with the keys, his hands trembling; they trembled more as he took out jewel-cases and loose stones. Some he tossed aside, others he dropped into his pocket, where they rattled like marbles. He opened case after case, but did not find the *Tear*.

He emptied the last one, and swung round.

"Where is it, you devil? Where is it?"

The murderer turned from the safe and began to rummage through the boxes, tossing them aside when he found them empty, and thrusting books away. He went to the desk and rummaged through every drawer, but found no sign of the *Tear*. He turned to Bernstein and stood glaring down; his voice was thick with fury, as if he could make a dead man speak.

"*Where is it?*"

He swung round and peered in every corner. His eyes were glassy, and he kept muttering to himself—swearing at the dead man, calling curses on his head, reviling him and all his race.

He went to the corner where the *Tear* lay between the pages of the book, lifted the books off the chair and examined it for a hiding-place. Then he pulled back the corners of the carpet; dust rose up, making him sneeze. He peered at the floor-boards, for any sign of a floor-safe, but the boards were old and none had recently been taken up. He went to the side of the room, bent down and ran his fingers along the wainscoting. Perspiration gathered on his forehead and began to trickle down his cheek, stood out in little beads on his upper lip.

Suddenly the quiet was blasted by a bell.

Brrrr-brrrr; brrrr-brrrr; brrrr-brrrr!

He swung round towards the telephone.

The ringing went on and on.

CHAPTER II

MANNERING IS PUZZLED

JOHN MANNERING put the telephone back on its cradle and looked across at his wife.

"That's odd, there's no answer."

"He hates the telephone," said Lorna.

"He doesn't hate it so much that he won't answer it, and he's expecting me to call."

"You could try again, darling."

"So I could. What should I do without you?" Mannering laughed at her, and she turned back to her book.

She looked contented. Her dark hair was burnished by the light of the standard lamp at her side; this also touched her beauty with softening shadows. Some said that Lorna Mannering's face had a sullen look when in repose, and beauty only when she was alert; Mannering knew better. He watched the fleeting movement of her dark blue eyes, the occasional frown of concentration which brought her heavy brows together, the quick twist of her fingers turning a page.

She sat in a winged armchair in the study of their Chelsea flat. It was always warmer in this room, and the autumn night was cold. The panelled walls and Jacobean furniture, each piece a treasure in itself, made the right background.

She looked up.

"Going to sleep?" she asked.

"Just worshipping."

"Fool!"

"Oddly enough, I meant it."

She put the book on her lap, where its bright red cover clashed with the dark red of her dress, and stared at him, a smile softening her full lips. A door downstairs slammed and broke the spell. Mannering stirred from his chair and took out cigarettes.

"I really believe you did mean it," Lorna said.

"Incredible, isn't it? A man in love with his wife!" He lit his cigarette and lifted the telephone.

"What do you want from Jacob?" she asked idly.

"One jewel of untold value."

"Which one?"

"Does it matter? I'm always buying jewels, selling jewels, and wishing I could buy them all and keep them for myself."

"I would still like to know which one it is."

"The *Tear*."

Lorna said : "*Oh*," and sat up.

"So you really are superstitious," murmured Mannering. "The tear of blood ! Jacob said something of the kind earlier this evening—what was his phrase? I remember I liked it. Oh, yes—'It is worth more than the blood of man and the beauty of women'—but he didn't add in a breathless voice that it is a famous jewel with a curse. So he probably believes it's won its fame because of the avarice of man rather than by the fatal quality in a piece of rock someone dug out of the bigger lump of rock in some hills belonging to the Maharajah of Wherever-it-was, centuries ago."

The ringing sound continued.

"When you're as involved as that, you're trying to hide something," challenged Lorna.

"I'm trying to kill an illusion—that if you possess the *Tear* you will probably die of a battered skull. And in any case, you needn't worry. I shall have it in my hands only for a few hours. Feel better?"

She frowned. "I suppose it is silly to feel jumpy."

Mannering said : "People who don't own the *Tear* have been known to die by violence. Odd—he still doesn't answer."

He dialled a third time, with the same result. Next he dialled O, and reported difficulty in getting Mayfair 01432. A pause, then : "The number is ringing, sir, but there's no reply."

"Thank you." Mannering replaced the receiver and stood up.

Standing, he was over six feet tall, handsome, with dark, wavy hair, cut short, and greying a little at the temples. A man whom many regarded, when they first saw him, as just handsome and dull. Others, who knew him well, still thought of him as a man-about-town, a *dilettante,* spoiled by too much money and a dash of blue blood. Few knew all the truth about him—either of his past or of what he did to-day.

"It can't be anything important," said Lorna.

"He's probably fallen asleep. He stays in that place of his alone far too much, for an old man. Care for a drive?"

"I don't think I'll come out to-night, darling, I want to be early in the morning, and it's nearly midnight."

"I won't be long," said Mannering.

Outside, he hurried towards his garage, five minutes' walk away, and wished that he had put on a coat. He switched on the heater of his Bristol before driving out of the garage—and switched it off before he reached Belham Street, where Jacob Bernstein had his shop. It was a narrow thoroughfare in the West End of London, a quiet place, with a few shops which were patronised by the connoisseur and the discerning. Not far away was Hart Row, where Mannering owned a famous shop called Quinn's.

Mannering avoided the main roads, and the headlights shone on walking couples, tall, grey houses, across spacious squares where history lived, on solitary women, lurking hopefully; and on policemen, doing their nightly rounds. At last he turned the corner of Belham Street. Then, with a caution which had become almost a sixth sense, he drove past Bernstein's shop and pulled up some fifty feet away.

While passing, he saw the dim light at the first-floor room where Bernstein spent most of his time. The glow came from a corner, as if the curtain had been lifted and not fallen back into place. Mannering thought no more than that Bernstein had been taken ill—until he saw the light go out.

The sudden dousing of the light filled him with disquiet. He stepped swiftly across the road and stood outside the tall, narrow door. This door led to the upstairs quarters; another led to the shop. He knew that the shop was a model of tidiness but that upstairs the rooms were neglected. He stepped to the window, placed one hand against the glass and peered in—the hand so placed to shade the light from a street lamp, some distance away. He saw the ghostly shapes of furniture; the dull glow of silver; the pale faces of clocks; he even fancied that he heard these ticking.

There was no sign of trouble there.

Then he heard footsteps from the stairs; not loud, not firm, but stealthy. He tried to laugh his fears away. Jacob's right ankle had been broken and never really mended—a legacy of brutality and Dachau. His shuffling walk would sound stealthy. Mannering stood to one side and waited while the footsteps drew nearer. He thought he knew the moment when the man reached the foot of the stairs. Then the footsteps sounded again.

Nearer; stealthy; nearer.

Mannering heard fingers touch the bolts, and the sharp sound as they were drawn back; he heard the heavy key turn. The door opened—not slowly, as Bernstein would open it, because it was heavy; but swiftly.

He saw a man with a Homburg hat pulled low over his forehead and a handkerchief tied over his nose and mouth. Before he could dodge aside the man kicked him in the pit of the stomach. Pain surged through him, driving thought out of his mind, made him double up and stagger backwards. He fell. He did not hear the man run wildly towards the end of the street, and did not see the killer again.

He lay on the pavement, doubled up, his knees almost touching his chin. He must do better. He staggered to a kneeling position, and the pain was like a gigantic spider with steel legs, clawing at his vitals. Sickness followed pain, but that gradually passed, and soon he could stand upright.

The door was open. A light glowed on the landing, showing the stairs with their strip of threadbare carpet, the plain brown walls and the door which led to the shop. In the distance a car started up; that might be his assailant. He clenched his teeth as he went forward, and had to hold on to the door for support, listening for other sounds, but hearing only the distant hum of traffic, as much part of London as the air. There were no plodding footsteps of a watchful policeman——

He left the door open and went to the foot of the stairs, leaning against the wall for support, feeling better as each second passed yet not trusting himself to walk naturally. He clutched the banister post, and called :

"Jacob !"

There was no answer; of course there would be no answer. He went upstairs, and by the time he reached the top he did not need to hold the banister rail.

"*Jacob!*"

The door of the front room stood wide open and he saw the corner of the littered desk, the shape of the angle-lamp beneath which Bernstein read, or worshipped his possessions. He also saw what might have been a dark shadow on the floor between the desk and the wall. He put on the other light and went forward. It was not shadow but a body.

He felt as if a bucket of icy water had been thrown over him as he stepped to the angle-lamp, stretched out his hand to switch it on—and drew his hand back sharply. The assailant had touched the lamp to put it out; he might have left prints. Mannering took out a handkerchief and through it pressed the switch carefully. The white light shone out on the desk and the closed black book. He moved it a little, so that it showed the old man's glazed, half-open eyes and the slack mouth; and he did not think that Jacob was alive.

There was little point in feeling for the pulse in the bony wrist.

First telephone Scotland Yard; then look at Jacob. He crossed to the far side of the desk, lifted the telephone, still using his handkerchief, but heard nothing when he put it to his ear. Then he saw that the cable had been torn from the tiny black box fastened to the side of the desk.

That explained why there had been no answer.

It didn't; the ringing sound had come, so this cable had been damaged since he had telephoned. He had probably been trying to get through while Jacob was being murdered, and in a fit of nervous rage the killer had silenced the telephone.

There was a kiosk five minutes walk away, and it would take more than five minutes to rouse neighbours and use their telephone. He turned back, bent down and straightened the frail body. He laid Jacob on his stomach, knelt astride him and pressed his hands into his ribs, gently at first, then harder.

After five minutes, he stopped, and tried the kiss of life, but there wasn't a spark of life.

Mannering hurried to the landing, swung round to face the stairs then stopped abruptly. A girl stood half-way up. She wore a dark fur coat and had wavy, bright fair hair. Startled blue eyes peered into his, bright red lips were parted.

CHAPTER III

GIRL IN DISTRESS

SHE was young; not beautiful, but vivid and attractive. The coat was slung over her shoulders like a cloak. She wore a black evening gown, the bodice glittering with sequins shimmering over her firm breasts from her agitated breathing. Her eyes, so blue and startled, were rounded. Her right hand moved and clutched the edges of the coat, drawing them together.

Mannering asked: "Who are you?"

She didn't speak, but held on to the banister rail with her left hand. She didn't move, and was obviously in great distress, and a false move would frighten her away.

"Can I help you?" Mannering asked.

She moistened her lips again. "I want to see Mr. Bernstein."

"I'm afraid he's out."

"I *must* see him."

"Then you'll have to wait." Mannering backed a pace. "Come and wait upstairs."

She didn't move.

"Who are *you*?"

"A friend of his." Mannering took out his cigarette-case, opened it and held it out; she would have to climb at least six steps to reach them. "He shouldn't be long." The words nearly choked him.

"I—I think I'll come back," she said, and turned. Mannering hurried after her, was just behind her when she reached the passage. He put his hand on her shoulder, but she slipped out of the coat, made for the front door, and turned right, clutching her skirt to run. She didn't look round again. Mannering flung the coat aside and raced after her, caught her up twenty yards from the shop, took her arm and gripped tightly. She struggled to get away, turned, and struck at him with her free hand; her small handbag caught his cheek.

They stood together in the darkened street, but the lamp-light was behind him, shining on to her face. He no longer thought of her as agitated but as terrified.

"Let—me—go. *Please*—let—me—go."

"Why did you come?"

"I've—told—you." She gasped each word out, as if it were an effort, and struggled to free herself again. She hadn't a chance. After a moment she realised it and went limp. "*Please* let me go. It isn't important, I—I can see him in the morning."

He wanted to let her go, as he would want to let a rabbit go from a trap. But soon the police would come and they would need to know everything about the night's events and certainly why this girl had come to see Jacob Bernstein and why she was so nervous. He ought to keep her here; yet something in him rebelled. Already he wanted to find the murderer himself; to pay a last tribute, and to do a final service for the man.

A temptation, born out of his secret past, came and whispered to him, while the girl's breathing quietened a little though the terror still lurked in her eyes.

He asked suddenly: "Do you know what's happened?"

"Happened?"

"Here. To-night?"

"Has—has anything happened?"

"Give me this." He released her and took the bag away. She realised what he was going to do too late, and snatched at it, but he backed away and opened the bag. She came at him, but he fended her off with one hand and looked into the bag. There were letters, a lipstick, compact and a purse.

"Give that to me!"

"What is your name?"

"I won't tell you." She snatched at the bag again and he took her wrist, pulled her suddenly so that she was in front of him and facing the direction of Bernstein's shop, then pushed her along and back into the doorway. He closed the door with his elbow—while outside, in the distance, heavy footsteps sounded, drawing nearer.

"You've no right——" She could hardly get the words out, but didn't try to take the bag away again.

He took out the letters but didn't look at them.

"If you want to get away, you will have to tell me your name and address. Otherwise you stay, and answer all the questions the police want to ask." His voice was harder, and his words shocked her.

"Has there been—a burglary?"

"Yes. And the police will soon be here. Who are you? Where do you live?"

"If I tell you will you let me go?"

She was young and strong enough to have killed Jacob; almost anyone would have been. She might have been here before, left something behind and come back.

She stretched out a trembling hand, the red nails glistening as she touched his arm.

"*Will you?*"

"Yes. But I shall want to see you again."

"I'll see you. I'll meet you anywhere you like, but—please let me go now. I'm—Fay Goulden. You can find me at 21, Clay Court, in Shepherd Street, near Park Lane."

He glanced at the letters. One was addressed to her at the Majestic Hotel, the others at 21, Clay Court, and each said "Miss Fay Goulden."

Outside, the plodding footsteps of the beat policeman sounded much nearer. Mannering turned the key in the lock and the girl exclaimed :

"You promised——"

"Be quiet !"

The handle of the door rattled and the door shook as the policeman tried it. The girl pressed her hand against her mouth. The rattling stopped and the constable passed by. Mannering said : "Don't raise your voice." He opened her bag again, took out the purse and looked inside; there were some pound notes, folded tightly, some loose silver, and a Yale key.

"You can have these later."

"Please——"

"If you want that policeman back, shout."

She said : "I know nothing about it, nothing."

"About what?" Mannering asked.

"You said there'd been a burglary."

"Have you been here before to-night?"

"No, I wanted to see Mr. Bernstein. It—it doesn't matter now, I must go. Don't keep me here any longer."

"Why? Don't you want me to keep these letters?"

"Oh, I don't care ! Just let me go."

He gave her back the bag and its contents.

She turned to the door and stretched out her hand towards the key, but he took her arm.

"I'll do that." He opened the door, using his handkerchief. She muttered thanks, and when he pulled the door wide, slipped out and hurried along the street.

.   .   .   .   .

Detective-Inspector Gordon was ginger-haired and freckled, with a big red mouth and a Roman nose. He was a tall, spindly man to whom police work was a mission. He looked at Mannering sourly and said: "So you're here, are you?" Mannering didn't answer. Gordon, at the top of the stairs, looked into the now brightly lighted room where Bernstein lay dead, and where two of his men were taking photographs. He pushed past Mannering, who followed him.

Gordon's pale grey eyes looked searchingly round the room everywhere, it seemed, except at Bernstein. Then he turned his head and glared at Mannering. "Did you move him?"

"Yes."

"Why will you always stick your nose in? It oughtn't to have been moved. Let's have an answer—why?"

"I thought I might bring him round."

"You *thought*! You'll think yourself into jail one of these days. Did you kill him?"

Mannering said: "Isn't it obvious? There's one dead jewel-merchant, and I'm another with a reputation that's dynamite. Of course I killed him." He couldn't hold his temper in check.

Gordon growled: "You're too smart."

"That's an improvement on not being smart enough."

"You can wait outside."

Mannering went to a chair, beside which was a pile of books, and sat down. Gordon tightened his lips, looked as if he were going to order him out, then turned to his men. There were four in the room. Two were measuring the distance between Bernstein's body and the wall and the desk, using an ordinary household tape measure. The photographers were folding their camera. They stood it against the wall and began to search. Mannering toyed with the books at his side, letting the leaves flutter through his fingers. The routine was boring; the police took it as a matter of course. Men kept breathing on shiny surfaces to see if prints showed up, smothering places where they did with black graphite which they applied with a small camel-hair brush, then leaving it and searching for other prints. Gordon himself sat at the desk and opened drawer after drawer.

When he pulled the top right-hand drawer open Mannering said:

"He usually kept a gun in there."

"If I want information I'll ask for it."

"What's got under your skin, Gordon?"

"You always get under my skin. You amateurs who think you're smart are a pain in the neck. And you're the biggest pain. How long after you found the body did you send for us?"

"About twenty minutes."

"That was nineteen too long."

"If I'd thought I could bring Bernstein round it would have been a couple of hours." Mannering let the pages flutter, then shifted the book and picked up another. He knew Bernstein had secret hiding-places in some of those.

"Know what the killer was after?"

"If you want me to guess, I will."

"All right, guess."

"Jacob had the *Diamond of Tears*—known as the *Tear*. Even you may have heard of it. I telephoned him about it to-night and promised to call him later. He didn't answer the second call and I came round to see if he was all right."

"Why shouldn't he have been?"

"Because he didn't answer an expected telephone call."

"How did you get in?"

"The murderer had opened the door for me."

Gordon stopped taking oddments out of the desk and piling them up in front of him, leaned back in his chair, stuck a thumb in the armhole of his waist-coat, and said: "Listen, Mannering, you were found on enclosed premises with the body of a murdered man. You had a chance to slip out and hide anything you lifted. We can hold you for that."

"I can tell you twenty other ways you can make a fool of yourself," said Mannering. The pages of the second book fluttered smoothly through his fingers as he watched the Yard man. "But go ahead, hold me. That will teach me to send for the police when a friend of mine has been murdered."

"*Friend*." Gordon sneered the word.

"Yes. And I choose my own."

Gordon lit a cigarette and flicked the match across the room; it fell at Mannering's feet.

"I asked you how you got in here."

"And I told you. The murderer opened the door for me. If he wasn't the murderer I'll eat my words."

"You *saw* him?" Gordon jumped up from the desk. "Why didn't you say so?"

"Because his face was masked and his hat pulled low over his eyes. And he kicked me before I knew what was coming. All I can tell you is that he was on the tall side, five ten or eleven, well-built, wearing dark clothes and a black Homburg. I gave the details to the constable two minutes after I spoke to him, and presumably they're going the rounds. Do you want me here any longer?"

Gordon growled: "Yes." He went out of the room, and Mannering picked up the third book and put it on his lap; the pages turned smoothly.

The police were working quietly, no one else took any notice of him. Downstairs, Gordon's voice was raised, hectoring the constable.

Mannering picked up the fourth book. There were a hundred books in this room and he had no reason to think he would find a hiding-place in any of the first few which came to hand.

The pages stuck.

Gordon came back, scowling. Mannering slid his forefinger between the pages, and touched the soft texture of cotton wool.

"Are you keeping anything back?" Gordon demanded.

"What should I keep back?"

"We can never tell, with you," Gordon said. "Are you sure Bernstein had the *Tear* on the premises?"

"Yes." Through the cotton wool Mannering felt something hard. The *Tear*? Or another jewel? He let the pages fall flat again, and kept the book on his knees while Gordon went to the safe; the keys were in the lock.

"Did Bernstein keep a record of what he had here?"

"I think so. In a little black loose-leaf book."

"See if you can see it on the desk, will you?" asked Gordon, and began to take the jewel-cases out of the safe. Mannering left the book on the chair and went to the desk, but he wasn't interested in the little black book. What should he do if he found the *Tear*? Hand it over? It would be held until Jacob's will was proved. Eventually the *Tear* would be sold, presumably at a public auction.

A man—or woman—wanted it badly.

Bernstein had told him that he was to have a visitor about the diamond; little doubt that the visitor had come and killed him but—had he found the *Tear?* If not— could it be used to trap the murderer?

He found the little black book and took it to Gordon, who gripped Mannering's arm without warning, looked straight into his eyes, and demanded :

"Who was the girl? Out with it—who was the girl?"

CHAPTER IV

THE WILL

GORDON's fingers were big and strong, and pressed painfully into Mannering's forearm. Two of the other men looked up. Mannering said: "Now what's on your mind?" but made no attempt to free himself.

"Who was the girl who was here when you came?"

"There was no girl here when I arrived."

"The constable said he saw a girl leave this place a few minutes before you shouted for him."

"He may be right."

"If he's right she was here when you arrived, because he didn't see her come in—and you must have arrived before he turned the corner. Your car was here. That girl *must* have been here. You've told us what time you got here, how long it was before you sent for us. Twenty minutes—remember? It takes the constable twenty-five minutes to do this street, both sides. When he tried the door here it was locked. You've made one of your mistakes—who was the girl?"

"Where was the constable when he saw her?"

"At the corner."

"Care to come for a walk?" asked Mannering.

"I want the truth out of you!"

"I want to get at the truth. Gordon, you know I didn't kill Bernstein, and you also know you can't stop me trying to find the killer. Come and see whether the constable can be sure that a girl left this house."

Gordon said: "He is sure."

"All right, let's see if we can shake his confidence."

Gordon let him go. "Bristow will probably be here soon, we'll see what he has to say."

The Yard man turned back to the safe and began to consult the little black book. Mannering returned to his chair, picked up the book and opened it near the front, where the leaves weren't cut. He began to fiddle with the leaves again until he could feel the shiny surface of the hidden stone. He fingered the cotton wool.

Soon he was able to feel the hard surface of the stone. With the book half open he felt round the wool with his fingers, gradually prizing the jewel up. At last he held it between his thumb and forefinger. The book was half-open now—if anyone looked his way they would surely wonder what he was doing. Seconds mattered.

The jewel was tear-shaped.

Gordon turned and growled: "Was his writing always as bad as this?" He looked into Mannering's face, and his gaze didn't fall to the book.

"Yes. He was an old man, you know."

Gordon grunted and turned away. Mannering kept the jewel between his thumb and forefinger and slowly withdrew it. Then he slid it into his pocket. It was easy to pull out the wad of wool and slip that out of sight. He sat back, the closed book on his knees, nerves and muscles tense. The excitement of having the *Tear* in his pocket affected him like strong wine, going to his head, numbing his mind. If Gordon looked at him he'd give something away.

He fought the excitement, got it under control.

Gordon took a folded document from the safe and said: "I wonder who gets his money?" He opened the document, glanced through it, and spoke without turning round. "Any idea?"

"No."

"I thought you were such a close friend of his."

"He didn't consult me when making his will."

Gordon said: "Maybe he didn't, but he made you——" He broke off abruptly. Gordon's weakness was his tongue; he couldn't keep quiet for long. "You're sure you know nothing about this?"

"Nothing at all."

"I *see*," said Gordon heavily. "All right, Mannering, we'll go and try that experiment you were talking about."

It was cold outside, and a keen wind blew from the corner round which Fay Goulden had disappeared. The uniformed man was young, small and pale-faced; his uniform fitted him loosely. He was outside, beating his arms across his chest.

They went briskly along the street. Suddenly Mannering stopped and said: "Wait a minute, the door ought to be closed, then opened."

"Why?"

Mannering fiddled with the jewel inside his pocket, wrapping the cotton wool round it again.

"The constable was at the corner. He looked round, saw a door open and a girl come out. Then the girl disappeared, walking away from him. That's right, isn't it?"

"That's it, sir," said the constable.

"And we have got to find out whether it's possible for you to be sure that the door was Bernstein's, or whether it could have been another door, nearby."

"Well——"

"Could it?" barked Gordon.

"I *thought* it was Bernstein's door."

"Do you mean you thought it was his door when you saw it open, or you assumed it to be when you knew there'd been trouble?" asked Mannering mildly. "It would be natural enough to jump to that conclusion."

If the constable were prepared to swear the girl had left Bernstein's, he was in for a rough night. Gordon was bad enough; if Superintendent Bristow arrived he would jump to the same conclusion—that Mannering knew about the girl. The result would probably mean a visit to Great Marlborough Street Police Station, and a search. They ought to search him, whether he were under suspicion or not; that was simple routine. But they could search him a dozen times now and he would have the laugh on them.

He wanted to laugh as he took the jewel out of his pocket.

"Wait here," Gordon said. He strode towards the shop, his long legs slightly knock-kneed, and the constable muttered under his breath and evaded Mannering's eye. The heady effect of the jewel remained while Mannering scanned the shop-fronts and the doorways.

He saw the empty milk bottle on a window ledge in the doorway.

He took out his cigarette-case, and flicked his lighter—the wind prevented the wick from catching alight.

He went into the doorway.

The constable followed, determined not to let him out of his sight. Mannering cupped his hands round the cigarette as he lit it; the pale yellow glow shone on the cotton wool. He had his back to the constable, and turned so that the man couldn't see his right hand, slipped the jewel into the neck of the bottle and poked it down.

Gordon came hurrying back.

"Now we'll see." They reached the corner and turned to look at Bernstein's doorway. It opened, and a dim light showed, a man came out, turned away from them and hurried off, leaving the door wide open.

Mannering said lightly: "You might like to swear on oath which door it was—I wouldn't."

"It was just about there," said the constable.

"About!" snorted Gordon.

"Is that exactly what you saw?" asked Mannering. He watched the detective who had helped in the experiment come back and wait in the lighted doorway.

"Oh, yes," the constable mumbled. "I suppose it could have been one of the other doors."

"I'll go further. That wasn't exactly what you saw."

The man snapped: "Oh, yes, it was!"

"You mean the girl left the door wide open? Didn't she close it?"

"I—"

"Did she close it or didn't she?" Gordon's voice was thin and angry.

"I only just happened to glance round," said the constable aggrievedly. "There was no reason why I should expect trouble, the door was locked when I tried it a few minutes before. Yes, and it *did* shut after the girl, sir. The light only shone out for a second or two. I didn't think of that, just now. I was concentrating on which door it was."

A car turned the corner of the street, its head-lamps shining on Mannering and the others as they walked back to Bernstein's shop—and it glowed on the milk bottle and the fluffy cotton wool which rested on the bottom, there for anyone who chanced to look.

The newcomers were Superintendent Bristow and the police-surgeon. Bristow was a spruce, grey man; grey-haired, grey-clad, with a clipped grey moustache stained yellow in the centre with nicotine. He didn't wear an overcoat, and a wilted gardenia drooped from his buttonhole. He nodded to Mannering, and led the way upstairs. The police-surgeon, stocky and pale-faced, got busy; Bristow and Gordon went to the safe. Mannering stood by the chair and the secret book. The effect of hiding the *Tear* astonished him. He felt as if he had just come through a spell of great exertion; was tired, yet still excited.

Bristow glanced through the Will and turned to Mannering. His voice was brisk but friendly; perhaps deceptively friendly.

"So you know nothing about this Will, John?"

"Not a thing."

"Bernstein didn't consult you?"

"Why should he?"

"It's a custom, when you name an executor," said Bristow dryly. "You and the *Midclay Bank*—you're going to have a nice time, sorting out this stuff! *Quite* sure you knew nothing about it?"

Mannering said: "It would be a nice change if someone here believed me once in a while."

He joined the two Yard men and took the Will. Gordon looked as if he wanted to stop him, Bristow followed the sensible course; as an executor Mannering had every right to see the document. It was typed, easy to read, and quite short. There were three beneficiaries: the Jewel Merchant's Benevolent Association; Lorna Mannering—and a name which Mannering didn't see at first, it was over the page. Shock after shock: the first that he had been named as executor, the second that Bernstein had left anything to Lorna. The gift was characteristic of the old man; a pair of emerald ear-rings, which Lorna had seen and tried on when she had been to the shop two years ago.

"That was a nice thought," he said.

"He was a nice old boy," said Bristow. "But John—you're not going to do it."

"Do what?"

"Try to find out who killed him. That's our job."

Mannering said: "We'll see," and then turned over the page, reading the final clause. Like the others, it was short and concise: "... *the residue of my estate, in its entirety, is bequeathed without condition to Fay Marianna Goulden, daughter of Joshua and Maude Goulden....*"

His fingers tightened on the Will, he continued to stare at it, but didn't read. The terrified eyes of Fay Goulden seemed to loom out of the black type. He didn't trust himself to speak, until he handed the document back.

"It shouldn't be much trouble, Bill."

"There'll be plenty of trouble before this is over. Do you know this woman, Goulden?"

"No."

"Sure?"

Mannering said: "I've never been called a liar so often in so few minutes in my life. What's on your mind, Bill?"

"The same thing that's on Gordon's mind. I'm not satisfied about your reasons for coming. If we let you go without looking through your pockets we'd be asking for trouble from the pundits. Care to come along to Great Marlborough Street? Or would you prefer the Yard?"

.   .   .   .   .

At the Yard Bristow smiled and said: "Sorry it was necessary, but you know how these things are. You aren't going to play the fool and start investigating, are you? This isn't a job for a lone wolf, even though he's a good lone wolf." Bristow, sitting in his office, lit a cigarette from the stub of one burned right down, and then remembered to offer Mannering the paper packet. "Smoke?"

They were alone. The office was small, with two desks, Bristow's at the end away from the door. Like everything about Bristow, neatness was the rule. Two or three files lay in front of the Superintendent, near two telephones and some reference books. Behind him were photographs of Scotland Yard football teams; Bristow, in his younger days, had been a useful player.

The room was already heavy with smoke.

Gordon had left, after the formal search of Mannering's clothes, and after Mannering's statement had been taken. Now, Mannering took a cigarette and accepted a light. The two men sat back, watching each other warily.

They were old friends; and old adversaries.

Bristow had known Mannering for many years, had been the first man at Scotland Yard to believe that Mannering was the Baron. But the Baron's day was over; now, the sensations which his escapades had caused were memories. Then, the Baron had been a jewel-thief, driven into conflict with the law and the community by an experience which had hammered the cold iron of bitterness deep into him. But the bitterness had gone with the years, during which he had turned from cracksman to collector, dealer and lone wolf investigator—as Bristow knew.

Bristow did not hold the past against him.

But none save Lorna and Mannering himself knew that two things struggled in him for mastery; love of precious stones which amounted to a passion; and love of adventure—of the chase. He had hunted down many a killer; as Mannering had won a reputation in the Press as great as the Baron's in the old days. Because of his past and his present business he knew and often mixed with expert cracksmen and shrewd fences. No man in England knew more about precious stones and the mania which obsessed some collectors; none knew more of the tortuous ways in which gems passed from one man to another.

"So no lone wolf?" murmured Mannering.

"That's it."

"Bill, it's early to talk about that yet. You don't know whether anything was stolen. If it was, if the *Tear's* gone, the job's going to take some handling. 'Worth more than the love of a woman or the blood of a man.' I'm quoting Jacob. Let's see what you've got to look for before we decide what I shall do."

"I've warned you," Bristow said. "And I'll warn you about something else. One of these days, when you're playing the fool, you'll get your past pinned on to you. I never knew such a man for playing with fire. Don't play with this one."

Mannering said meekly: "No, Bill. Any reason why I shouldn't go home now?"

"No reason at all. You'll be wanted at the inquest, of course—you won't leave London, will you?"

"No."

"Right!" Bristow stood up. "Thanks for calling us at once. Don't keep us in the dark about anything—about Fay Goulden, for instance."

The words came easily, seemed to hold no hidden significance; but Mannering felt his heart thump, and stared into the detective's mild eyes.

"Why her?"

"It shook you when you saw her name as chief beneficiary," said Bristow. "Funny thing, as you don't know the lady!" He laughed, and opened the door—and Mannering walked quickly through the wide stone passages of the Yard, with the laugh and the gleam in the mild eyes clear in his mind.

As he stepped out of the building nearby Big Ben chimed: *one, two*. He looked up into the lighted face of the huge clock and at the shadowy outline of the great pile of the Houses of Parliament.

Two o'clock; and the milk roundsman would begin his journeys early. When? Five o'clock, or six? Was Belham Street early or late on his round? Best assume that it would be early, possibly between five and six o'clock. Mannering had to get that bottle before five, but it wasn't going to be easy. The police would be going in and out of Bernstein's shop all night; everyone who passed along the street would be scrutinised.

He found his car parked outside; Bristow had had it brought round.

He drove out of the Yard and went slowly along the Embankment, across the top of Parliament Square and then along the Embankment again, on the other side. This was the shortest way to Chelsea, and Lorna. But he wasn't thinking about Lorna; only of the *Tear*, the murder of Bernstein, and the significance of Bristow's warning.

Another car followed.

CHAPTER V

THE BOTTLE

MANNERING thought: "All right, Bill—I'll give you a run for your money!" and he turned right, away from the river.

The thought went through him, like the touch of the *Tear;* more heady wine. Defying Bristow, skating over the law's thin ice, hunting a killer and finding out the truth about the terrified girl. As he swung off Victoria Street he was smiling broadly, as if all were well in a wonderful world. He drove along the narrow streets to St. James's Park, where there were no lights, and switched on his headlights.

The twin orbs of the following car's sidelamps shone in the driving mirror.

He drove fast, leaving the Park by Admiralty Arch and turning left up Cockspur Street. He took corner after corner swiftly, always slowing down in time for the pursuing car to appear again. It was not far behind him when he turned into Belham Street.

An ambulance stood outside the shop, and the two men in white carried a stretcher. Mannering slowed down in front of the ambulance, seeing Jacob Bernstein in his mind's eye; alive—and dead. He drove past slowly. A constable came up, waving to him to stop. Behind the constable was a slight, fair-haired man wearing an old raincoat which sagged open, and with a trilby hat on the back of his head. The slight man had a pale, eager face, and a cigarette drooped from the corner of his mouth.

"Your licence, please," said the constable formally.

Mannering produced it.

"Thank you, sir." The constable stood back, to study it. The slight man lunged forward, a laconic grin on his full lips.

"Well, well! If it isn't the great sleuth on the trail already. How did you get to know about this, John?"

"Doesn't the Press ever sleep?"

"Not this part of it, when there's murder in London. Got anything for me?"

"Sorry, Chitty," Mannering said.

"Any purpose for your *return?*" asked the constable in a stilted voice.

Mannering said: "Yes, I've lost my lighter." He opened the door and got out, but to his surprise Chittering, of the *Daily Record*, turned and backed away. Gordon came out of the shop, and Chittering hovered in the background.

"Why don't you go home?" growled Gordon.

"I lost my lighter. Have you come across it?"

"I've had something better to do than look for your lighter. It's a wonder they let you go."

Chittering was still in the background.

"Anything missing?" asked Mannering.

"A hell of a lot has—" began Gordon, then checked his runaway tongue, turned on his heel and went back. A sergeant loomed from behind him.

"We've been through that room with a comb, Mr. Mannering, and didn't come across any lighter."

Mannering frowned. "I know I had it when—oh, yes! I lit a cigarette along here, didn't I? It might have dropped in the shop doorway." He hurried along the pavement, pushing past Chittering, who watched him with his head on one side. He turned into the doorway and looked at the milk bottle. There it stood, with the little tuft of cotton wool at the bottom. He actually touched the bottle, then drew his hand back sharply. With Gordon in his present mood he couldn't be sure of getting away quickly. And the diamond would remain safe so for a while.

"Found it?" Chittering had a cheerful voice.

Mannering produced his lighter, as by sleight of hand. "My lucky night."

"Not Jacob Bernstein's."

The words were like a douche of cold water. "No."

"On the hunt?" asked Chittering. "It would give me a nice headline. Gordon is like a bear with a sore head, I can't get anything out of him. I'll miss the final edition if I don't send something in soon."

"Mr. Mannering had no statement to make."

Chittering grinned. "Thanks! I'll be seeing you." He hurried off towards the telephone kiosk.

On the journey to Chelsea Mannering was followed again, but he drove more slowly. The car behind him passed the end of the street.

He left his car outside the flat.

There was a light in the front room, shining through a gap in the curtains. Lorna was still up. He went quietly upstairs, hearing no sound as he approached the front door. Perhaps she'd gone to bed and left a light on. He let himself in stealthily, tiptoed across the hall and looked into the study.

Lorna, asleep, sat in her winged armchair.

Mannering went across, looked down at her, smiled faintly, and kissed her forehead. She started and blinked dazedly.

"John! You scared me."

"I have my rights."

"What happened? Has the *Tear* been stolen?"

Mannering said: "Yes." He backed away, taking out cigarettes, suddenly bleak.

Lorna's eyes clouded with growing alarm.

"What is it?"

Mannering said: "About as bad as it can be."

"Jacob's not—" Her voice broke.

"He is."

"Oh, how awful!" She stood up, now very wide-awake. "Where have you been? What have you been doing? Do the police know? Have they caught anyone?"

"Last first; no. The *Tear's* gone, with a lot of other stuff, as far as I learn from Gordon, who is in a sour and hostile mood. I've seen Bristow. Chittering of the *Record* was hovering around, and will probably put me in headlines."

"Have you done anything yourself yet?"

"Want me to?"

Lorna said: "I ought to say no." She turned away, went to the cabinet in the corner and poured drinks. She looked pale and shocked. "Poor Jacob! There wasn't a better man living."

"There are mysteries." Mannering sat on the arm of a chair and told her much of what had happened; omitting only what he had done about the *Tear*, and about the Will. When he finished she stretched out her hand and he gave her a cigarette and lit it.

"What have you done that you've forgotten to tell me?" asked Lorna. "Playing the fool over that girl was crazy enough, but it's not all. I can tell that from the look in your eyes."

"Can you think of anyone we could ring up and send out on a little mission? Such as collecting a milk bottle off a window-ledge at 17, Belham Street. It isn't that I need the milk bottle, but there's some cotton wool in it."

Understanding dawned and her eyes blazed. She raised her hands and moved towards him. "The—*Tear?*"

"That's it."

"I hate that stone! Why on earth didn't you let the police find it?"

"Did I tell you that Jacob left you a pair of earrings?"

Lorna said: "Oh!" And suddenly she cried: "Not those emeralds?"

"Yes. I forgot to tell you another thing, too. He named me as an executor. No one has a greater right to that *Tear* than the executors, have they? Provided it's kept in a safe place and can be produced when everything's ready for probate, no one need lose any sleep. How well do you know the milkman?"

Lorna said huskily: "And he remembered that!" Slowly: "*I* could go for that bottle."

"Oh, no, my darling that won't do."

"Who else is there?"

Mannering went to the telephone and lifted the receiver, his finger resting on the dial.

"Larraby, I think. He probably won't be recognised, and if he is—well we've got to take a chance. That bottle must be off the window-ledge before the milkman arrives in the morning."

•   •   •   •   •

Larraby worked for Mannering at Quinn's. He was not only an assistant and odd-job man in the shop, but the night-watchman, who liked sleeping on the premises. He slept with a telephone and the bell of a burglar alarm system in his small room. No glimmer of light came in at the window, although in the far distance stars twinkled above the roof-tops. He slept like a child, on his back, with his arms above his head, and when the telephone began to ring he started but did not immediately wake. Sleeping, he looked youthful, in spite of his grey hair and his lined face.

The bell kept ringing.

He woke, at last, stretched out his hand and switched on the light. Then he sat up and groped beneath his pillow for a gun;

finally he said: *"Fool!"* and stopped groping. "That's the telephone. . . . Hallo. . . . Good morning, sir !"

He listened. . . .

"Yes, I will go at once," he said. "Shall I bring it to you at Chelsea, or bring it back here? . . . Very good, sir, I will keep it under my pillow. . . . You did say 17, Belham Street, didn't you?"

Hart Row, and Quinn's, was exactly seven minutes walk from Belham Street. Larraby, yawning in the early morning air, stepped out briskly. He took nine minutes to reach the street, because Mannering had told him to approach from the corner nearest Number 17, so that he would not have to pass Bernstein's shop. It was anyone's guess what was in the milk bottle. If you worked for Mannering you had to know when to ask questions and when to be discreet.

Number 17—good !

He counted the doorways as he walked quickly along. Thirteen—fifteen—ah, 17 was painted clearly on a hanging sign which jutted out from the top of the doorway. He glanced along the street and saw that two constables stood, with their backs towards him, by several parked cars. He chuckled softly. He would get away without being noticed, and—

Milk bottle?

There was no bottle here.

. . . . .

Lorna was in bed. Mannering had a hand on the light switch, ready to put it out, when the telephone bell rang. The night was full of ringing sounds and lights. There was an extension on the bedside table. Lorna mumbled: "Shall I go?" as Mannering lifted the receiver.

"This is John Mannering. . . ."

"Yes, Larraby."

He sat heavily on the side of the bed, and Lorna pushed back the clothes and sat up, affected by his tension. Larraby was still explaining. He had looked in all the doorways up to Number 29, but there was no milk bottle with a piece of cotton wool in it; none had been broken, or he would have seen the glass. There was no doubt, both cotton wool and bottle had been removed. The policemen hadn't seen him at close quarters, he was quite sure of that. . . . Was there anything he could do?

Mannering said : "No. You get back to bed."

Mannering replaced the receiver and looked bleakly into Lorna's eyes. The room was silent; nothing stirred anywhere. He had made an utter fool of himself, had thrown away a jewel which was almost beyond price. He must have been watched; perhaps from a house opposite—no, that wasn't the explanation, no one had seen him put the jewel in that bottle. Yet it hadn't been taken away by chance.

Lorna said : "They didn't believe your story of the lighter and went to look in the doorway."

"Yes, probably."

"Darling." She took his hand. "Perhaps it's a good thing. I don't want you to have that diamond."

He pulled himself free and picked up his cigarette case from the bedside table. "Clever and bright, wasn't it? Get the *Tear* out of the shop, then put it anywhere. The police are blind fools, never mind the police. Astute John Mannering! That *Tear* might have led us to the killer, and I—"

"John, stop going on like this."

"I like it. It does me good to know how bad I am. Teaches me not to sit on top of the world."

Another bell rang, the front door. It jarred through the quiet, making Lorna catch her breath, and he knew that the thought which sprang to his mind had its echo in hers. The police had found the *Tear*, and wanted to know why he had put it there.

The bell rang again.

"Oh, well," said Mannering. "It could be Larraby. He probably thinks that he can be helpful." He forced a smile. "Be in a nice deep sleep, no need for you to be worried by Bristow or his boys."

Mannering slipped into his robe and tied the sash as he crossed the hall, then switched on the light to make sure that he had a clear view of the caller. He opened the door. Chittering stood there.

•   •   •   •   •

The reporter came in, smiling. "Not in bed yet? Or were you? Apologies, Mr. Mannering!" He saw Lorna at the bedroom door, also in her dressing-robe. "Has he been telling you a fairy story? Any hope of a drink John? I always get thirsty listening

to Gordon telling me where to get off." He had to look upwards
to meet Mannering's eyes. "What about a real story, too? This
reporter won't be put off by the brush-off. You're going to make a
statement for the *Record*—persuade him, Mrs. Mannering. You
know our motto: the inside story of every crime in London, by
ace reporter Chit Chittering. I've my reputation to think of.
Speechless, John?"

"What's this? Blackmail?"

"My dear chap! You must have been in a dead sleep."
Chittering strolled across to the study, for he was no stranger to
the flat, and pushed open the door. "Mind if I switch on the
light?"

"Where is the jewel?" asked Mannering.

Lorna said: "Do you think—"

"I don't think, I know. Come across, Chittering, or you'll be
crossed off the visiting list." He tried to sound flippant, and
succeeded in sounding pompous. He had no doubt that Chittering had gone to Number 17

"Too bad," said Chittering. "I can't imagine what the great
John Mannering is after. Mind you, I might guess. I'm no good at
guessing, though, and the *Record* only deals in facts. You
should see the tears our readers cry, sometimes!" He looked
quite boyish. "I'll try to guess, if you'll give me the story of your
visit to the shop, John. Were you first on the scene? Mr. Mannering got there first and the police came tumbling after—we like a
rub at the Yard every now and again. How about it?"

Mannering said: "Oh, no. Not yet."

"So there is a story?"

"It would make your mouth water."

Chittering put his hand into the pocket of his raincoat; where
something bulged. Then he drew out a milk bottle, full of
milk.

CHAPTER VI

21, CLAYCOURT

CHITTERING held the bottle up to the light.

"Isn't it lovely? Does it matter what glass I use, Mrs. Mannering? Nice stuff to drink, milk. Can't understand what's come over John. Going to talk, John?"

Mannering said: "Yes."

"I *thought* you'd see my point of view." Chittering's grin became cherubic—until Mannering went to the telephone. When it changed to a frown. "Oi! What's the idea?"

"I'm going to talk."

"You don't have to telephone me."

"They have people on night duty at Scotland Yard."

"You wouldn't tell Scotland Yard about to-night's little escapade if I tried to make you. Joke over. Did you find Jacob's body?"

"That's not what I'm going to say to Bristow. I'm going to tell him that a certain reporter who was hanging around Belham Street to-night disappeared with a bottle of milk. Milk snatching in London has become as prevalent as bag-snatching. I can't make you show me what's in that bottle, but Bristow will. Or I might try Gordon, as he's in a bad temper. And all the other national newspapers will have lurid headlines: *"Record Reporter Held On—"*

"Your trick," sighed Chittering. "Bring a jug, Mrs. Mannering, and we'll see what came out of the cow."

"Not so fast," said Mannering. He took the bottle and stood it on the mantelpiece, behind him. "Let's see what's happened so far. You were after a story about Jacob Bernstein, didn't know that I'd been involved, followed me when I went to look for my lighter, found a bottle of milk—"

Chittering said: "An empty bottle."

"Then where did the milk come from?"

"The *Record* canteen."

"You found an empty bottle—"

"Let's have the facts. There was some cotton wool at the bottom of the bottle."

"Did you take the wool out of the bottle?"

"I thought you'd like to do that."

"You thought I'd put the cotton wool inside, too, but even reporters make mistakes. Supposing we told Bristow about this: would you be able to swear that I'd put anything in that bottle? Or wouldn't you have to state that I bent down and picked up a lighter, and you afterwards examined the bottle?"

Chittering sighed: "Let's hear the rest."

"It all depends on what is in the bottle. You think it's a jewel which came from Jacob Bernstein's. If it is such a jewel and you found it, you've a certain duty. What would your editor say if he discovered that you were running round with a piece of property stolen from the shop where a man had been murdered? What would the police say?" Mannering paused, but Chittering made no comment. "They would say you'd been a very bad boy, that you ought to have rushed with your discovery and your knowledge straight to the police. That is expected of all good London reporters. Wouldn't it be much safer if you didn't *know*? No one can stop you from guessing, and you don't have to report guesses."

Chittering went to the desk and took a cigarette from a beaten brass box. He lit it slowly.

"Mrs. Mannering, your husband is first cousin to the Devil."

"But isn't he right?" asked Lorna sweetly.

"Now if you really want a story—" began Mannering, and Chittering laughed; then listened to Mannering, glancing occasionally at the bottle of milk.

Mannering finished: "Now you can give him a drink, but don't let him go until I've checked on that milk." He took the bottle and hurried into the kitchen, poured the milk into a basin until a sodden piece of cotton wool stuck in the neck of the bottle. He pulled it out, and caught his breath as he touched the hard surface of the jewel inside. He unwrapped it. Milk smeared and dulled the facets. He dried it on a tea towel, and the kitchen seemed to blaze with multi-coloured lights. He took a pen-knife from his pocket and scratched the surface of the *Tear;* it was just possible that this was a paste stone.

The scratch didn't show.

This really was the *Diamond of Tears;* and its beauty set his heart hammering and his eyes glistening; and he seemed to hear Jacob's cracked voice:

"Worth more than the beauty of
woman and the blood of man."

The beauty was there, in all its glory; and the rounded end
glowed, as with blood. It was set in platinum and tiny diamonds, in the shape of petals.

He slipped it into his pocket and went slowly back to the
study. Chittering finished a drink, put his head on one side, and
said: "That must be some stone. Mind if I go now? I'm in with
you all the way on this job, John."

.   .   .   .   .

Lorna said: "Let me see it." Mannering put the *Tear* into her
hand; she didn't look down immediately but held it as if its fire
hurt her. Slowly she opened her hand and glanced downwards;
fiery streaks of light shone into her eyes. She caught her breath,
stared at the jewel for a long time, then looked up and said:

"It frightens me."

Mannering said: "It's a diamond. There are hundreds of
thousands of diamonds, and they don't frighten anyone. They
have nothing more than their intrinsic value. The stone hasn't a
blood-curse—it just brings out all the avarice in man, and some
will commit murder in order to possess it. Don't blame the
diamond, blame the men."

"It still frightens me. I don't want you to keep it for long.
And not here. Not here, John, please."

.   .   .   .   .

At half-past ten next morning Mannering drove the Bristol
through the crowded streets of the West End and, out of curiosity, turned into Belham Street. A crowd was surging about
Jacob's shop, outside which were four policemen to keep people
away from the window. Another policeman had to clear the way
for Mannering. He drove on to Hart Row and Quinn's.

Hart Row, off New Bond Street, was narrow and short, with
old shops on either side except at the far end, where a desolate
empty site, legacy from the air-raids, was utilised as a car park.
Mannering parked the car near the exit and walked to Quinn's.
The narrow-fronted shop looked as if it belonged to a London
three centuries past. The roof was red-tiled and covered with
dark green lichen, the chimney stack was crooked, the grey walls
mellowed with age. There was one window; and in that a single

picture, a tiny miniature on a velvet background, worth a fortune.

Inside was little Larraby and a middle-aged, courtly and portly man who had recently joined the staff.

" 'Morning, Benson."

"*Good* morning, sir."

"Come into the office, Larraby, will you?" asked Mannering, and Larraby followed him into the small windowless office at the back of the narrow shop. Mannering switched on the light.

Larraby looked tired and bright-eyed.

"Is everything all right, sir?"

"Yes, I found it. Have the police been here?"

"No, thank goodness! You know how difficult the police can be."

"If they question you, you didn't go out last night, and I didn't telephone you."

"That's understood, sir. Is there anything I can do?"

"There may be, later."

Larraby ran a hand over his greying hair. "I was horrified to hear what had happened to Mr. Bernstein. Were you there, sir?"

"Yes. I found him."

"And you're going to—"

"I don't know what I'm going to do yet, and you're not to guess."

"I know *nothing*, Mr. Mannering. But if there is anything I can do to help avenge Mr. Bernstein's murder, you have only to tell me. *Anything*." Larraby bowed gravely and turned to go.

"Just a moment." Mannering took a small packet from his pocket, wrapped in brown paper, stamped and heavily sealed. "Post this for me, will you? And see where it's going first."

Larraby took the packet and read aloud: "*James Milton*, c/o *Poste Restante, Strand, London*. I shall remember. Ought I to register it, sir?"

"No, just slip it into a post box."

Larraby went out, and Mannering watched him until he disappeared, then touched his forehead; it was damp with sweat. In the past he had often sent gems *poste restante*, believing that safer than in a safe deposit or a bank vault. Now he was on edge; was it another mistake to let the *Tear* go again?

He waited until Larraby returned.

"All right?"

"Yes, sir."

"Now forget all about it until I jog your memory," said Mannering. "Here's another job for you, and you'll have to be away from the shop most of the day. I want you to find out everything you can about Jacob Bernstein's customers. He had several assistants—you know them, don't you?"

"Very well, sir, we often have a drink together."

"I want a list of all customers who might have been in the market for big stuff—really big stuff. The police probably won't be able to get much out of the assistants, you ought to have better luck. Don't take any notice of what you read in the newspapers or anything the police say. "Just dig deep, and find those customers."

Larraby's eyes glowed.

"I'll find them *all*," he promised, and went out, his squared shoulders declaring him a man with a mission.

.   .   .   .   .

Mannering looked up at the massive concrete pile and did not greatly like it. Stark modernity seemed loud and ugly among the graceful buildings of Shepherd Street. Behind him was Park Lane; beyond that, Hyde Park, green and friendly beneath a watery autumn sun; and here, in the heart of London, Clay Court seemed to sneer at the age of the streets and the tradition in which they were steeped. A commissionaire, resplendent in royal blue and silver braid, stepped forward.

"Good morning, sir."

" 'Morning. Flat 21?"

"Third floor, sir, I will take you up." The commissionaire led his generalissimo's way to the lift. It shot up and then stopped. "The second door on the right, sir."

"Thanks."

Mannering pressed the bell outside Flat 21, and the lift whined as it went down. No one answered the bell. Mannering pressed again, and stepped to a window which overlooked the backs of houses and, in the distance, the plane trees in Park Lane.

Still no one answered the bell.

He pressed for a third time, and rapped on the door—and then he heard a faint click. He stood back. The lift was silent, and no door opened. He studied the deep cream paint of the one in front of him, concentrating on the letter-box. It was set on a level with his shoulders. He turned to the window again—and the faint sound was repeated. He looked out of the corner of his eye, and saw the flap of the letter-box lifting.

He lit a cigarette.

The flap clicked again, louder this time. He had heard no other sound, no hint of anyone approaching the front door. He lit a cigarette and said audibly: "Someone must be in." But although he rang twice again there was no answer, no further indication that he had been heard.

He said: "Oh well, I'll come back this afternoon."

He pressed the lift button and the lift came up, without the commissionaire. When he reached the hall the man was in earnest consultation with a fat woman wearing a mink coat and carrying a Pekinese. Outside the sun shone into his eyes and made him blink. He strolled to his car, sat at the wheel, and surveyed the street. No one watched him; Bristow had called his bloodhounds off. He let in the clutch and drove slowly towards the nearest corner, and parked there so that he could see the entrance to Clay Court.

The woman and the Pekinese came out.

Two cars passed swiftly along.

A man came out, sped by the commissionaire's loud "Good-day to you, sir." The man was of medium height, broad and powerful. He looked up and down quickly, almost nervously, then walked quickly towards Park Lane.

Mannering turned the car and drove slowly after him, catching him up when he stood at the kerb, waiting for the traffic to pass. He made a sudden dash towards the other side of the road. A huge red double-decker bus loomed up, driving him back. Mannering slid the nose of the car into the traffic as he turned the corner. He caught a glimpse of the man's face. It was red, chunky, with a bristling brown moustache. He was a man in the middle thirties, Mannering judged—and he also looked like a man with a mission. Mannering went straight across Park Lane and into the Park, pulled up at the side of the road and watched. The man from Clay Court reached the Park, crossed the road, and walked briskly towards Rotten Row.

Mannering waited until he had gone a hundred yards, then drove slowly after him. Near Rotten Row the man stepped off the path, over the little fence and on to the green parkland. He stopped near an oak tree which spread protecting branches over his head.

Mannering drove past him, went out at Hyde Park Gates, had luck with the traffic lights and re-entered the Park. Now he was on the same side as the man, who still waited, looking right and left; obviously he had a load on his mind. Mannering pulled up some way behind him and adjusted the driving mirror so that he could see him clearly. Two or three women on horseback moved towards the dirt surface of Rotten Row, as well-groomed as their horses. A few straggling sightseers watched them. The man beneath the oak tree lit another cigarette and now glared rather than looked about him. He paid no attention to Mannering.

A policeman stood on the other side of the road, doubtless preparing to tell Mannering that this was no place for parking. Before he could get across a small car pulled up a few yards behind Mannering. The red-faced man hurried forward. When the policeman arrived he had two victims; he chose Mannering first.

Mannering beamed at him.

"I know I shouldn't, but I've got a touch of cramp in my right leg. Better to stop where it's forbidden than crash into something, isn't it?"

"Oh, I *see*, sir."

"Glorious morning," said Mannering. "Couldn't be better. I shall be all right in a few minutes." The red-faced man walked quickly away in the other direction. Who mattered most? Mannering didn't take much convincing that his interest was in the driver. The small car went to Marble Arch, swung round it, then went along Oxford Street. Mannering drove close to the kerb. Immediately in front of him was a taxi, and he craned his neck, saw that the "For Hire" sign was up. Brakes squealed as they came to traffic lights. Mannering swung the car close to the kerb, jumped out and hurried to the taxi; a bulky man at the wheel hardly deigned to look round.

"Feel energetic?" asked Mannering.

The man half-turned, and grinned, showing a brick-red face. "Depends."

"Double fare for following that Morris Ten, a fiver if we're still in sight when the driver gets out."

"That fiver's mine, Guv'nor!"

Mannering settled back on his seat. Horns protested stridently at his car, parked in Oxford Street. The lights changed, and the driver of the Morris did not once look round. Mannering showed no interest in him, the taxi-driver yawned but kept close to the bumpers of the car he was following. Oxford Circus, Regent Street's wide curve—and then the Morris turned off into a side street. Soon they were driving through the narrow streets of Soho, past dozens of obscure little restaurants with foreign names and boasting foreign cooking, or past espresso bars and little shops, until the Morris driver pulled up in Wine Street.

"Straight past, next corner," said Mannering.

The taxi-driver grunted.

He turned the corner while Mannering looked through the tiny rear window. The man sat at the wheel of the Morris looking at something which Mannering could see—the packet. Mannering thrust a five pound note into the driver's hand and said: "Wait." He stood by the corner, in the doorway of a shoe shop. The man from the Morris got out, carrying the packet. He went into a restaurant, outside which hung a sign: "Toni's Italian Restaurant." Toni did not seem to believe in painting his premises or keeping the outside clean.

After five minutes the driver came out; for the first time Mannering had a good view of him. He was pale and thin-faced, with high cheekbones, dark eyes and a small black moustache. He took off his hat and smoothed down his sleek black hair, looking satisfied and smug. Twice he patted his breast pocket. Then, strutting, he climbed back into the Morris.

Mannering hurried back to the taxi.

"Same again."

"Suits me. You a copper?"

"Do I look like one?"

"Okay, okay, it's yer money I want, not yer life 'istory." The driver swung the wheel on that remarkable lock which enables London's box-like taxi to turn almost in their own length. They reached Wine Street again while the Morris was in sight. It pulled up at a parking meter near a tall, narrow building, one of a grey terrace, which was marked: "Pandora Hotel."

"Same again?" asked the cabby.

"Wait ten minutes, in case I want you."

"Okay." The cabby tucked the second note into a pocket somewhere in the hinterland of his three overcoats. Mannering walked past the Pandora Hotel and caught a glimpse of a single wilting palm tree in a brass-ribbed barrel, a red carpet and several easy chairs, an ash-blonde at a reception desk—but no sign of the little man. Inside, he saw a box-like booth marked "Telephone," squeezed in, and dialled the *Daily Record*. It was five minutes before Chittering came on the line. No one entered or left the hotel.

"Mannering," said Mannering.

"Hal-lo!"

"There's a Morris Ten, black, parked near the Pandora Hotel, in Wine Street."

"Someone giving it away?"

"You might care to follow it if you want to be in this job."

"Try to stop me," said Chittering. " 'Bye!"

Mannering left the booth and approached the desk.

"Can I help you?" The ash-blonde had a friendly eye for dark, good-looking men.

"The question is, do you want to?"

"Oh, don't *come* it," trilled the ash-blonde, but looked delighted. "Want a room?"

"No. I'm a busy."

"A *busy*? What on earth is that?" She wouldn't see forty again, and she talked as if she hadn't yet seen seventeen. She pressed her billowy bosom against the edge of the desk, and looked at him from bright eyes made brighter by blue eyeshade.

"Detective, to you."

"Oh, *really!*"

Mannering produced a pound note, leaned forward, and was rewarded by a whiff of cheap scent. "A man came in just now, a few minutes before I arrived."

"Supposing he did?"

"Is he staying?"

"Yes, *and* he's alone, we don't go in for divorce and all that kind of thing *here!*"

"Oh. Pity. Has he been here long?"

"Only two days," said the woman. "At least, I *think* it's two days. I've been away, I had a dreadful cold, could hardly breathe with it, I couldn't." She pulled the open register towards her and ran her scarlet-tipped forefinger down it. "Yes, there it is—Tuesday. And he's going to-day, paid his bill before he went out. Anything else you want to know?"

Mannering pushed the pound note towards her.

"What does he call himself here?"

"You don't mean he uses a false *name?*" She giggled, and

read aloud : "T. E. Benoni, so he can't be English, can he? But he *speaks* like an Englishman, ever such a nice voice he's got. Thanks everso." The pound note disappeared down the deep plunge of her dress.

Mannering pulled the register towards him. Benoni had given his last address as Birmingham, which wasn't much help. And Benoni would be leaving soon; he had probably gone upstairs to collect his bags.

"You must have a *thrilling* life," said the woman. "I—oh, excuse *me*." A telephone bell rang. She turned on a swivel chair and leaned across, cat-like, to the tiny switchboard at her side. "Hallo. . . . Well, the porter isn't here. . . . Well, I'll *see* what I can do." She plucked the plug out. "That was him, he wants a taxi. And I can't leave the desk with no one here, can I?"

"I'll see if there's one passing," Mannering offered. Her "Oh, thanks everso" floated back to him as he hurried to the doorway —and saw the bundle of overcoats leaning back in the taxi smoking and reading a newspaper. The newspaper drooped, bright eyes grinned.

"Thought I'd give you a bit longer."

"Thanks. You've another fare. A man's coming out of the hotel in a few minutes—I want to welcome him."

"What *is* this, guv'nor?"

"Nothing that can make trouble for you."

"Well, yer money's good. Okay." The driver moved the cab towards the hotel as Mannering went back and called : "I've found one." He went to the other side of the cab and stood behind it, waiting until footsteps came from the hotel.

The thin-faced man got into the taxi. "Waterloo," he said, and sank back in his corner. You didn't go to Birmingham from Waterloo. The engine whined—and Mannering opened the door of the cab and scrambled inside. He felt a hand on his shoulder, but didn't look at the man.

"You can't come in here." It was a trained voice; rather arty and stagey. "This is my cab."

Mannering murmured : "Can't I?" He sat down on one of the tip-up seats, thrust his left hand into his pocket and poked the finger against the coat. "I shouldn't make a fuss, Benoni, I've been wanting to see you for some time."

Benoni shrank back. Opening his mouth wide, he looked quite as terrified as Fay Goulden once had.

CHAPTER VII

NAME OF FIORI

"Nice day," said Mannering.

"Who the hell are you?"

"A man who knows a little and wants to know a lot about you, Benoni. What have you got in your pocket?"

The cab moved off with a jerk, throwing Benoni against the glass partition separating him from the driver. Mannering, his back to the partition, wasn't affected. His finger poked ominously against his coat. Benoni glanced down at it.

"N-n-n-nothing!"

"Let me have a look." Mannering pushed his finger hard into Benoni's side, pulled the coat open and slid his hand into the pocket; he felt paper. Benoni sent a frightened glance at the back of the driver's head.

"I'll have the police—"

"Forget it." Mannering tugged at the paper and pulled out a wallet. Inside was a wad of one-pound notes, at least a hundred. He put the wallet into his pocket, and waved the money in Benoni's face. "How come?"

"That's mine!"

"Where did you get it and why did you get it and where are you going to take it?"

"None—none of your business." Benoni tried to look defiant. He glanced out of the window, as if he had given up all hope of getting help from the cabby. They were in a side street, where few people passed, and opposite a large empty site.

Mannering said: "You only have to talk, Benoni. I'm not after you. Who gave you this money?"

"You can't—"

Mannering opened a window, and made as if to throw the money out. Benoni lunged forward and grabbed his wrist.

"That's mine, I tell you! Give it to me!"

"When you've talked."

"I—I did a job for a man." Benoni collapsed in his corner when Mannering withdrew his hand. He eyed the notes as if they were the beginning and the end of his existence. "I just did a little job for a man."

"What man?"

"I can't give a pal away!"

"Ever heard of those people who light cigars with pound notes? Care to see it done?" He pulled out his cigarette-case, opened it one-handed, and dropped half of the notes. Benoni darted to pick them up. Mannering jabbed his forefinger harder against his side, then bent his head, took a cigarette with his lips, slid the case back and fished out his lighter. "These will do for a start." The flame came at the first flick.

The cab went slowly on, turning corners slowly.

"No! No, don't burn them, I need that money. I got to have it, I—" The veneer of culture in Benoni's voice began to crack; he licked his lips again, "I did a job for Toni."

"Who is Toni?"

"Toni Fiori. He—he's got a joint in Wine Street, a caffe, he asked me to pass on a message for him."

"A valuable message," Mannering sneered. "Let's have the truth. Toni's a fence. You took some sparklers from a man in Hyde Park and passed them on to Toni. What do you think the police would have to say about it?"

Benoni said: "I—I didn't know what was in the packet. I tell you I didn't know."

"But you know Toni paid you a hundred pounds for it. Why do you need the money?"

"I'm in a jam. With a girl, she—"

"You can keep the cash," Mannering said. "But if you warn Toni that we've had this little chat, I shall talk to the police and you and your girl friend will have to find another way out of the jam. Or she will—you'll be inside."

Benoni muttered : "I won't tell him."

"I'll take a chance," Mannering said, and tapped on the glass. The driver pulled up. "I'll find another cab, and I'll post your wallet back to the address I find inside."

He got out, and gave the driver his third bonus. "Waterloo. If you have any trouble from the boy-friend, just mention the police. He's got plenty of money, it's all over the floor of the cab."

The driver turned his head and saw Benoni scrambling on the floor for the notes, muttering to himself; and Mannering walked quickly away.

He was near Shaftesbury Avenue when he hired another taxi, reached Oxford Street ten minutes afterwards and meekly apologised to a large constable who was standing by his car. When he drove into the thick stream of traffic Benoni's wallet was lumpy in his pocket.

When he reached Clay Court again the resplendent commissionaire welcomed him as an old friend.

.   .   .   .   .   .

A maid opened the door of Flat 21. She was elderly, timid and nervous. Her swift sideways look when she saw him, the quiver of her thin lips, gave that away. Beyond her was a square, pink wall; on the wall a picture with colours as vivid as Picasso's.

"Yes, sir?"

"Miss Goulden is expecting me," Mannering said.

"Is she? She didn't say anything; I don't know whether she's in."

Mannering smiled. "She's in to me." He stepped past the maid and across a long, narrow hall, where black and gold striped the walls and ceiling, dazzling and harsh. One door was ajar. In front of it a shadow darkened the gold-coloured carpet. He pushed the door open wide, and Fay Goulden cried:

"Oh!"

"And how are you this morning?" He went in and she backed away. She wore a pale grey dressing-gown, high at the neck, flowing in deep folds from her tiny waist. Her hair, parted carelessly in the middle, rippled untidily to her shoulders. Without make-up she looked girlish, and her skin was fair and clear. Obviously she was as frightened now as she had been the night before.

"Don't say you've forgotten me already." Mannering smiled at the maid. "Go out and shut the door, please." The maid hesitated, until Fay nodded. The door closed with a snap.

"Poor, frightened Fay!" Mannering said.

"I'm not frightened!" She turned away and groped for a cigarette-box on a low, glass table. It wasn't just glass-topped, but solid. Everything in this room seemed made of the same clear material—plastic—not glass. Chairs, sofa and cushions were silvery in colour, giving the room a brittle look.

She took a lighter off the table and fumbled until it glowed. The cigarette bobbed up and down in her lips.

She said: "Who—who are you? You've no right here, I've nothing to say to you. Go away!"

"Not until I know more about your problem," Mannering said.

She backed further away.

From outside, there came a sharp *ting!* as of a telephone bell. Mannering moved swiftly, opened the door, and heard the maid say:

"Hurry! Oh, hurry!" After a pause, she went on in a tense voice: "Is that—"

The girl was now by Mannering's side.

"You've no right—"

He gripped her hand, silencing her, but had missed the name. The maid said:

"Yes, he's here, yes, come quickly!" Then the ting! came again, and Mannering, still holding Fay's arm, drew her back into the room and closed the door again. On a chair were several morning newspapers. He picked up a *Record*—and saw his own photograph, as well as Jacob Bernstein's.

"Fay, I'd like to help." he said. "You're in a nasty spot and you know it, and I think you also know that you can't trust your friends."

"You've no right here. Go away!"

"Someone's drilled you well. Last night you were willing enough to promise to see me. You gave me the right address, too."

"I don't know where you got the address! I—oh, I wish you'd go." She drooped, sat down on a straight-backed chair and stubbed out the cigarette. "I've a terrible headache and hardly slept last night. Please go away."

"If I were a policeman, I'd take you off for questioning. Murder's been done, there's a limit to what I can keep from the police. And a time limit, too."

He heard a sound at the door and thought the maid was back again, to protect her mistress; but although it was a woman who spoke, it wasn't the maid. The voice was deep, husky, laughing; a voice which promised much.

"You're already too late, Mr. Mannering."

Mannering stiffened, but did not turn round. Fay raised her

hands and ran past him eagerly, as if towards salvation. Mannering slid his cigarette-case from his pocket and moved forward. In a long, narrow mirror, silvered or chromiumed at the corners, he saw the rest of the room—and the woman in the doorway. Fay reached her and cried: "Oh, Julia!" The woman put an arm round the girl's shoulder protectively, while Mannering went nearer the mirror, until he could see the woman's face in it.

"Julia!" sobbed Fay. "Julia, make him go away. He frightens me."

"He won't frighten you for long, dear."

The voice which had mocked Mannering soothed the girl. It was as lovely and unusual as her face, yet it did not strike Mannering that she was beautiful. He had seen no one quite like her before and was not likely to again. There was sweetness, wisdom and maturity, such a face as a supreme artist might draw to depict an imagined madonna. Raven-black hair was coiled round her head, her cheeks were the colour of lilies touched by pink.

Her eyes met his, in the mirror, and she smiled.

"Are *you* frightened?" she asked him.

"Of what?"

"Of facing me."

He said: "Yes. I don't want to be disillusioned. I'd like to remember you as you look now, not as you really are. But I'll face you." He turned slowly and looked into her dark eyes.

She was taller than Fay; deep-bosomed; wearing a black dress of simple cut, and a mink stole. Her smile had faded and she frowned, as if his words both hurt and puzzled her.

"Make him go," sighed Fay.

"Fay doesn't want me to go," Mannering said. "Look at her, Fay. Stop letting others tell you what to do. You think you can trust Julia, but you can't—not her nor any of your friends. You can trust me."

He broke off; another word would be too many, he had said enough to make the woman Julia wonder how much he really knew. He lit a cigarette, easing a tension which was only partly of his making. For as Julia looked at him, ignoring Fay, it was as if a mask had dropped, to prevent him from seeing her as she really was.

She said: "Fay, go and get dressed."

"Julia!"

"Hurry." Julia took her arm, pushed her out, and said, "Everything will be all right." She closed the door on Fay's protest, turned the key in the lock, then moved slowly across the room towards him.

"You're not what I expected, Mr. Mannering. Be guided by me. Don't probe into the murder of Jacob Bernstein or try to find the *Tear*. Just make your peace with the police and read all about the case in the newspapers. You'll be much, much safer. I don't want you to get hurt."

"I take a lot of hurting."

"You're as vulnerable as anything made of flesh and blood. There's been enough hurt already, too much blood spilt. You'll make the situation worse for Fay, too. You're a married man and you lead a full life. Don't throw it away." She put out her hand and took his; her fingers were cool, their pressure firm. "You'll be sorry if you ignore my advice. You've kept certain facts from the police too long to divulge them with safety now."

"A man I was very fond of was brutally murdered last night."

"Let the police do their work."

"And a diamond beyond price was stolen."

Her eyes flamed, and the mask was torn away.

"*Stolen?* The *Tear?*"

"Yes."

"No!" she cried. Her fingers dug into his hand; she swayed, as if from shock. She stood there for a long time, then turned away, swept across and out of the room, with Mannering close behind her.

"Julia!" cried Fay.

Julia said: "I'll come in for a moment," and went in and closed the door. Mannering heard the key turn in the lock, then an undertone of voices.

He tried to remember Julia's expression when he had announced that the *Tear* had been stolen. Alarm, dread, disbelief —she had shown all three. He tried to decide what to do next—follow Julia, or try to make Fay talk.

The maid watched him furtively from a doorway.

Soon Julia came out and passed Mannering without a word or look. She didn't speak to the maid, who hurried to open the front door for her.

The door closed; and Mannering stayed.

He went to Fay's door and tapped. She didn't answer. He tried the door; it wasn't locked. He went in, and found her sitting at a dressing-table, her robe round her shoulders, her eyes rounded with dread.

"Fay, you'll be much safer if you tell me all about it. Don't pretend any longer. You were at Bernstein's last night."

"I wasn't there! You didn't see me! I wasn't in London, I was with friends!"

Mannering moved forward swiftly, caught her shoulders and shook her.

"Don't lie, Fay. I made a bargain with you, and now you'll keep your side of it." He shook her again, slowly. "No cheap tricks, no lying, Julia isn't here to help you now."

She *laughed* at him.

It was a giggle at first, with a touch of hysteria, and her eyes were feverishly bright. Although he shook her she couldn't stop laughing. She swayed to and fro, then began to shake her head. She said something that he couldn't catch, because she was convulsed with laughter. He let her go, and heard:

"She is. She is. *She is!*"

Mannering snapped: "Be quiet!" But Fay went on laughing.

A frightened Fay he could have managed: even had she been sullen, or shouted and threatened, he could have coped with her; but this laughter defeated him. He slapped her face hard enough to sober her if this were hysteria, but she went on laughing.

Why was she laughing?

He turned suddenly and went to the door; it was not locked. He half-expected to see someone else outside, perhaps a man; but no one was there. Puzzled, on edge, with Fay's laughter still in his ears, he went back to the bedroom. She lay on the bed facing him looking tired and relaxed.

Five minutes later she was asleep.

.   .   .   .   .

Mannering shook her, she didn't stir. He raised her eyelids. The pupils had contracted to pin-points, so she had taken a morphine drug. It explained her laughter, and what she had meant by that "she is." Julia had given her dope to make sure she couldn't talk to him. And he'd chosen to stay for just that!

Mannering glanced through the drawers in the dressing-table, wardrobe and tallboy. He found nothing of interest, but there was a large box with photographs of Fay inside. He selected three copies of the best likeness and put them in his pocket.

.   .   .   .   .

The maid was sitting in the kitchen, sewing. She looked up, tight-lipped, when Mannering entered. By her side was a tea-tray, with a red knitted cosy over a teapot. Mannering took a cup and saucer from the dresser and poured out a cup of tea, while she watched furtively, almost too scared to look at him.

"The visitor has a flat here, hasn't she?" Mannering knew she had, or Julia couldn't have arrived so quickly. The maid's expression was an answer in itself.

"Who is she?" Mannering asked.

She didn't answer, so he said sharply :

"Tell me, or tell the police."

"You can't—"

"I can tell the police, and will, if you don't tell me the truth. What is the woman's other name?"

The maid gasped : "She—she's Mrs. Fiori, from Flat 23."

.   .   .   .   .

Toni Fiori owned a cheap little Soho café. Did his wife live in a luxury flat two doors away from Fay?

CHAPTER VIII

MRS. FIORI'S JEWELS

THERE was no stopping the maid, now that she had started talking. She didn't know anything, it wasn't her fault, there was no reason why her past should be brought up against her, supposing she *had* served time? You couldn't go straight once you'd been in jail, unless you were lucky. Miss Goulden was a very nice young lady. She'd worked for her for five weeks—Mrs. Fiori had introduced her, Mrs. Fiori was wonderful, she wasn't going to get Mrs. Fiori into trouble. . . .

"What makes you think you could?" demanded Mannering.

"I can't! I don't know anything, she—she's been a good friend to me, that's all I know." The thin nose and pinched cheeks were ashy pale. "She found me this job, she knows I've been inside and doesn't hold that against me."

"Nor will I," said Mannering. "Take it easy, Lizzie. Or have you got a name?"

"My name's Ethel, Ethel Grayson. I've never done anything wrong since I came out."

"Keep up the good work and you'll be all right. How long has Miss Goulden been as edgy as this?"

"She—she's been jumpy ever since I came."

"But not so jumpy as to-day?"

"No, she—she's worse this morning."

"Where were you last night? Did you help her dress?"

"Yes. She went out to dinner. Mr. Kenneth took her, she was very happy last night, but this morning—"

"Kenneth who?"

"I don't know. She always calls him Kenneth, he's been here several times."

"Is he young, or old?"

"Oh, *young*. Ever such a nice boy. They're in love, head over heels, they are. I went to bed at midnight, like I always do. I didn't hear her come in, but when I went in with her tea at nine o'clock she was in an awful state."

"What did she say?"

"She didn't say anything about what happened or why she was upset! She said she'd had too much champagne last night, but I knew there was something else. Then—then a man came to see her this morning, but he didn't stay long. He told me to send for Mrs. Fiori if you came."

"How did you know me?"

"Your picture's in the paper."

Mannering believed that she told the truth, even when she said that she didn't know the name of the morning caller. He had just said that Mrs. Fiori had sent him, and the name Fiori was *open sesame* in this flat. She didn't know whether anything had changed hands, she hadn't heard anything that the visitor had said to Fay. When Mannering had called the first time she had gone to the door, peered through the letter-box, then told the man who was there.

"What was he like?" Mannering asked.

She burst out:

"I'm no good at describing people, but he had a red face and a big moustache!"

That fitted the man who had set Mannering off on his morning trail.

"I'll take your word for it," Mannering said. "But if I catch you out in a lie you'll probably know what the inside of a prison cell is like again. You're mixed up in a nasty business."

She jumped up from her chair, dropping the sewing, stretching out her hands towards him. "You won't tell anyone I've talked, will you? I might lose my job. Then I'd have to go back to the old life again. You don't have to tell them, do you?"

"No. What were you in for?"

She passed her tongue over her lips. "I did a bit of shop-lifting."

He took her chin in his hand and forced her head back.

"I may want more from you before this is over Ethel. If you help me, I won't let you down."

He released her, turned, and went out of the flat. He stood by the closed front door, listening; she didn't come into the hall after him. No one appeared to be watching, so he went softly down the carpeted stairs to the next floor; no one was about. He came back, and went to Mrs. Fiori's flat. He rang the bell, but there was no answer. He rang again, keeping his finger on the bell-push for a long time, but no one came. He drew back, hand in pocket, feeling for his knife. One blade was broad and not made of steel but of mica. He opened it, and began to work on the lock. Here in the broad daylight streaming through a landing window, and in full sight of anyone who came up the stairs or from the lift, it was an invitation to trouble, but he might not have a chance like this again. The mica crept between the lock and the door, gradually pushing it back; there came a sharp click, the sound he wanted to hear. The whirring of the lift sounded clearly. He left the door ajar and walked swiftly to a recess which was large enough to hide him.

The lift stopped at a floor below.

He went into the flat and closed the door. The lock wouldn't catch properly, the disadvantage of this method of lock-picking, so he shot a bolt. The flat was planned on exactly the same lines as Fay's. He looked into every room and found no one, but received a dozen vivid impressions. There was no futuristic nonsense about Mrs. Fiori. This was a well-furnished apartment, full of charm and good taste. The furniture was modern but distinctive, each room furnished in dark, shining walnut. In the main bedroom there were twin beds, but apparently only a woman was using it for the time being. There were no man's brushes on the dressing-table, only women's clothes in the wardrobe which stretched across one long wall. In this were two fur coats—a brown mink and a Persian lamb—several fur wraps, a dozen evening gowns, afternoon dresses by the dozen. Only a really wealthy woman could afford such clothes.

One drawer in the dressing-table was locked. Mannering pushed in a skeleton key attached to the knife; a quick flick of the wrist and it was open. Inside were trinkets hardly worthy of the name jewels. He passed them over quickly; bangles, necklaces, ear-rings, all imitation gems, beautifully made but worth very little; it was hard to imagine Julia Fiori wearing paste jewellery. He came to a long, narrow jewel-box, which wasn't locked, opened it and started back.

Inside lay five diamonds set in platinum petals, each exactly alike, large and gleaming; and each might have been taken for the *Diamond of Tears*.

.   .   .   .   .

Not one was real; he had been a fool to think one might be.

Yet each was beautifully made, and approximately the right measurements for the *Tear*. He took measurements of two with a pair of pocket calipers, jotted them down on his notebook and put the gems back. The discovery had slowed him down. He locked the drawer, went to the hall and listened, but heard no sound outside. Back in the bedroom, he searched every piece of furniture, but found nothing of any significance. He went into the drawing-room, where quiet blues and golds were restful, glanced through an unlocked bureau and all likely hiding-places. Nothing he found told him anything about Julia Fiori or her husband.

Was there a safe?

He didn't find one, but on top of a cupboard in the kitchen was an old deed box; unlikely hiding-places were the safest, and this box was locked. He used the skeleton key again, but had much more difficulty opening this lock. At last it opened. Inside were important-looking legal documents, some tied round with red tape. They were mostly title deeds, in the name of Julia Fiori, who owned houses and flats in the West End of London. Then one address caught his eye—47, *Wine Street, London, W.*1.

Toni Fiori's café was in Wine Street, and his house and shop was owned by Julia. The deed of transfer was dated five years ago. Mannering put this with the others, finding smaller documents beneath it—certificates of birth and marriage. Five years ago, about the time of the transfer, Julia Howlett had married one Enrico Fiori, who was described as a "British-born Italian."

At the time of her marriage Julia had been thirty-one, which put her in the middle thirties now. Other papers held no significance, but at the bottom of the box was a small loose-leaf notebook. He looked through it. Only a few pages had been used, and on the last of these he saw the name of Jacob Bernstein. He read swiftly, and discovered that these were extracts from the old man's will.

•   •   •   •   •   •

There was nothing here that he need take away, but much of vital interest. Mannering relocked the box and put it back on the top of the cupboard, then hurried to the front door. Anyone who knew the ways of cracksmen would know how the flat had been entered, but he had to face that. He opened the door cautiously, and immediately heard the lift. He saw the top of the lift appear, then Julia's braided hair.

He closed the door but didn't bolt it, slipped quickly through to the kitchen, then stepped on to a fire escape which also served as a tradesmen's entrance. He went down quickly, glancing at the windows of the other flats, from which he might be noticed. He tucked his chin on his chest and hunched his shoulders, reached the paved backyard and went quickly towards an open door. It led to a narrow passage, thence to a cobbled mews, which gave on to Park Lane.

No one followed him.

He took a taxi from the corner, went to Victoria, and took another taxi to his Chelsea flat.

The folly and the value of that visit to Julia's flat were equal. Julia would guess who had been there. She had warned him, and talked of sudden death; would she be given to idle threats? It wasn't likely. But he had discovered in an hour more than the police could have found in a week. There was no room for regrets, but—

The taxi turned the corner and he saw a small car parked outside his flat, facing him; on the windscreen was a single notice: "Press."

Lorna was out, but Chittering was in the study, which was filled with a blue haze of tobacco smoke. He wore the same old raincoat, battered trilby and bright shining brown shoes. His broad grin was friendly.

"Welcome, hero!"

"What have I been doing now?"

"Something you wouldn't want Bristow to know," said Chittering. "What did you expect from that little Morris?"

"How much did you get?"

"I'm not yet sure," said Chittering, wrinkling his nose. "I hung about for an hour. Then a little chap came and drove it off, Italian or Spanish—I wouldn't know which. You know the type. Dark hair, sallow face, wasp waist, spiv written all over him. He left the car at Green's Garage, Charing Cross Road, and then walked to a café in Wine Street owned, I'm told, by a certain Toni Fiori. Know anything about Fiori?"

"No. Do you?"

"I gathered from a newsboy at a nearby pitch that Toni Fiori thinks no end of himself, and doesn't make his fortune from that café. Not that you can tell, there's a fortune in food and the food is good—or so I'm told. I've asked my research department to find out what it can about Fiori. How much will you give me for the report?"

"A tip. This job is dangerous."

"How dangerous?"

"I don't know how far this goes but it isn't as simple as it looks—not just murder of Bernstein for robbery."

"Evidence?"

"You'll have to take my word. But you can give your research department another job."

"It's just waiting for jobs."

"There is a nice young man named Kenneth. I don't know what he looks like, whether he's dark or fair, rich or poor, and I don't know his surname. But I do know that he's supposed to be in love."

"I said research, not romance department."

"He's in love with a young woman who will inherit Bernstein's fortune; and there is a large fortune. That's off the record, don't go writing sensational articles about it."

"Where does the sweet young thing live?"

"At Clay Court Mansions—Number 21. She was out with Kenneth last night, and I doubt if he'd take her to Lyons Corner House or the Trocadero." Mannering took out one of the photographs of Fay. "There she is—will you get some copies made and then have a talk with your Society gossip columnist and find out all you can about her and Kenneth?"

Chittering studied the photograph.

"*Very* nice."

"She's scared out of her wits, and she's probably frightened that something drastic will happen to her. You can do this research much more easily than I can, and the police won't be surprised at you probing. I don't want them to know what I'm up to yet."

"I shan't tell them. Have you seen this?" asked the reporter, taking a folded copy of the *Daily Record* from the pocket of his raincoat. "All the latest news; if you want the facts read the *Record*." The headline was about Bernstein's murder, and the sub-heading ran: "Murderer Gets £100,000-worth of Jewels." There was a picture, not of man or woman but of the *Diamond of Tears,* and in a heavy black type a potted history of the diamond and of the three men and one woman who had owned the *Tear* and died violent deaths. The *Tear* was valued at £55,000; the other jewels were listed. Bristow and Gordon had made good use of the little black book.

"Not bad," said Chittering.

"What else do you know?"

"London's being turned upside down. Every man the Yard and the Divisions can spare is on the job. Every fence in the City and the West End is being checked, jewel dealers everywhere have a description of the stolen stuff, a full release has been made to the Press. The official statement is that the police are following up an important clue and expect to make an arrest shortly. Unless they're going to arrest you."

Mannering said : "Not just yet."

"Is the *Tear* still here?"

"Was the *Tear* ever here?".

"I am not normally a cautious man," said Chittering, his blue eyes rounding, "but I sleep sometimes and I've slept on this. I was a fool not to take that jewel to the police last night and you'll be a bigger fool if you hide it for long. They mean to get the man who has the *Tear* because they think the man who has the *Tear* killed Jacob. Go warily, John."

"Thanks."

"Meaning you'll do exactly what you want to. I admit being relieved that I can't give evidence of seeing the *Tear* in this flat. How's Lorna taking it?"

"As you'd expect."

"You're a dangerous couple when roused," said Chittering. "When will the inheritance of lovely Fay be made public?"

"Bristow will probably want to keep it secret—and don't forget he's almost certainly watching Fay."

"According to what I was told at the Yard, a woman was seen to come out of Jacob's shop or one near it, John. Could she have been Fay, I wonder? If she's going to inherit a fortune she'd have a pretty big motive for killing Jacob. Also, according to a whisper from the garrulous Gordon, you're suspected of knowing that the girl was at the shop and letting her escape. Gordon breathed the word 'accessory.' What have you done to Gordon? He hates your guts."

"That's because of what I haven't done for him," said Mannering. "Don't worry about Gordon. Thanks for all you're doing. You'll find it's worth the trouble."

Chittering grinned. "It's a good job I've a soft spot for your wife; if it were only you I'd stand by and watch them catch you." He slouched towards the door, hands thrust deep into the pockets of his raincoat, curly head bare and untidy. "When you get anything I can print don't sit on it, will you?"

"No."

"How convincingly he lies," marvelled Chittering. "How Lorna lives with you I don't know. I—"

The front door bell rang, cutting across his words. He murmured: "Bristow, maybe," and moved back into the study.

Mannering opened the front door—and saw Julia Fiori.

She was alone.

CHAPTER IX

JULIA WARNS

Julia Fiori didn't speak, but gave Mannering time to collect his thoughts. He whispered: "Come back in ten minutes," and then raised his voice so that Chittering could hear; blocking the doorway with his great frame. "Oh, thanks. Yes, I'll sign." He took out his wallet, extracted a slip of paper and made it rustle—and Julia made no attempt to force her way in. She turned away and he closed the door and slipped his right hand into his pocket. Chittering came bobbing out.

"No police?"

"Just a letter by special messenger."

"Love or secret?"

"Both. What's your editor's mood these days?"

"It depends on the international situation. If it's bad he's as happy as a lark. If it's good, and he can't scratch up a headline, he makes life miserable. Why?"

"You might find one or two specially written articles helpful," Mannering said, and went to the door. Julia would have had time to reach the street by now, and Chittering obviously suspected nothing. "You can sign them."

"Not if you wrote them—they'd be dynamite." Chittering left, waving from the head of the stairs. Mannering went to the kitchen and poked his head inside.

"Make tea for two, Susan."

Pretty fair hair on a broad head, and an attractively freckled face, turned from the dresser towards him.

"I didn't know you'd both be in, sir."

"We shan't. I'll answer the bell when it rings next."

"Very good," said Susan.

Mannering went back to the study and stood looking over an empty site where there had been gracious Georgian houses. He could see as far as the Embankment, where traffic crawled, and to the River Thames, sluggish and silvery in the afternoon sunlight. He could also see the end of the street, but there was no sign of Julia Fiori. He hurried upstairs to the attic which was

Lorna's studio. A faint smell of paint met him. Hair cord carpeting was spread over the boards, a dozen or so unfinished canvases stood with their faces to the wall, an empty canvas was on the easel near the great skylight from which the north light came. Here Lorna spent much of her time; on a rostrum covered with blue carpet her sitters sat for weary hours—famous and unknown alike.

Julia Fiori was walking from a corner, alone. No one else was in sight, and this was a good spot for seeing most of the street. Had she really come alone? Another window of the attic overlooked the back garden of the house; that was empty of watching eyes. As he turned away the front door bell rang, and rang twice again before he opened it.

"Thank you, Mrs. Fiori," Mannering said mildly. "I thought you'd prefer not to talk with the Press present."

Mannering led her to the study. She used a costly perfume, walked with delightful ease, was dressed in a black two-piece suit, in the height of fashion. Her wide-brimmed hat stood out beyond her shoulders.

She didn't look round.

"What did you take?" she asked.

"Nothing. From where?"

"I don't believe you. From my flat."

"Have you missed anything?"

"Not yet," she said, and went to sit down. She was superbly confident; a superb woman, showing no hint of annoyance or exasperation. "I told you as clearly as anyone could that you were asking for trouble, Mr. Mannering. Why didn't you take my advice?"

"Perhaps I like trouble."

"You won't like this kind. What did you find out—apart from what Ethel told you? She's told me all about that."

"Enough to make me want to find out more," said Mannering. "Wait for a minute." He went to the door and Susan wheeled in a tea trolley, smiled and bobbed to Julia, and went out. "Tea?" He began to set out plates and cups and saucers on small tables. "Now if you threatened to take away my afternoon tea you might frighten me."

"You will be frightened if you go on with this."

"Not so frightened as poor Fay. I think she is in the hands of what they call a heartless adventuress, and I don't think it's good for her." Mannering poured out. "Milk and sugar?"

"Thank you. Fay will be all right if you leave her alone, but might not be if you harass her too much."

"Do you travel with knock-out drops in your pocket, or have you a variety of ways for silencing the talkative and the inquisitive?" His hand was steady as he poured out milk. "I'm still worried about Fay. She's nearly a rich young woman, and I should hate to see Jacob's money get into the wrong hands."

"Nearly," Julia said softly. "Why nearly?"

"Probate hasn't been granted yet. And some obscure relative of Jacob may turn up and claim that he wasn't in his right mind when he made that will. As an executor I think I can make sure that it is several months before Fay inherits, and that should give me time to find out all you don't want me to know. You're taking on a lot more than me, Julia. You're taking on the law in its most tedious form. You won't be able to hurry it, any more than you'll be able to stop me from probing. And you've whetted my appetite. I haven't been so hungry for information in years." His eyes laughed at her. "I'm glad you called, it makes you human and tells me that you're also frightened. Have a sandwich."

She took one.

"What will make you forget Fay?"

"I can't forget her. Jacob Bernstein made me an executor of his will, so I have to see the thing through. Don't waste time trying to scare me by threatening to tell the police how much I haven't told them."

"I'm afraid you're a fool," said Julia gently.

"My wife would agree with you."

"And yet I think you've some common sense, and you must know that I'm serious." She leaned back, and he saw that her eyes were a deep blue, almost violet. She looked more lovely now than when she had been at Fay's flat. "Where have you put the *Tear?*"

Mannering almost gave himself away, looked down at his tea and stirred it earnestly, then looked up as if he had just understood what she had said.

"*What's* that?"

"I asked you where you've put the *Tear.*"

"That's hardly funny." His voice grew harsh, he looked at her with sudden, cold hostility. "Your friend the murderer took big risks to find the *Tear;* I'll take bigger ones to get it back.

She said: "He didn't take it because he couldn't find it. You wouldn't let Fay go in. You were there from the time he left until the police arrived, and if the *Tear* had been at the shop they would have found it. Where have you put it?"

"You should use a more reliable burglar."

"He reported immediately that he hadn't been able to find it." Julia Fiori finished her tea and put the cup down, and said softly: "Four people have died because they had possession of the *Tear* but had no right to it. Money doesn't give you, didn't give Jacob Bernstein and doesn't give anyone, the right to own the *Diamond of Tears.* Three men and a woman have died because they thought they could keep it from its rightful owner. Others will try and others will die, *if* they hold on to it. I shouldn't feel safe walking along the street if I were in your position."

"So you've committed all the murders," Mannering said drily.

"I've committed none. I know the history and I know the truth about that diamond. I know that whoever wants the *Tear* will stop at nothing to get it. He'll brush you aside as ruthlessly as he did Jacob Bernstein. Where is it?"

"If I knew, you'd get it over my dead body. I don't." He gave a short, convincingly bitter laugh. "I thought I did, but the thief was smarter than Jacob, and knew his pet hiding-place. I was anxious about it—I have a prospective customer."

"I've told you that money can't buy the *Tear, or* the safety of anyone who owns it."

"You've told me a lot of odd things and I don't believe half of them." He stood with his cup in one hand, saucer in the other, and made every word count. "I shall find the killer of Jacob Bernstein; I shall find the *Tear.* If Fay Goulden wants to keep it I'll make sure that she can, safely. I know the strength of the police and of the other side. I know there are a lot of things I can do that the police can't, but before it's over the police will catch the foul brutes who commit murder for that stone."

Julia Fiori opened her handbag suddenly, and Mannering started back, half expecting her to show a gun—but all she had in her hand was an envelope. "Look at these."

"What are they?"

"True stories about the murder of the other people who owned the *Diamond of Tears*. Read them, and see whether you enjoy your tea afterwards."

He slipped the envelope into his pocket.

"Later. We're at war, Julia. More tea?"

"No. Do you remember telling me that you're a married man?"

"Well?" He spoke more sharply.

"If you don't care for your own safety, think of your wife's." She looked straight into his eyes, which had gone bleak again. "You think you know a great deal, actually you know little. *I* don't want the *Tear*. I should be afraid of it. But I know something about those who do, and how far they'll go to get it. You'll understand more when you've read those reports. They're confidential police reports, the full story was never told in public. Jacob was lucky. He was killed quickly. But they will make you suffer, and not just physically. Mannering, you *must* listen." Her voice was composed, her earnestness touched with desperation. "I've told you that if I had the *Tear* I shouldn't feel safe to walk along the street. Every minute of every day I should be afraid—for myself, my relatives, my friends. I've never been more serious. I'm helping Fay because she needs help badly. I want you to forget the *Tear*—let them have it, and then wash your hands of it, not because I've any regard for you or your wife, but because I'm fond of Fay."

She stood up quickly. Although he wanted to scoff at her he felt on edge. She turned to the door, reached it first, crossed the hall and opened the front door. She didn't speak again until she was on the landing. Then:

"Get rid of the *Tear* to-night. They'll come here and search for it. Let them find it. That's your only hope."

She turned and walked down the stone steps, her footsteps ringing clearly. She did not look back, but Mannering stood by the open door until he heard her go out of the house.

.   .   .   .   .

The telephone bell rang. . . .

"Oh, darling," said Lorna, "I can't get away for several hours yet. I just have to stay here, unless—"

"You stay," said Mannering. "Where are you?"

"At the Richmond Gallery. It's the Exhibition Committee, and it would be unforgivable if I left now."

"You must certainly stay!"

"Has anything happened?"

"Odds and ends, they'll keep until I see you to-night." He wiped his forehead, surprised to find it cold and damp; he hoped his voice didn't betray the effect of Julia Fiori's last words. "I may not be in until late. Chittering is making himself a busy bee. I haven't seen the police for some time, I think they've given me a clean bill."

"How late will you be?"

"Not a minute later than I can help," said Mannering. "I—here's Chittering now. I'll be seeing you."

He rang off, dropped into a chair, and called himself a fool. Because a woman had threatened him with unknown horrors he shouldn't feel like this, but he did. Or was it because of what he already knew about the *Tear*? He touched the envelope in his pocket as Susan came in briskly. "Shall I clear, sir?" He nodded. He lit a cigarette and went across the room to the cocktail cabinet, poured a stiff whisky, sipped and drank.

"I'm crazy!" he told himself.

But he went back to the telephone and dialled Whitehall 1212, and was impatient until Bristow came on the line.

"Hallo, John. Going to confess?"

"Yes. The *Tear* has got under my skin."

"Well, where is it?"

"I'll send you a postcard. Bill, someone who wants the *Tear* badly thinks that I know where it is. I can't give you names, but I've had a nasty jolt."

Bristow said slowly: "Yes, you sound as if you had. What is it?"

"Threats. Against Lorna."

"Perhaps that will teach you not to make a fool of yourself. What kind of threats?"

"Can you put a good man on to watch her? She's at the Richmond Gallery in Bute Street, and in committee for the next hour or so. After that she'll come straight here. I have to be out. I'd prefer not to have this on my mind."

"I've never known you impressed by threats before," said Bristow. "Well, I was going to have your flat watched, anyhow. John, don't get your fingers dirty. I tried to warn you earlier, but you wouldn't take me seriously. You've taken the other people seriously, which is something. This is a foul job."

"Meaning?"

"Come round here one day and I'll show you the unexpurgated reports of what happened to the earlier owners of the *Diamond of Tears*. 'Bye."

.   .   .   .   .

Mannering read the reports of how three men and a woman had died; and as he read he seemed to be withdrawn from this friendly room and friendly city, to be exposed to bleakness and horror which sent a chill along his spine and brought a cold sweat to his forehead. They were written in straightforward language, with no effort to make the flesh creep—and the effect was greater than if he had been reading some vivid narrative of imagined murder.

Each man had died the same way.

Not one had been recognisable afterwards; each had been identified after long investigation by the police. The medical reports, brief and revealing, told what had happened to them before death; and the quiet room seemed filled with dark shadows.

He turned to the story of the woman's death—and started back, dropping the papers, sheering away from them as if the horror had come into the room. For fastened to the last story was a photograph of what had once been a woman; mutilated, despoiled. He steeled himself to pick up the papers again, to turn the photograph over and to read of what had been done to a wealthy woman of renowned beauty and intelligence—and then he made himself study the photograph.

Darkness fell slowly, yet it was a long time before he stretched out a hand and switched on the light—and as he touched the switch the telephone bell rang. He let it ring and jar through his head, then took off the receiver and said harshly:

"Who is that?"

"I'm glad you've read them," said Julia Fiori. "Now will you believe me when I tell you you must give up the *Tear?*"

CHAPTER X

THE FAT MAN

He could fetch the *Tear* from the post office, leave it in some obvious place, go out and keep both Susan and Lorna away from the flat until the thieves had been and gone. Or he could tell Bristow what he had done, and leave a note to tell the thieves that for the *Diamond of Tears* they must apply to Scotland Yard.

Or he could go on as he had started.

The first method would remove all fears, real and imagined; and betray the memory of Jacob Bernstein. The second might well anger the thieves, make them suspect that he still had the jewel. Even if they believed him they might call off the hunt until Fay inherited everything, including the *Tear*, then strike again.

That amazed him most; his absolute conviction that at all costs they would get the *Tear*. He might save himself, yet leave Fay a potential victim of a great horror.

Only fear would allow him even to consider that.

Questions crowded into his mind.

Why had Julia kept five imitation *Tears* in her jewel-drawer? Why had she kept a note of Bernstein's will? How had he obtained it? Would he be wise to see Bristow again, tell him everything, leave him to tackle the job? Would it really help Fay or anyone if he himself persisted? There must be a limit to pride, was there really anything stronger than pride tormenting him, urging him to carry on?

Better see Bristow, now, while the mood was on him. He needed to conjure up only two pictures in his mind's eye; Lorna, as she was, and the woman as she appeared in that photograph.

He started at a tap on the door.

"Yes?"

"I'm just going, sir, is there anything else you want?" Fair hair, confined in a tiny hat above a freckled face, appeared at the door.

"No thanks. Have a good time." It was Susan's evening off-duty.

"Oh, I *will*. I'm going to a dance," said Susan. The front door slammed. The only sounds came from outside, a hum of traffic, the mournful hoot of a tug on the river. He stood at the window, looking out over the lighted streets on both sides of the Thames, his resolve weakening even now. But for Lorna he would take a chance. While he had the *Tear,* and while the others had a chance to get it from him, he could draw their fire and perhaps lure them into a mistake they wouldn't make with Bristow.

He put on his hat and coat, slapped his gloves against his thigh, and went out, pulling the door behind him, shutting out the light.

Two figures loomed out of the darkness; one in front, one behind him. He saw the first, drew back, felt his hat tipped over his eyes and a blow smash on the back of his head. He was unconscious before he hit the ground.

.   .   .   .   .

There was too much light. It hurt his eyes, no matter how tightly he kept them closed, and the pain spread from his eyes to the back of his head, his head and shoulders seemed to be on fire. He heard a strange grunting, groaning sound, which stopped abruptly as he realised he was making it himself. The light was like fire, too—the fire of lightning, white and brilliant but there all the time; it didn't fade.

It hadn't come suddenly, but slowly and with increasing effect, like the remorseless pressure of a tightening vice. He heard the drumming of the blood in his ears. He could think of nothing else, gave no thought to where he was or how he had got there, or to what had happened before. There was no past; only the agonising present and a menacing future.

Then other sounds came; a muttering, as of voices. They seemed far away. There was a shadow over his eyes, which gave him slight relief. It disappeared, and the light blazed mercilessly down on him. The voices drew nearer, as if someone were talking to him.

A new pain streaked through his head; he knew that fingers were touching and probing. That stopped, and he realised that he was gasping with mingled pain and relief. He could not distinguish the words, but knew that the speaker was close to him. Someone touched his arm, pulled up his sleeve until it tightened about his forearm and the blood pumped vigorously through the veins, pain in another place. He felt a sharp prick in his forearm and a lingering pressure which made his arm swell until the shirt and coat sleeve were like iron bands round it. He had been given an injection.

The light went out; blessed darkness came.

Gradually the pain dulled. He could move and feel ordinary things, and even begin to think. He didn't think far back yet; only about the men who had talked, the injection and the relief from the glaring light. Slowly he began to wonder where he was and what had happened to him. Then he remembered Julia Fiori, and a flood of other recollections came. The most vivid was a picture of what had once been a woman, and it struck a new note of horror. It soon faded. He felt relaxed and free from pain and full of a new confidence, as if he knew that all would be well.

He moved his hands and legs.

He was lying flat, on something soft; a bed, of course. He could touch the sides without moving his hands far, so it was a single bed. He was warm, beneath an eiderdown. He pushed it back. His feet were cold, he couldn't understand that for a while, but at last it dawned on him that his shoes were off and his feet weren't covered; he drew them up beneath the warmth of the eiderdown. He was quite comfortable now, and drowsy—but it was the drowsiness before full wakefulness, not of sleep.

He heard music, a waltz played some distance away, perhaps from a radio. Footsteps drew near but passed the door which he could not see.

He sat up, slowly, expecting pain to surge through his head, but although there was stiffness there was no actual pain. He groped in his pocket for his lighter, and found it; a tiny flame flickered, showing the bed, a table and a lamp by it. He let the flame go out, groped for the lamp and found the switch. He closed his eyes against the light, but whatever they had given him had driven all pain away.

This was a small room.

The bed was in a corner, opposite a white-painted door. Alongside the head of the bed, in front of a curtained window, was a small walnut dressing-table, against another wall was a wardrobe; it might be a bedroom in any suburban house, cheaply furnished but with no little taste. There was a woolly fringe on the shade of the lamp, and by the lamp his cigarette-case, an ashtray and a glass of water. He took the glass and put it to his lips, then hesitated; was it safe to drink this? Drink up! There was no need for his captors to drug the water, they could do what they liked with him in his present condition. He drank deeply.

Soon, with a cigarette between his lips and leaning back on his pillows, he began to think more naturally. The sense of dread was missing, although he felt vaguely that it should still be with him. He caught a glimpse of his face in a side mirror of the dressing-table, leaned forward to get a better view. He looked pale, but saw neither bandage nor adhesive plaster. What had caused the pain? Where had that powerful light come from? He glanced up and saw the pale cylinder of fluorescent lighting in the ceiling; that explained it.

He laughed.

There wasn't anything to laugh about. He was a prisoner, and his captors meant business. They wanted the *Tear*—and for a while he had forgotten it. Ought he to wish that he had never seen it? Then the door opened and a fat man came in.

.   .   .   .   .

The newcomer wasn't simply fat, he was huge, but there was nothing gross or flabby about him. He was well-dressed, his pale face was impressive and handsome. He had big eyes with drooping lids. His black hair was curly and glistened in that poor light. He closed the door and crossed the room quietly, almost as if he were walking on tip-toe. He had a small cupid's bow of a mouth, red as if with lipstick. He stood by the bed looking down at Mannering.

Mannering said : "Good evening."

"Good evening. How are you?" It was a smooth, cultured voice, with no trace of accent.

"Counting my blessings," Mannering said.

"You have some to count?"

"I'm alive."

"Yes, you are alive." The man ought to smile, but didn't. "It is a good thing to be alive. Do you know me?"

"No."

"I hope that is true," said the fat man. "I do not want more difficulties. I come to talk to you." His phrasing was too precise, it was strange that he had no accent. He drew up a small chair and overlapped the sides when he sat down. He placed his hands on his knees; they were small, pale hands, and on the left little finger was a huge signet ring; he wore no other jewellery, and was dressed in excellent style. "This diamond, the *Tear*. You have it?"

"No."

"I do not want you to lie to me."

Mannering felt as if part of his mind were asleep; that there were things he had said in the past that he ought to repeat now, but he couldn't be sure that he remembered everything; in particular there was something he had told Julia Fiori—ah! He remembered and felt easier.

"You understand," the fat man said. "It will help you to tell me the truth "

"I haven't got the *Diamond of Tears*. It was stolen from Bernstein's shop before I got there."

"That is what you said before, but I do not believe you," said the fat man. "Tell me what happened when you reached the shop, why you went there—everything, please."

He sat like Buddha in modern clothes while Mannering told him; and in the telling became much more certain of himself. He described his meeting with the man who had come from Bernstein's, described how he had searched the shop before the police had arrived, looking for the *Tear*. He even talked of a book in which he thought it had been hidden, but said that the hiding-place was empty. He believed he spoke with conviction, but as he went on he became more and more uneasy beneath the steady scrutiny of those big eyes.

When he finished, the man asked :

"And this man whom you met at the door, you saw him?"

"Not clearly. It was dark, and he had a handkerchief over his face."

"You would recognise him again?"

"No. I remember his size and build, that's all."

"Perhaps it is enough," said the fat man. He leaned towards the dressing-table and touched a bell-push which Mannering hadn't noticed. There was no sound, but the door opened and a man came in. The first glimpse made Mannering start back, for it was almost as if he were reliving the past. The man had a Homburg hat, pulled low over his eyes, was stocky and broad,

and had a white handkerchief over the lower part of his red face.
He came in quickly and closed the door, approached aggressive-
ly—and he might easily be the man who had come out of Jacob's
shop.

It was the man he had followed from Fay's flat.

The fat man said : "You have seen this man before?"

"It could be the murderer."

"You are not sure?"

"I can't be sure."

"At least that is the truth." The fat man turned to the other
and contemplated him from beneath his lashes, and now Mannering saw that the blunt-fingered hands of the masked man
were trembling. Yes, the fat man's gaze could be frightening.
Mannering's own nerves were dulled with the drug, his in-
difference artificial. He would be frightened of the fat man if his
senses weren't dulled. He did not question the danger and the
horror and the capacity to frighten of this man.

"Mannering tells me again the *Tear* was not there when he
arrived."

"It must have been !"

"Tell me again, why is that so?"

"I called Bernstein up an hour before. He said he had the *Tear*
there. So it must have been there. I searched everywhere and
couldn't find it. Then Mannering arrived and I had to run. Who
else *could* have found it?"

The fat man said : "One of you is lying."

"It's Mannering !"

"Yes, perhaps it is Mannering, but I am not sure. I am not sure
whether you can be trusted. The *Tear* is a great temptation and
you have always been a greedy man. Go and wait for me."

"I tell you—"

"Go and wait."

The other turned and, still shivering, went out of the room.
The door closed silently behind him. There was still no vestige
of any expression on the big face.

"It is a bad thing to lie to me, Mannering. You understand, I
must obtain the *Tear*. I will do anything to obtain it. I will not
be harassed by the greed of little men or the persistence of men
like you. Already you have been a great nuisance. That must not
be allowed to continue, so you will stay with me until everything is finished. If you have not the *Tear*, you will not suffer. If

you have—" He shrugged. "You will tell me. It is easy to make men talk. You understand me?"

Mannering said slowly : "Yes."

"Remember the photograph," the fat man said, and stood up with unexpected grace of movement. At the door he looked back. "Do not forget that photograph, Mannering, or that I must have the *Tear*. It is not important what you consider right. It would have been better had you not gone to that shop, because then Fay would have inherited all that Bernstein left, including the *Tear*, and all would have been well. I can afford to wait. But now the diamond is stolen and I must find it again. Again," he repeated, and the word was like a sigh.

He went out. From the passage he called : "You will listen. In a little while you will understand what I mean."

The door closed.

Mannering sat looking at it, and felt as he had done when Julia Fiori had left his flat. Cold, frightened. The effect of the drug was working off. There was a dull pain at the back of his head and an ache across his eyes.

"You will listen. In a little while you will understand what I mean."

What had the fat man meant? Who was he? A name sprang to mind immediately—Fiori. If you saw him and Julia together you would have to agree that they shared something more than looks and a good presence; they shared self-confidence. This man had threatened unnamable things so quetly. He felt able to talk in such a way, to kidnap a man from his own doorstep, to bring him safely here and to behave as if he could keep him prisoner for as long as he wished. He knew exactly what he wanted and did not doubt that he would get it. He treated the law as if it did not exist.

Was he Fiori?

A sound broke the quiet of the house; a cry, not far away. It plucked at Mannering's nerves, made him sit up abruptly—and then it came again, longer, high-pitched, a cry of pain and fear.

"You will listen," the fat man had said. "In a little while you will understand."

A third scream, wild and uncontrolled, brought sweat to Mannering's forehead and a chill to his spine—and as he got out of bed more screams came and merged with one another in a continuous shriek of agony.

CHAPTER XI

TORMENT

THE door was locked; and the screams went on. They came from the next room, now high pitched and shuddering, now little more than moans; soon there was only the moaning, followed by a steady voice which might be the fat man's. Mannering could not hear the words but guessed that Bernstein's killer was being questioned with the cold-blooded cruelty that the secret police reports had revealed in the affair of the *Diamond of Tears*.

Then Mannering distinguished shrill words.

"*No!*" A murmur of questions followed. "*It wasn't there.*" Another murmur. "*I didn't take it!*" Silence, and then a cry of dread: "*No, don't do it again, don't do it again! I didn't take the stone!*"

The man was suffering like this because Mannering had lied; even the fact that he had killed Bernstein could not justify that. Mannering could hear his sobbing, and tensed himself to withstand more screaming; none came. Slowly he relaxed—and gradually the obvious dawned in his mind so obvious that he hadn't given it a thought.

He must get away.

He turned swiftly to the window, pulled aside the curtains— and faced green-panelled steel shutters. The rounded heads of the rivets stood out all round, and there was no keyhole; they must be electrically controlled. He backed away slowly and turned to the door.

There was a lock on the door.

He thrust his hand into his pocket to get his knife, but it wasn't there. Everything else was; keys, silver and copper, the oddments he always carried; he went through his other pockets quickly, but the knife wasn't anywhere.

He sat heavily on the foot of the bed. Why couldn't he *think?*

Slowly he bent down and put on his shoes, forcing himself not to fumble with the laces. He would get nowhere if he went on like this. He was too susceptible to the atmosphere, the mental torment. But he couldn't argue with physical facts and his hands were unsteady, his nerves aquiver. He stood up and went to the dressing-table, opened the drawers, found a nail file but nothing else remotely like a tool.

There were some reels of cotton; red, white, green—many colours. You could use cotton in more ways than one.

He heard a footstep, shut the drawer and spun round, his right hand in his pocket, holding his cigarette-case. That was the only thing he had for a weapon, except the chair on which the fat man had sat. He leaned forward and held the chair top, ready to raise it as a club—and all the time he argued with himself. You couldn't defeat the fat man by blunderbus methods, you had to match his cunning. First pain, then the drug had sapped what cunning he had, reduced him to elemental thought of brute force and—

The door opened.

Mannering swung the chair, but did not need to use it. A man was pushed into the room, a sobbing wreck of a man. The Homburg hat, still perched on his head, supplied an added touch of horror. His eyes were bloodshot, two burns showed livid on his cheeks, blood dripped from the top of one of his fingers as he thrust out his hand to save himself from falling.

The fat man said from the door: "Look after him, Mannering."

Then the door closed.

.　　.　　.　　.　　.

You had to match cunning by cunning.

The tortured man lay on the bed, his eyes wide open as he stared towards the ceiling.

Mannering had found a salve in the dressing-table, applied it to the burns and to the little finger, the end of which had been crushed and the bone probably broken. He had bandaged that with his handkerchief, there was little else he could do, the man must see a doctor to have that finger put right. Doctor! Now the man lay sullen and resentful, smoking one of Mannering's cigarettes.

You took a deep breath and accepted facts as they were; this devilry was part of the fat man's technique and you couldn't stop it by ordinary means. You just accepted the position, then, and tried to deal with it. If you concentrated on what was likely to happen when the door opened again, you would only be in a state of funk and nerves. So you thought further ahead, looking at the mystery from the beginning. You planned what you would do when you were away from here, not whether you would ever get away—and you wondered how you could take advantage of this situation.

You knew what the fat man was planning.

Mannering hitched his chair nearer the bed and the bloodshot eyes turned towards him.

"Feeling any better?"

"I feel like hell."

"You've a nice employer."

"I'd like to smash his face in."

"Worked for him for long?"

"Too long."

"Why don't you get out of it?"

"Have you ever tried to get out of a padded cell? That's what this is—a padded cell. You *can't* get away from him."

"Is he Fiori?"

"Supposing he is?" A glint shone in the man's eyes, as if he realised that he was talking too freely. "You'll get yours. If it wasn't for you I wouldn't have had this."

"What makes you so sure I took the *Tear*?"

"*I* didn't."

"Someone else could have taken it. Bernstein might have found a specially safe hiding-place for it. The police might be foxing, and have it at the Yard. I told Fiori the truth. I didn't expect him to work on you like this, and there was nothing I could have done about it if I'd known. Why does he want the *Tear*?"

"He's crazy about that diamond. It isn't the first time he's tried to get it. He'll do anything for it but he doesn't make us take risks for anything else, he's smart most of the time. The *Tear* makes a fool out of him."

Mannering said: "If I were in your shoes I wouldn't get a laugh out of anyone."

The man snapped: "Shut your trap!" He stared at the wall, his uninjured hand clenching, as if with sudden pain. The cigarette was nearly finished and burning close to his lips.

"Why did you kill Bernstein?"

"I had to kill him."

"There's just one thing that might save you from a life sentence," said Mannering. "Well, two things. Fiori might kill you first. The other—" He broke off. "Another cigarette?"

The man pushed out his lips. Mannering took the stub away, lit him another and stuck it into his mouth; he didn't grunt thanks. Mannering sat back and looked at the wall, then the door, wondering how long he would be left here, whether it was possible that Fiori could listen to their conversation. There were no holes in the wall, nothing to indicate a speaking tube or a microphone. Even if one were hidden somewhere it wouldn't help much to find it. He closed his eyes, and blotted out ugly thoughts, until the man on the bed said harshly :

"What's the other way?"

"Other way to what?"

"Don't stall! You reckon the busies will get me, that I haven't a chance of dodging them except—"

"Oh, that. Queen's evidence. Ever heard of it? You did a foul job with Bernstein, but maybe you were acting under pressure from someone else—from Fiori. That wouldn't save you, but if you tell the police all you know about Fiori, it would go a long way towards helping you."

"I'm not a squeaker."

"I didn't think you were so fond of Fiori."

"He'd never let the police get me."

"He's not so clever as all that. You could have gone to see Bristow at the Yard this morning, instead of picking up that stuff at Fay Goulden's flat and taking it to Benoni."

He said "Benoni" carelessly; the glitter in the other's eyes, the tensing of the man's body, rewarded him. They looked at each other, intent, hostile, before the man on the bed growled :

"What do you know about Benoni?"

"That he was paid a hundred pounds for the job, that he's got a girl in trouble, and the girl lives at Woking, or somewhere in Surrey. Also, that he's a frightened little rat who would squeal if the police got him. He would give you away, wouldn't he? Maybe he has by now. What did you do with the stuff you took from Bernstein?"

"To hell with you !"

The man turned his head again, but Mannering did not think he would keep quiet for long.

He was sitting here talking calmly to a man who had committed murder; a man who would hang and for whom he felt no pity at all—but one who might save him. How much time was there?

The man said abruptly: "I took it to Fay's flat."

"Why not to the café?"

"I took it to the flat and left it. Then I was told to pick it up and give it to Benoni. That's how Fiori covered his own tracks. I didn't want him to use me this morning, but you can't argue with Fiori."

There were two things wrong with that reasoning. Fiori hadn't covered his own tracks by having the jewels delivered to the café. And he invited trouble by sending the killer as a messenger.

"Why didn't you hide?"

"He wanted to see if the cops had me covered."

"Had they?"

"Not on your life."

"What is Fay worried about?" Mannering asked.

"You'd be worried if you had to work for Fiori."

"Does she know him?"

"Sure she knows him."

"Do you know her boy friend, Kenneth?"

"That dude!" The man laughed. "He couldn't see trouble if you stuck it on the end of his nose. He doesn't know she's mixed up in anything, doesn't know she can hardly move out of doors without being frightened. I'd like to wring his neck!"

"Who is he?"

"She goes around with him. I can't tell you anything else. And I don't have to tell you anything. It won't do you any good anyway. When Fiori gets a man he doesn't let him go. You've got in his way, see? He'll rub you out when he's finished with you. And you'd better tell him where to find the *Tear;* if you don't your own wife wouldn't recognise you afterwards."

Mannering was getting on, but not fast enough, nothing like fast enough; Fiori wouldn't leave him here for ever. More haste, less speed.

"Fiori has a lot coming to him that he doesn't expect," he said. "Do you know his wife?"

"Maybe I do, maybe I don't." The man was steadier, talking had done him good. Mannering went over everything that had

been said, keeping his thoughts off the moment when that door
would open again.

"Why did he send you to Bernstein?"

"I knew the shyster."

"So you're in the trade?"

"I've been in the trade all my life." The man caught his
breath. "I started off on the level and then got mixed up with a
mob, and here I am."

"Wasn't Bernstein on the level?"

The man turned and looked at him, hatred in his eyes. He
looked as if he were trying to burn Mannering up; yet his hatred
wasn't for Mannering.

He rasped : "No Jew is on the level."

"I thought Bernstein was."

"So did a lot of people."

"Did he fence for you?"

The man said reluctantly : "No, he didn't buy any hot stuff.
I've got a good connection in the trade, I'm well represented in
New York. Bernstein was too fly to buy hot stuff, but no Jew's on
the level. I wouldn't trust one as far as I could see him. I hate
the whole ruddy race."

You couldn't argue with a man who thought and felt like
that; against prejudice and hatred which had been instilled into
him over the years; against a man who was a natural Jew baiter,
who could see no good in any one of them and who had no
evidence that Bernstein had been crooked, just assumed that he
was. This hadn't anything much to do with the main job, but it
had an important bearing. Fiori had wanted Bernstein dead, and
sent along a man who would be glad to kill him just because of
Bernstein's race. You didn't argue with this man for whom you
had no pity—only loathing.

Mannering said : "Do you know where we are?"

"Supposing I do?"

"I'd like to get out."

The man said harshly : "So you'd like to get out ! You invited
yourself in, now you'll stay. Fiori will never let you get
away."

"Where are we?"

"We're not at the café, if that's what you think. We're at the
other joint."

"West End?"

"Yes, it's in the West End. Right now people are dancing over our heads, having a hell of a good time, and making money for Fiori. If he wasn't crazy over the *Tear* he'd be sitting pretty. He's in nearly all the rackets, but not many people know about it, because he's clever. He's so clever he'll get himself slugged one of these days."

Mannering asked: "How's your face?"

"It's still burning like hell."

The burns were inflamed and the angry red area seemed to be spreading. Mannering got up and applied a little more of the salve.

"Is there a way out of this room?" he asked.

"There's the door."

"Have you got a knife?"

"If I had a hundred knives you wouldn't be able to get out of that door; Fiori knows what he's doing. He keeps all of his friends here. And next door he gives them the works. That's where he worked on me. I've heard of the cell, I hadn't seen it before to-night, and—" The man broke off and closed his eyes. "I've heard screaming coming from it. They all came here—all four of them. The woman was the worst. I shall never forget—"

He broke off again.

Mannering said: "No one who's ever been in that cell has lived for long, have they?"

There was no answer.

"If I can get out, you can get out."

"You haven't a chance, Mannering, you can save your breath."

You just had to face facts. They might shriek against reason; it might be impossible to believe that there was such a man as Fiori, that he had committed his crimes in the cell next to this room. But the secret reports and the photograph bore it all out.

"What about that knife?"

The man turned over. "It's in my pocket. I can't get my hand in." So the knife was in his right pocket. Mannering slipped his hand inside and felt the knife, larger than an ordinary pocket knife. He drew it out and examined it, opening every blade. His own knife was much better, but there was a long button-hook attached—and it wasn't intended just for doing up buttons, no burglar's kit was complete without one. He weighed the knife in his hand.

"What's your name?"

The man said: "I'm Harry Green. What the hell?" Green couldn't keep his gaze away from Mannering and the knife as Mannering turned to the dressing-table and opened the drawer, took out the reels of cotton and selected a red one. His eyes widened. "Do you know *that* trick?"

"You can't catch crooks without knowing how they work." Mannering went to the door, bent down and peered into the tiny lock. If he were right about its construction he could get it open—and suddenly he was in a fever of impatience, angry with himself for having waited so long, for wasting time in talking. Fiori surely wouldn't leave him much longer, he'd need time for this. He pulled at the end of the cotton, made a little ball of it between his fingers, and pushed it into the keyhole with the hook. Then he poked at it, pressing tightly, unreeled more cotton and squeezed it in. He was conscious of Green's tense gaze, could guess Green's thoughts: this wasn't the first time he had tackled a lock in this way. He took the nail file now. The cotton sped through his fingers and was packed tightly into the lock round the hook blade, but before it was half full the reel was empty.

Mannering started on another; blue.

The second reel was empty before the lock was jammed tightly with the cotton, and the knife jutted out. He drew back. His forehead was filmed with sweat and he realised that his mouth was open, he was breathing through it. His fingers and wrists ached, but he hadn't been aware of any ache before.

Green said hoarsely:

"It might work."

The bed creaked as he got up.

Mannering rubbed his right wrist slowly as Green drew near him, looked round, made sure that no violence threatened; but Green did not appear to have thought of violence. His breath came in short, wheezy gasps, his burning cheeks made him look a sick man.

"Mannering—"

"Well?"

"If we get out I want a break!"

"If we get out I've more to worry about than holding you." Mannering went forward, gripped the knife handle, poised himself, and then began to turn. It wasn't easy, the cotton didn't seem to yield. If the trick worked it would get round the barrel of the lock and gradually force it backwards. The cotton might be too tight, you often had to try half a dozen times. His wrist ached with the strain, he felt Green's breath on the back of his neck.

The knife was turning slightly.

He grunted, held it in position with his left hand, rested his right.

"Let me have a go," Green hissed.

"I'll manage." Mannering began afresh, straining every muscle, grunting with the effort, feeling pains shooting up his arm to the shoulder, and pain came again at the back of his head. But he felt the hook turning, twisted harder, twisted until his wrist felt as if it were breaking. He tried the handle and pulled; the door didn't budge. He rested again, holding the handle tightly with his left hand, afraid that it would slip back.

"Don't waste time!" Green muttered. "Fiori might—"

Mannering said: "That would be our bad luck." He gripped the knife with his right hand again, felt the hooked blade move a little more freely, strained himself for a final turn, and thought he heard a muffled click. Green exclaimed aloud, snatched at the handle and pulled.

There was light in the passage outside.

CHAPTER XII

NIGHT CLUB

GREEN said : "We've made it !"

"We've started to make it, there's a long way to go. What floor are we on?"

"Basement." Green stood in the middle of the passage and looked left; several doors opened from the passage. The ceiling was high, the walls papered expensively in yellow, and a thick brown carpet stretched from wall to wall. Mannering glanced right; only one door was in that direction, standing ajar. He moved towards it, and Green muttered :

"Don't waste time !"

Mannering said : "This is going to be rough on you." He jabbed his clenched right fist at Green's chin, snapped the man's teeth together, and struck again. Green's eyes rolled as he sagged backwards. Mannering stopped him from falling, supported him and dragged him along the passage to the door on the right. He kicked the door open. The passage light shone on a small, bare room, with whitewashed walls, a chair, a small table. On a table was a large crucible, which glowed red even now. It was electrically heated, and the branding iron which stood on top of it had been made red hot in there before Green had been burned.

There was a key in the lock.

Mannering came out, closed and locked the door, then walked cautiously along the passage. There was a faint sound of music to which people were dancing, if Green had told the truth. He didn't worry much about Green. If he got out the police would soon raid this place; they would have Green free before he could come to more harm from Fiori.

If he got out.

He paused by the first door, tried the handle and found the door unlocked. He switched on the light in a small office, severely modern but untidy. Papers were strewn over the desk, some had fallen on to the floor, drawers had been left open, and he could see right into a continuation wall safe.

His heart started to hammer against his ribs as he went out, passing the next rooms. No light shone beneath the doors. There was a blank wall at the end of the passage, and he found himself at the foot of a short staircase which led up to a closed door; at the head of the stairs a single electric light burned dimly. He should have made sure that no one could come from behind him. He raced back. Both rooms were empty; one was a bedroom, the other a small lounge, where a table was set for dinner for two, and a bottle of champagne stood in a silvered ice bucket.

Fiori *had* flown.

Mannering reached the door at the head of the stairs, and tried the handle. The shock of disappointment at finding it locked went through him like a physical pain. He stood back, sick and giddy, his head was swimming; the tension of hope had kept him going. He leaned against the wall, staring at the door. The small key-hole was exactly like that in the bedroom; he could get this open, but it would take as long again, perhaps longer— and he wouldn't be able to pull that button hook out easily. He licked his lips, felt physical nausea—and then saw the handle of the door move.

It turned slowly.

He gritted his teeth against the swimming pain in his head and stepped behind the door as it opened. A man said : "Get a move on!" and another grunted. Then Benoni stepped through, glanced neither right nor left but hurried down the stairs. Behind him came another man, tall, bulky, with a trilby hat pulled over his left eye, keys in his right hand. He stepped towards the stairs, then glanced round and saw Mannering.

He cried : *"Ben!"*

Mannering sprang at him, smashed a right to his nose, brought up his knee and drove into his stomach. The keys fell. Benoni swung on his heel at the foot of the stairs. Mannering caught a glimpse of him while pushing the big man sideways. He grabbed the keys, then jumped through the doorway. He heard the sharp report of a shot, heard a bullet strike the ceiling, felt tiny pieces of plaster fall on to his head.

He slammed the door.

Ahead stretched a wide empty passage, more elaborately decorated, with easy chairs and sofas by the walls. The sound of music became much louder. A heavy thud shook the door as he hurried. The passage widened into a hallway, swing doors led to a foyer where half a dozen people in evening dress stood staring towards him; one woman in scarlet had her hand up to her mouth, as if to stifle a scream. A short man with a completely bald head pushed open a door and strode forward importantly. Beneath his importance there was fear, which made his voice shrill.

"What are you doing here?"

More heavy thudding shook the door behind Mannering.

"Get the police!" he said urgently.

"Police!" echoed a young man who was pushing open the swing doors. "What's up?"

"Get them." Mannering turned and ran after the little man, who had reached the door and had a set of keys in his right hand. Before he could insert a key Mannering took his shoulder and swung him round. "They can stay where they are," he said.

"You've no right—"

"Fiori isn't your boss any more," said Mannering, "The police will soon be here. If you're smart you'll know when to change sides." He looked at the door. Any moment Benoni would shoot at the lock, to force it. Mannering pushed the important little man in front of him as several men in evening dress came hurrying. Among them was a tall, fair-haired youngster.

Mannering said: "Careful. They'll try to shoot their way out."

The muffled report of a shot came from the door; then two more. The fair youth rushed past Mannering, grabbed an easy chair and wheeled it swiftly towards the door. Three more shots were fired in quick succession. The door shuddered so the youngster pushed the chair to block the path. Others went to help him. The fear in the eyes of the fussy little man increased.

"This is outrageous. Outrageous!"

"Tell the police all about it," Mannering said.

His head was beating like a trip-hammer. The nausea in his stomach came from hunger. Pretty, well-dressed women eyed him askance, elderly men came up—and then a welcome figure appeared. He was welcome because he was Chittering; wonderful because he was spruce in evening dress. He pushed through the crowd by the swing doors, reached Mannering and said:

"So you found him, too?"

"Fiori? Yes, but—"

"Fiddle on Fiori, I mean Fay's boy friend. Our Kenneth."

"Is *he* here?"

"And I thought you were good! He's the fair-haired Apollo running around like a lost duck because his Fay hasn't kept an appointment."

"Where is she?"

"I came here to meet her, too. She had a date with Kenneth, telephoned to put it off an hour and said she would meet him here."

"Where are we?"

Chittering put his head on one side. "You're certainly not yourself. This is the Hula Club. The one night club in London with a blameless past and pure present, John, John, what's happened to you? You ought to recognise the Hula from the top, middle and bottom, and—but if you don't know where you are, how did you get here?"

Mannering said: "I rubbed Aladdin's lamp. Chitty, call Bristow, have him send men to Fay's flat at once—Fiori might take her away. And tell him that Green, one of the three men behind that door—the one with the burned face—is Bernstein's murderer. Look after this little man, he might try to run."

Chittering gasped: "Is that *all*?"

"It'll do." Mannering hurried through the swing doors and into the foyer and upstairs. Several people called out to him; he smiled vaguely, pushed his way to the head of the stairs and hurried down. He wanted to get to Toni Fiori's café quickly. A cab pulled up as he reached the front door, depositing a young couple who held hands even as they got out. Mannering got in, said: "Wine Street," and leaned back, closing his eyes.

With immediate tension over, pain surged through his head again; it was tender against the back of the cab. He sat forward, trying to think. Fiori was on the run—why? Fiori probably wouldn't go without Fay; if he had to go into hiding he would want to take Fay with him—and, presumably, his wife. That was guessing, one guess was as good as another.

"What number?" asked the cabby.

"Forty-seven, I think—Toni's Café."

"Oh, Toni Fiori's." The man made it sound as familiar as Buckingham Palace. "Nearly there." They crawled along a few yards, and a lighted window sign showed in the gloom of the narrow street: "Toni Fiori for Good Food." Mannering jumped out, said, "Wait," and then as an afterthought: "If I'm not out in a quarter of an hour, fetch the police."

From the outside the café seemed a squalid, dirty coffee shop, where one would expect to find a quick-lunch counter, gleaming tea and coffee urns, probably vulgar and appalling murals. Inside, it was small but neat and comfortable; little alcoves were built round the walls, a waiter in evening dress came up and bowed, ignoring Mannering's dishevelled appearance.

"Good evening, sah."

"I want to see Toni Fiori."

"Yes, sah, Mr. Fiori is here," said the waiter. "You will wait, please." A dozen couples, sitting in the alcoves, looked at Mannering curiously. On each table was a bottle of wine; at two, bottles of champagne. Three other waiters stood about, methylated lamps glowed at two corners, a chef wearing a tall white hat stood at a covered trolley near a doorway at the far end of the room. The waiter who had spoken to Mannering didn't go to the doorway but towards a flight of stairs; Mannering followed him. There was an appetising smell, making him feel more hungry than ever.

They reached a small landing where there were three doors, all of them closed. One was marked "Ladies," the other "Gentlemen," and the third: "Toni Fiori." The waiter went forward to tap on the third door. Mannering held his arm and said: "You needn't announce me." The waiter didn't protest now, and that was remarkable. Mannering opened the door.

This was a small sitting-room, a pleasant room, with a coal fire; in a corner a radiogram was playing soft chamber music. The only occupant was a man who sat in an easy chair with the *London Evening News* open on his lap, a cigar in his mouth, an expression of surprise which could not quite hide his contentment on his round, rosy face.

"Ze gentleman to see you," said the waiter.

Toni Fiori said: "So," and made an elephantine job of getting to his feet. He was fat; flabby; frowning when he saw Mannering's condition. He wasn't Fiori of the Hula Club.

. . . . .

Toni Fiori was not so tall as Mannering and had to look up at him. His frown had changed to an indulgent smile, as if he were telling himself that he must humour this visitor. The music came faintly, as from a long way off, reminding Mannering of the bedroom he had recently left. The room was warm—and a bottle of cognac stood on the table by Toni's side.

"Good evening, sir, you are good to call." Toni's English was good but with a marked accent.

Mannering felt his head swim, and put out a hand to steady himself. Toni gave a little popping exclamation, gripped his arm, helped him to sit down in the big armchair. He turned to the table, and poured out a little cognac.

"A little drink, please. It is verra good." He held the glass under Mannering's nose. The bouquet was stimulating, and Mannering sipped, "I am Toni Fiori, I have not the pleasure of knowing your name, signor."

"Mannering. John Mannering."

"And I can help—" began Toni, only to stop abruptly to send a startled glance over Mannering's head to the waiter. Then he turned and picked up the newspaper, flattened it out, looked at the front page and then at Mannering. He breathed: " *This* Mannering?"

Mannering thought: "Chittering will do what he can for Fay. I'm beat." He stretched his legs. "That's right. Is your brother the owner of the Hula Club?"

"That is so, signor. My brother Enrico, and it is a fine club, the best in London. Always we say: For the best dancing, Enrico: for the best food, Toni." He bowed—and shot another startled, perhaps warning glance over his shoulder at the waiter. "You expect to find Enrico here, perhaps?"

"I did."

"It is not often Enrico visits me. He is so rich, so important, I am poor. But there is a difference. *I* am happy. Is there a way I can help you, Mr Mannering? It will not be to find Enrico, we do not live the same lives or go to the same places. Certainly we do not. I can help—yes?"

"I'm hungry."

"You are hungry," echoed Toni, and threw up his hands. "It is a good place to come when you are hungry, signor. What would you like?"

"I leave it to you."

Fiori backed away and spoke in an undertone to the waiter, who hurried off.

"Signor, if you are not too hungry perhaps you will wash," said Toni.

Mannering allowed himself to be led into a bedroom, leading off which was a small bathroom; Mannering saw himself in the mirror—and laughed while Toni stood gravely behind him Mannering washed his hands, the first washing turned the water almost black. How had he got so dirty? His hair was dishevelled, there were streaks of dust on his cheeks, and there was also a scratch; he didn't remember getting his face scratched. He washed three times, towelled gingerly because his head was tender, and then gently combed his hair. Toni watched with bright eyes.

In the living-room a table was laid, cutlery and damask glistened, a bottle of Chianti in its little basket lay waiting; a dish of spaghetti arrived. As Mannering began to eat, he heard voices downstairs, voices raised excitedly.

"Everything happens at once," he said.

"Always it is the same. You will please excuse me." Toni went out, and as the door opened the voices became louder. One was that of a waiter, the other a deep, heavy voice, as English as London itself. Then Toni joined in—and suddenly Mannering remembered what he had told the taxi driver, and knew what was happening downstairs. He stood up as Toni came hurrying in, an indignant and flushed Toni.

"Signor, you send for the police?"

A constable loomed behind him.

"Yes," said Mannering. "It was—" No, it wouldn't do to say that it was a mistake. He smiled at the constable. "You've probably got a call out for me—Mr. Mannering."

"Haven't heard of one, sir."

"Oh. I thought Superintendent Bristow wanted to know where I was."

"I was at the call-box five minutes ago and heard nothing, sir. Are *you* Mr. Mannering?"

"*John* Mannering," murmured Toni. "It is, then, the mistake. There is nothing the matter with the signor, and this is a respectable restaurant. So. You will forgive me, signor, while I take the constable downstairs?"

Mannering smiled at the policeman, who nodded and went off.

The meal was perfect.

The arrival of Bristow, on the heels of coffee and liqueurs, did nothing to spoil it.

Toni ushered the Superintendent in, said that he was honoured, insisted on opening another bottle of wine, and asked them if they would excuse him, he had work to do downstairs. Bristow sat in an armchair opposite Mannering, with a glass of wine at his side, a cigarette jutting from his lips.

"I'm told you've got a crack on the head."

"I have, Bill."

"You deserved it. Why the devil can't you listen when I warn you?"

"I couldn't help this one. I was shanghaied on my own doorstep, five minutes after asking you to look after Lorna." Lorna! "Is your man—" Anxiety sharpened his voice.

"Lorna's at Chelsea, and I've a man back and front. I'm not playing with this business."

Mannering relaxed. "Thanks, Bill. Did you find your prisoners at the Hula Club?"

"Yes. What's this about Green?"

"To tell you that I have to tell you everything." Mannering stretched out his legs, lit a cigarette and began to talk, until there was little about that night's events which Bristow didn't know. Toni Fiori kept out of the way, Mannering spoke in a low voice so that there was no fear of being heard outside the door.

Bristow said: "*Hmmm*. One of these days you will really get yourself into a mess that you can't get out of. But I suppose it was unavoidable to-night." What he really meant was: "You've got results which we couldn't have got in a week, and I'm not going to complain about it."

"Enrico Fiori's queer notion that I have the *Tear* really began it," said Mannering. "Have you any idea why he wants it?"

"No. We've always known that he sailed close to the wind at times. Do you know what scared him away?"

"Have you discovered anything about Fay Goulden?"

Bristow said slowly: "She's the daughter of a Professor of Medicine, who was at Bonn University for twenty years before the war. She was brought up in Germany. Her father disappeared under the Hitler regime. Bernstein looked after her for a few months and then sent her to England. I don't know any more than that and can't be sure that it's all there is to know. It might explain why Bernstein made her his heiress, but—" Bristow shrugged. "Do you know where she is?"

Mannering sat up sharply.

"Isn't she at her flat?"

"No. She left at half-past seven, according to her maid. She was to have been at the Hula Club at nine o'clock, but no one saw her there. Enrico Fiori left at half-past nine, alone and in a hurry. He was tipped off about something, but we can't find out what. If you've the slightest inkling as to where we might find that girl, you've got to tell me. Fiori may think that she has the *Tear*; you know what happens to people he suspects of having that. Was she the girl at Bernstein's shop that night?"

CHAPTER XIII

NO TRACE OF FAY

"I've no idea where she might be," said Mannering. The picture of a dead woman hovered in his mind's eye, and he seemed to hear Harry Green screaming. "Find her, Bill."

"We'll find her—sooner or later." The qualification sounded ominous. "And don't evade my questions. Was she at Bernstein's shop when you found him?"

Mannering said; "No." That was true. "Does it matter?"

"She could have killed Bernstein."

"Work on Green carefully and he'll confess."

"And she might have taken the *Tear*," Bristow said. He stood up abruptly. "I've taken plenty of chances with you, holding back information is bad; deliberately lying to us is going too far. Did you see the girl at Bernstein's?"

Mannering said : "Nothing I've done has hampered you."

"So you saw her." Bristow looked aggressive and angry—but it was simulated anger. "How long have you known her?"

"Twenty-four hours or less."

"That's a lie."

"Gospel truth, Bill."

"You've been lying from the start. You knew more about Fiori, Fay Goulden and the *Tear* before you went to the shop. It wasn't chance that took you there. Why did you go? Who else is interested in the *Tear*? Who are you acting for?" Questions flashed out as Bristow stood towering over Mannering, forcing the issue because he believed that Mannering's power of resistance was at a low ebb. "I'll pull you in for questioning if you don't answer. Forget the 'all friends together' business. Remember that this is a murder investigation, and we've been after Fiori for years—since the first *Tear* crime was reported. This isn't a simple business. It's big. We can't have you withholding information. I'm serious—do you want to spend a night at the Yard?"

"I knew nothing about the *Tear* that I couldn't read in any newspaper and I've a customer who wants it for his collection. A reputable customer—Lord Amman. I've told you all I can and all that matters. Stop wasting your time with me and find Fay."

It may have been chance; it may have been because Bristow's voice was raised and could be heard outside. Whatever the reason, Toni Fiori chose that moment to come in, apologising, hoping that the superintendent and Mr. Mannering had nearly finished; he had work to do here.

"I want to go home to bed," Mannering said. "Have you time to drive me home, Bill?"

Bristow growled: "I'm going back to the Yard. I shall come and see you again later."

Mannering sat in the back of the taxi, which had waited for him outside, and the real danger to Fay was menacingly close. Mannering felt cold, not just because of the chilly night or the fact that he was tired, his head still ached and he was near the limit of his physical resources.

Would it help to go to Fay's flat?

Or would it be best to try to see Julia Fiori? Had she gone with Fiori? Questions—dozens of questions which he couldn't answer, and underlying all of them the simple fact that he had helped to put Fay Goulden in danger. But, he wouldn't go to Clay Court; the police would be there. And the police would question Julia.

A car stood outside his flat. Lights blazed from the front window, and he thought he saw Lorna looking out. He didn't want to talk to anyone except Lorna, and not much to her. He paid the cabby. By the time he reached the front door it opened; Lorna appeared.

"All safe," said Mannering. "No great harm done."

Lorna looked at him intently, and startled him by saying:

"Chittering says—"

"He's here, is he?"

"Yes." Lorna drew him inside, closed the door, and stood looking at him in the dim light which came from the landing above. He put his arm about her, and they stood very close together; he could feel the beating of her heart. She was frightened. She would be until this affair was over, whatever she said and whatever she did.

Chittering called from upstairs: "Break it up!"

"We'd better go," said Lorna. "You do look dreadful."

"I'm all right. How much do you know?"

"All that I know," said Chittering cheerfully. "Read it in the *Record* in the morning." He stood at the door of the flat, still in evening dress, like a smiling cherub. "So romance is not dead. Been baiting Bristow?"

"He's been baiting me."

"You can't have your own way all the time." Chittering's smile lingered as they went inside, but there was no smile in his eyes. "Have you heard about Fay?"

"Yes."

"Bad business. Her Kenneth is distraught."

"Where is he?"

"Looking for her in all the familiar places. He wouldn't wait for a police escort, but one of the brighter young men of the *Record* is going the rounds with him, and I'll have a report before long. Did you go to Toni's café?"

"There are two Fioris."

"I wondered when you'd catch up with that," said Chittering. "Toni the Restaurateur seems a nice little man, but I wouldn't take him at face value if I were you. Has Bristow any idea where the *Tear* is?"

"He can only guess. Chitty, will you run the story of Fay's disappearance very hard. Get a good photograph, splash it on the front page, and ask for your readers' help. If you can, persuade the news agencies to feature the story. We've got to find that girl."

"Leave it to me, John." Chittering said seriously. "I'll see you."

When he had gone, Lorna said grimly: "You're going to stay in to-night, if I have to tie you to the bed."

Mannering grinned. "Just hold me down," he said, and yawned—and now his head was throbbing and seemed likely to split. He couldn't even worry much about Fay, not as much as he knew he should.

He woke at eight o'clock next morning.

Lorna's bed was empty and he could hear voices, probably coming from the kitchen. The only other sounds came from outside the flat. A pain at the back of his head told him that he wasn't going to have a good day. He sat up, and the throbbing grew worse. He pressed the bell at the side of the bed, and the ringing had hardly stopped before Lorna came in.

"Good morning, darling," said Mannering. "Sleep well?"

"If you mean, did anyone call, no." Lorna came and sat at the side of the bed and took his hands. "You look as if you spent the night on the tiles. How's your head?"

"Only cracked."

"We ought to have had a doctor last night."

"It isn't a big crack."

"You might get concussion—anything. Let me see." He moved his head gingerly forward; she stood up and parted his hair, searing his scalp with pain. "It's a big bump! Does anyone in this establishment know how to make tea?"

"Susan's bringing it in. And you're to have breakfast in bed." She was sharp-voiced, as if holding herself in check only with a great effort. Then she went on tensely, "Chitty told me about that secret police report, and what happened to the women. I've always hated the *Tear;* I hate it even more now. Have you told the police that you have it?"

"No," said Mannering and jested, "I forgot." Then his manner changed and he reached out for the telephone. "There's something else I forgot—in fact I didn't even think about it. If ever I tell you I'm good, explain in words of three letters how bad I am." He began to dial. A detached voice answered his call, while Susan came in with a tea-tray. "Is Mr. Chittering in the Reporters' Room?" asked Mannering.

Soon Chittering said: "Who's that?"

"It's nice to know you never go to bed," said Mannering.

"I've slept like a top, and have just looked in. Have you seen the blatt this morning? We've had thirty-seven people on the line already, telling us that they've seen Fay, from Land's End to John O' Groats. Anything new?"

"Yes. Can you get the *Daily Record* to play ball?"

Chittering laughed. "There isn't an editor in London who won't. What's the new idea?"

"Will you run this: Has the *Diamond of Tears* been smuggled out of the country? Produce a mysterious Frenchman, Brazilian, Portuguese, anything you like, who was after the *Tear,* and known to have been negotiating with Bernstein for it. Suggest that it may not have been at the shop after all, that Bernstein may have been lying when he said that he'd still got it. See the idea?"

Chittering paused, then said: "Not bad. Not bad at all."

He rang off, and Lorna handed Mannering a cup of tea and

said: "At least you can still think. What do you hope to do?"

"Persuade Fiori that Fay hasn't got the *Tear*. Anything that might stall him for twenty-four hours would be a help. Darling, look up Mrs. Fiori, of 23 Clay Court, in the telephone book and find out if she's in, will you?"

"Who *is* this woman?" asked Lorna. If he didn't know her too well he would have thought her almost jealous. "Did she come here yesterday?"

"Yes." Mannering pulled her forward, but she still yielded only to humour him. "She's enough to make you turn green with jealousy."

Lorna pulled herself free, and dialled while Mannering sipped tea. He could hear the ringing sound faintly, but was much more worried by Lorna's frown. Her manner was beginning to disturb him. Then the ringing stopped.

"Is Mrs. Fiori there?" asked Lorna. She paused, then handed Mannering the telephone.

.   .   .   .   .

Mannering said: "Good morning, Julia," and Lorna bit her lip, and continued to stare at him, tense and on edge. It was a long time before Julia Fiori said:

"Who is that?"

"And you can't even remember my voice," said Mannering, reproachfully. "How's Enrico?"

"I think he must be losing his touch, as you're still here," said Julia.

"I want a word with you about Fay," Mannering said. "Don't let anything happen to her. That's extremely important. If she gets hurt then strange and violent things are going to happen. People like you will get messed up in the process. Look after Fay."

The pause which followed seemed to become ominous. When she spoke her voice was low-pitched and expressionless, yet he was vividly reminded of the way she had talked as she had left the flat. She even sent tension into the room. Lorna stood very still, as if she were aware of it, too.

"If anything happens to Fay Goulden, John Mannering," Julia said, "it will be your fault, and if he thinks that she took the *Tear* I don't think we shall see her again," said Julia softly. "If you've got it, let him know."

"How can anyone tell him anything, now that he's on the run?"

"You could tell me, and I'd find a way." She lowered her voice until it was little above a whisper. "I'm serious. There's one way to save Fay Goulden—by proving that she hasn't the *Tear*. If you really want to save her tell him you've got it, or take it to Scotland Yard."

Mannering said: "It's a pity I haven't got it, you create the note of horror so well."

"I've known him for some time," said Julia, and rang off.

．　　．　　．　　．　　．

Mannering had breakfast in bed, but ate with little appetite. It was a bright, sunny morning, and the world was fair, but the threat hovering about Fay Goulden crept into the flat, shadowed him and shadowed Lorna. He got up just after nine o'clock, and dressed by half-past. His head wasn't as bad as he had feared; he took aspirins.

What was the best thing to do?

Lorna joined him in the study, went to the window, stared towards the river, and spoke without turning round. She looked grave, but lovely enough to make him catch his breath, to wish that he had never heard of the *Tear*, that he could wave his hand and spirit all anxiety from her.

"You've got to help her," she said.

"Yes. How?"

"Even if it means letting Fiori have the *Tear*."

"I needn't go as far as that," Mannering said gently. "If he's convinced that I've got it, that will do."

Lorna swung round. "If he's sure you've got it, then he'll never leave you alone."

"I can't just hand the diamond over, wish Fiori luck, and let him get away with it. The *Tear* has a place in this affair, as bait—good, strong bait. Fiori will take risks to get it, and I've got to make him take a risk too many."

"Or he makes you."

Mannering said: "There's so much we don't know. Why Fiori wants the *Tear*, where he is, what else he does, why his wife—if she *is* still his wife—takes such interest in Fay. Whether his wife—let's just say Julia—is involved as deeply as she appears to be. One argument against it is that she's still at the flat—hasn't been scared away."

Lorna said in a hard voice: "You can give the *Tear* to Fiori or to Bristow. Either way it will help the girl and take a load off you. You can't keep it yourself and hope that it will lure Fiori into making a mistake. You might want to, but you can't." She turned and faced him and he had never seen her show more intensity of feeling. "Because I won't let you. If you don't decide to do one or the other, soon, I shall tell Bristow everything. I'd rather see you in prison than at Fiori's mercy."

She turned away abruptly and stared out of the window.

It was very quiet in the flat, but there was tumult in Mannering's mind. He should not be surprised by this, yet it appalled him. She was in deadly earnest, and he knew why she had seemed so strange; this had been heavy on her mind last night.

She said, without looking round: "I mean every word."

"I know you do," Mannering said quietly. She knew as well as he that if he surrendered the *Tear* he lost his chance of finding out the truth, but nothing would change her, except some new turn that would make nonsense of his calculations.

The telephone bell rang.

He answered it, looking at Lorna's back. "Yes?"

Bristow said: "Well, have you come to your senses this morning?"

"I'm about normal," Mannering said, "Any news of the girl?"

"No."

"Fiori?"

"No."

"Have you been to see a Mrs. Julia Fiori, who lives next door to Fay?"

"In spite of your low opinion of us we don't spend most of our time sleeping," Bristow said. "Yes, I've seen her. And I've had an interesting talk with a woman named Ethel—remember all she said to you?"

"Julia Fiori was mentioned, that's all. Julia Enrico Fiori, his wife."

"Ex-wife. They were divorced two years ago."

Because he was so surprised he didn't notice that Lorna moved from the window and came towards him.

"So there's no love lost between her and Enrico. That might

be a help." It might explain why Julia was protecting Fay, or trying to protect her, or pretending. "No, Bill, there isn't anything new this end."

"There is," said Lorna.

She took the telephone from him, catching him unawares. She was very close to Mannering. Her black eyebrows were drawn together.

"Mr. Bristow, my husband John does want to tell you something else. If he doesn't, I will." She held the telephone towards Mannering, and their eyes still met. She whispered: "John, don't play with fire any longer. Tell him."

Mannering said: "I've nothing to tell him. You please yourself." He backed away, forced himself to look out of the window, felt his nerves tautening, was afraid of what she would say. Nothing like this had ever happened before. He had had too little warning to decide what best to do.

Would she tell the Yard man?

He heard Bristow's voice, faint, impatient and hopeful. Lorna put her lips closer to the mouthpiece, and Mannering heard her draw in her breath.

The front door bell rang.

Mannering swung away, went to the door and into the hall. Susan came hurrying out of the kitchen, drying her hands, saw him and beamed: "Will you go, sir?" He nodded, straining his ears to catch what Lorna said. The front door bell rang again, drowning her words. Susan looked back over her shoulder, as if his expression puzzled her.

He opened the front door and Larraby came in.

CHAPTER XIV

NEWS FROM LARRABY

"I REALLY am sorry that I've been so long, Mr. Mannering," said Larraby. "I think I can tell you much of interest about Jacob Bernstein's customers, I do indeed."

He smiled gravely.

Mannering could still hear Lorna speaking on the telephone. Larraby, realising that not all was well, drew back. "There's nothing wrong, I hope, sir? I haven't had an opportunity to see the newspapers this morning, although I was told that you had some misadventure last night."

"Nothing to worry about. Go into the drawing-room, will you? I'll be with you in a minute."

"Very good, sir." Larraby hurried away, reminding Mannering of the important and fussy little manager of the Hula Club. Normally Mannering would have been on edge to hear what Larraby had to say; now nothing mattered except what Lorna had told Bristow. It went far beyond that, cut across the almost perfect understanding that there had always been between them. From the early days of the Baron Lorna had never failed him, had believed that he was right to take his own course, had trusted his judgment. Now, fear of Fiori and the history of the *Tear* so obsessed her that she was prepared to betray him. Betray? Was that the word? He knew that it was, knew that if Bristow could prove he had taken the *Tear* Bristow would be compelled to take action, there was nothing else the Yard man could do. Did Lorna feel desperate enough to take the chance? Had she meant it when she had said that she would rather see him in jail than in possession of the *Tear*.

What a name : *The Diamond of Tears!*

He heard the ting of the telephone being replaced, rooted in his pocket for his cigarettes, lit one and went towards the study door. Lorna stood by the telephone, staring into space. Was this the moment to ask questions? He felt his nerves at a screaming edge, did not trust himself to behave rationally, for anger was storming inside him—the unheard of thing, anger against Lorna.

Yes; have it out, now.

He went in and closed the door. Still she didn't look at him. He drew nearer, and said in a low-pitched voice :

"Was he glad to hear about it?"

She turned and looked at him, catching her breath.

"I'm a fool!" she said bitterly. "I should have told him, but I couldn't bring myself to it. But—I shall. If you haven't told him or Fiori to-day I shall make a statement."

"Lorna—"

She said savagely: "I'm tired of it—tired of wondering whether you'll come back safe, tired of seeing you hurt, tired of having you risk your life for people whom you hardly know. You're not in this because of Jacob—oh, I suppose it's not because of Fay or any person, it's because you like it—you love it. I've tried to help you. Time and time again I've forced myself to wait, pretending that sooner or later you would get tired of it, but it's never ending. We have a few months' peace and then something like this happens. Even if you win through this there will be others. I can't stand it any more. It's useless to pretend, I just can't stand it!"

There was nothing Mannering could say.

"And I'm not going to stand it," Lorna went on tautly. "Day in, day out, worry, anxiety, fear. You'll go off soon and I shan't know whether you'll ever come back. You make light of it, pretend that it doesn't matter, behave like a fool, and have the nerve to say that I'm driving *you* crazy. Driving *you!*"

"Lorna—"

She swung round, rushed past him, out of the room and into the bedroom. The door slammed.

.   .   .   .   .

Larraby was waiting with his budget of news. Bristow probably suspected what Lorna had meant to say, would try to break her down. Somewhere, in mortal danger, was Fay Goulden. Behind them there was the dead Jacob, and the four other people who had been tortured and cruelly murdered because of the *Diamond of Tears*. And there was Lorna, overwrought but justified in everything she said.

He went to the drawing-room and paused outside. The door was ajar, Larraby stood by the piano. What *had* he discovered?

Mannering suddenly wanted to know that more than anything else. Lorna was right; there was nothing he could do about it; the hunt was part of his life.

Was a choice to be forced on to him?

He went in and Larraby turned round, eagerly.

"I hope you're fairly well, Mr. Mannering. I've just looked at the *Record* and heard what happened last night. Things have moved very fast, very fast indeed. No doubt our friend Bristow is annoyed because you have stolen a march on him, but I don't think that Bristow has ever really acknowledged his debt to you, sir."

Mannering said mechanically : "Debt?"

"I mean that seriously." Larraby's clear blue eyes were earnest now. "Each man has his own particular and peculiar gift, and you—have you ever marvelled at the number of times you have been able to help the police?" The words were spoken softly. "I remember only too well the time when I was in grave danger of being imprisoned for a crime which I did not commit. I am quite sure that but for you I should be in prison now. The evidence was strong, and there was little I could do in my own defence. There are many others who owe you a great debt, and Bristow is certainly not least of them. I—but I am rambling, sir! Forgive me." Larraby smiled and came forward, taking a sheet of paper from his pocket. "I have the list of wealthy customers, and some of them are extremely interesting—*extremely*."

Mannering looked at Larraby, not at the list. Had the little man heard what he and Lorna had said? Was this his way of trying to help.

Mannering took the list. "I began to wonder whether you had got yourself into trouble."

"No, it was all quite straightforward, just a matter of patience," said Larraby. "I could do little at Bernstein's shop because of the police, but I spent the evening, and indeed part of the night, talking to his assistants. I think they are all quite reliable, loyal to Jacob and upset and distressed by what has happened. I didn't finish with the last until nearly three o'clock this morning, and I felt sure that you wouldn't wish to be disturbed at such an hour. Then I'm afraid I overslept."

Mannering ran his eye down the list, frowning when he saw: "Toni Fiori." What had Toni bought from old Jacob? The next name had a black cross against it—and the name was Harry Green, with an address in Hatton Gardens.

"Why mark Harry Green?"

"To draw your attention to him. He is a man of good reputation but I have reason to believe that he is not all that he seems. I have been told that he buys 'hot' stones, and is not above smuggling jewels out of the country. And moreover, he has bought a great deal from old Jacob in recent weeks and sent most of it to America. According to all the assistants, Green has been to the shop more often than any other individual during recent months. I hope I was right to mark his name."

"You were. He killed Jacob."

Larraby gasped: "*What?* You've caught him?"

Mannering said drily: "Don't confuse luck with genius." He looked further down the list, saw familiar names of dealers and collectors who often bought from Quinn's. The extent of Jacob Bernstein's business was quite remarkable—known and unknown people famous and notorious. Near the end of the list another name caught his eye. He glanced up sharply:

"What do you know about Kenneth Yule? I've never heard of him."

"And I hadn't until I talked to old Jacob's assistants," said Larraby. "He is a very presentable young man, who appears to be very rich. There is something a little mysterious about his association with the trade. Whether he buys as a collector or for someone else, it is impossible to be sure. The opinion is that he loves jewels for their own sake. He was not among the most frequent visitors to the shop but has made several large purchases. I particularly noted him because he made inquiries about the *Diamond of Tears*. I thought you would be interested in anyone eager to obtain the diamond. Is it still at the post office, sir?"

Mannering said "Yes," and Larraby almost purred with satisfaction. Mannering looked through the list again, saw no other name of interest and slipped it into his pocket.

Green's visits to old Jacob weren't news: Toni Fiori's and Kenneth Yule's could have an important bearing.

The front door closed.

He heard it faintly at first, and it had no significance—until suddenly he thought of Lorna, swung round and hurried out. He went into the bedroom; Lorna wasn't there. He hurried to the front door, and heard her in the passage leading to the stairs. He didn't call out, but ran after her. He saw a taxi drawing away from the kerb. When he reached the street the taxi was near the corner. He stood there, tight-lipped, heavy at heart.

He went slowly upstairs. Larraby was sitting on a sofa reading the *Record*. He jumped up.

"What would you like me to do next, sir?"

"This Kenneth Yule—do you know what he's like?"

"He is a tall, powerful young man, aged—well, about thirty, rather less than more according to my informants. He is good looking, fair-haired, and—"

"That's good enough. Where does he live?"

"Here is a second list, with the names *and* addresses," Larraby said, and took out a sheet of paper. "I will gladly find out more about him if I can."

"Find out whether he knows Toni and Enrico Fiori, how long he has known Fay Goulden, whether he buys for himself or for a third party. Draw what money you need from the shop, and report to me twice a day."

"Very well," murmured Larraby.

Mannering said: "You've read the *Record;* you know what kind of job this is. Be careful."

"I will indeed, sir."

"Has Mrs. Mannering asked you where you sent that package? Does she know it's at the Strand Post Office?"

"Why, no, sir."

"Good. Don't tell her."

"I certainly will not, sir. Is there anything else?"

Mannering said: "No, not now. Thanks, Josh, you're doing a good job—a very good job."

.   .   .   .   .

Outside the house one of Bristow's men stood and smiled across at Mannering. Further along the street a small car was parked, with no one at the wheel. A postman rat-tatted at a nearby door, and Mannering watched him after he had delivered his mail and came plodding nearer. The C.I.D. man came across the road and said:

"Lovely morning."

"Yes. Wasn't the idea to watch Mrs. Mannering, not me?"

"Both, sir !"

"And are they both being done?"

"Yes—we had strict instructions not to let Mrs. Mannering out of our sight. We'd a patrol car at the end of the road, it's following her taxi. I don't think you need worry about her."

"Thanks. Anyone hanging about?"

"Not that I've noticed."

"Thanks," said Mannering again, and went towards the postman.

"I've something for you, Mr. Mannering, several in fact." He ran through his bundle, produced three unsealed and one sealed letter and handed them to Mannering. "I'll take them up if you'd rather."

"No, don't trouble," said Mannering, and smiled and walked towards the Embankment end of the street. He was more likely to get a taxi from the other end, and didn't intend to use his car. He knew that he turned in this direction because he and Lorna often walked here at the end of the day and watched the gentle, rippling river. He crossed the wide road and stood at the parapet looking at some barges, a few oddments of flotsam bobbing up and down in the tide and, across the river, a crane working slowly, swinging round with a load of boxes for a small wharf. Bargees stood on their barges, dockers bent strong backs to their task, and the faint noises came floating across the river.

He put the three unsealed envelopes away and studied the fourth. The postmark was London, W.C.1, and it was type-written. He slit it open with his forefinger, took out a single fold of paper—and saw at a glance that there was neither address nor signature; and there were very few words. A man strolled past, taking no apparent interest in him.

He read : "*Your good fortune will not last. It is easy for you to give me what I want. You can make it easy for others, too. Fay is a charming girl, I do not wish to hurt her.*"

Fiori might have been talking to him; looking at him with those heavy-lidded brown eyes, putting no feeling into his voice, and thus making a deeper impression. Mannering read the words again, then folded the paper and put it back into his pocket. The man who had passed him was leaning against the parapet, not many yards away. Mannering walked on—and was followed. Was this another C.I.D. officer? Or did the man work for Fiori? Mannering quickened his pace, then crossed the road; the man followed, never far behind. Mannering looked in vain for a taxi; none came along. He walked very quickly, feeling the warmth of the sun on the back of his head, turned down a side street, and was still followed. He reached the main road where there were buses, saw one approaching an official stop, raced for it and jumped on board.

The man behind made no attempt to follow, but stood grinning at him. There was something in the grin which made Mannering think of Fiori; yet Fiori hadn't smiled.

Mannering got off the bus at Victoria, walked along Victoria Street, where there were more people, most of them in a hurry. Traffic was noisy and smelly, and there were plenty of taxis here, but he wanted to find out whether he had really shaken the man off or whether he was still being followed. He turned off the main road towards Caxton Hall and crossed the churchyard. He was followed only by two girls and a fair-haired boy who whistled shrilly.

He took a taxi to Piccadilly, and strolled along Shaftesbury Avenue. He saw no one whom he recognised. He was free enough now; safe enough. The word "safe" crossed his mind, he couldn't reject it; and he understood more clearly what Lorna felt. He stood at a pedestrian crossing, waiting for the lights to change—as he started off he felt a sharp prick in his left arm. He turned, saw a man move back and double across the road. Mannering swung round to follow. He cannoned into a big woman who said: "*Really!*" There was no pain in his arm, but an imagined sense of numbness. Imagined? He reached the opposite pavement but lost the man, who didn't look round but dived into a subway leading to the underground; it would be a waste of time searching for him. He rubbed his arm gently; the numbness wasn't imaginary. He raced along the narrow pavement into the Regent Palace Hotel and made for the cloakroom, stripping off his coat as he went. White-clad attendants stared at him. He fumbled with his cufflink; the link fell to the floor. He rolled up his sleeve and looked at his arm.

There was a small puncture and a tiny smear of blood.

CHAPTER XV

FEAR

AN attendant came up and put a towel by the side of the handbasin in front of Mannering, looked at him curiously, and hovered near. Raising his arm, Mannering could just touch the spot with his mouth. He squeezed it between his teeth, and sucked vigorously, knowing that everyone else in the cloakroom was watching him with increasing curiosity. The attendant came closer: "Anything I can do, sir?" Mannering shook his head, went on sucking, then spat into the handbasin. The numbness seemed to be spreading, but that might be because of the pressure of his teeth; teeth marks showed clearly on his arm, the little puncture was on top of a red ridge.

"*Sure* I can't do anything, sir?"

"No, thanks."

He could go to a doctor, there would be one in the hotel; or to a chemist, there were several nearby—but would either be able to help? Would anyone be able to judge what this was until the symptoms began to manifest themselves? They could only guess at what had been injected. The simple fact was that someone working for Fiori had jabbed a hypodermic needle into his arm—well, some kind of needle or pin. There hadn't been time for the man to press the plunger for long, whatever had gone in was likely to be quick acting. He should soon know.

The wise thing was to consult a doctor.

"If there *is* anything I can do, sir—"

"You're very good. Where can I find the hotel doctor?"

"First floor, sir, I think it's room—Charlie!" The attendant shouted across to another. "What's the number of the doctor's room?"

"One-o-nine," answered Charlie.

"Hundred and nine, sir. Send someone up with you, if you like." The attendant, a small man with an anxious, worried face, helped him on with his coat, and offered to take him to the lift. He preferred to walk. He fancied that his arm was stinging, but that might be because of the bite. He walked quickly along the first bedroom floor, and found the door of Room 109 open, with a man coming out, another saying:

"Yes, look in to-morrow." The speaker was genial, plump, prosperous-looking. He smiled at Mannering. "You're lucky, I was just going on my rounds."

"Thanks." Mannering entered a small reception room, followed the doctor into a surgery, wondered if he were making a fool of himself. The doctor waited for a few seconds, then asked:

"Well, what's the trouble?"

Mannering said: "Wind up, chiefly." He took off his coat and remembered that he had dropped a cufflink downstairs. "Can you tell me whether this was made with a hypodermic or an ordinary needle?" He bared his arm, and the doctor shot a surprised glance at him. "And if you can guess what shot was put in, I'd be happier."

A few seconds seemed an eternity.

"Hypo," pronounced the doctor. "Just a moment." He took a long-handled glass off his desk, switched on a small electric light attached to it, and studied the puncture. "Yes a hypo—and it was done through your shirt; I can see one or two tiny pieces of fluff attached to it. It's a subcutaneous injection, which usually works very quickly. Are you trying to tell me you know nothing about it?"

"I felt a jab."

"Is there any reason why—" began the doctor, then gulped and drew back. "I *thought* I recognised you. You're Mannering. Has this anything to do with the case?"

"It could have, and be intended either to frighten or to kill."

"Have you told the police?"

"I couldn't get up here fast enough."

"I see you've been sucking it. Probably as good as anything I can do. I'll cauterise it, that may help if there's anything venomous there. It hasn't gone straight into the blood stream through a big vein. Do you feel anything?"

"A numbness—more imaginary than real, I think."

"It could be. Almost anything jabbed in there will give you a sensation of numbness. Does it hurt?"

"No."

"Do you feel anything at all—giddiness, anything like that? Sleepiness?" The doctor laughed. "You certainly aren't falling asleep!" As he talked he was opening a bottle, dabbing the puncture with cotton wool. He rubbed Mannering's arm briskly; now the place stung badly. "Hurt? That's good! How long ago did it happen?"

"Ten to fifteen minutes."

"Then it wasn't any drug with an almost instantaneous action, like some of the barbitones. It may prove to be nothing at all. You know—" the doctor laughed again, not with humour— "almost anything could have been put in, bacteria, any drug in solution. The proper thing is to have you under supervision for a few hours or even longer. But you won't want to sit back and do nothing in case symptoms develop."

"No, I shan't."

"Then stay here for twenty minutes or so. I've a couple of people to see at once, and then I'll come back. If you're still all right you can get off, but see a doctor the moment you feel any symptoms—that is, as soon as you feel anything at all unusual. Nausea, giddiness—but I needn't teach you your A.B.C. Use my telephone if you want to. It would be wise to call the police."

"Thanks."

"Sorry I have to leave you on your own, my receptionist is down with influenza." The doctor picked up his black case and went out. A good chap; deliberately casual, doing nothing to add to nebulous fears. Mannering lit a cigarette and picked up the magnifying glass, studied the puncture, and saw nothing remarkable about it. The sting of the cauterising liquid was much worse than anything he had felt before. He put the glass down—and the telephone bell rang

He hesitated; it pealed again. He lifted it, and wondered what the doctor's name was—and nearly dropped the telephone, for a man said quietly:

"Mannering?"

A pause; and then insistently: "Is that Mannering?"

Mannering said: "Yes."

"He means business. I shouldn't lose any time getting rid of the *Tear*," said the man. His voice seemed vaguely familiar, yet there was nothing remarkable about it, no hint of emphasis. "Don't forget, he means to have it."

The line went dead.

.   .   .   .   .

So they'd not only followed him here but knew when he had come upstairs and where he was, had probably seen the doctor go out.

°   °   °   °   °

The doctor was back in thirty-five minutes.

Mannering felt no different, except that the sting had gone out of the puncture.

"That's fine," said the doctor. "It was probably nothing to harm you. Have you told the police?"

"Not yet."

"You must, and I'll have to report it."

"You go ahead," said Mannering. "Thanks very much, you've been a great help. How much do I owe you?"

The doctor shrugged : "Well, say a guinea."

Mannering remembered his cufflink; the anxious attendant had it.

Outside on the pavement in front of the hotel Mannering looked right and left and saw no one he knew, no one he had noticed earlier in the morning. But he was sure that he was watched. He walked slowly to Piccadilly Circus, eyed the traffic circling, tried to decide what he had better do. Lorna was one anxiety, Fiori the other; there was Kenneth Yule, too—he ought to see Yule soon. Perhaps Chittering had discovered more than Larraby about Fay's young man.

He called Chittering from a call-box but the reporter wasn't in the office.

"Any idea where I can find him?"

"Who is that?"

"John Mannering."

"He said if you called I was to tell you he would call you at Chelsea. He isn't sure where he'll be except that he'll look in at Great Marlborough Street, where Green and the other two from the Hula Club will be up before the beak."

"Yes, of course. Thanks."

Mannering stayed in the box. No one was near, no one appeared to be taking the slightest notice of him. A crowd of people passed; when he was jammed in a crowd someone might jab another needle into him—next time a poison which might work quickly. Fay was terrified; Lorna so frightened that she had lost her nerve; and he wasn't free from fear. He had panicked after that prick.

What to do now? He dialled the Chelsea flat. After a pause Susan answered him brightly.

"Is Mrs. Mannering there, Susan?"

"Oh, *no*, sir, she hasn't come back. And she didn't say whether you would be in for lunch, either of you. What do you think I'd better do?"

"Get something ready, in case we turn up, and tell Mrs. Mannering I called. Don't forget that."

"I won't," said Susan. "Good-bye, sir."

It was hot inside the kiosk, but a cold wind swept along the street as Mannering stepped out. A taxi came along slowly, its "For Hire" sign up. He signalled it, jumped in before it had properly stopped, and slammed the door. No other taxi followed him, there were several private cars behind but none started off from the side of the road. *Could* he be followed now? The taxi drove on for a few yards, then the driver pulled up, looked over his shoulder and said laconically:

"Just going for a ride?"

"Eh? Oh—sorry. Clay Court, Shepherd Street."

Of course, he must see Julia again; it was the obvious thing to do, the trouble with the obvious was that you so often failed to do it. He felt more rested and less prone to fear. Had there been anything lethal pumped into his arm he would surely know by now. An hour and a quarter had passed and he could feel nothing at all. It had been evidence of menace; like the letter and like the telephone call, just to show how easily he could be killed. Julia Fiori had told him that if she were he she wouldn't feel safe walking along the street. She'd meant it.

And *Lorna* was out.

He asked the cabby to wait, was told curtly: "Can't do it, Guv'nor." The resplendent commissionaire greeted him with a hearty good morning, and a C.I.D. man standing in the hall looked at him with a faint smile. Mannering took himself up in the lift, and found another C.I.D. man outside Fay's flat.

"Anything new this morning?" Mannering asked.

"I wouldn't know, sir."

The lift bell rang behind him, and the lift began to move slowly down. Mannering passed Fay's flat and remembered how badly the girl had been scared when he had first met her, terrified the second time; her danger now was chiefly due to what he was doing. All reason argued against him, but he wasn't convinced he was wrong. He rang the bell at Julia's flat and immediately heard footsteps and a voice—Julia's. He stood back, but was ready to thrust his foot in the door if she attempted to close it in his face.

She greeted him like a long-lost friend.

"Hallo! We've been expecting you." She stood aside for him to pass, but he hesitated. The "we" was significant; someone might be there who would carry on with Fiori's good work. Nonsense! He mustn't let himself be harassed by these nameless fears. The police were actually on the doorstep, nothing could go amiss here.

He went in, Julia closed the door—and he heard the lift stop as the door latched.

"I've had the lock replaced," Julia said, and led the way to the charming drawing-room. Mannering saw no one else outside; whoever was included in the "we" was probably in this room.

Lorna, standing in the window, looked at him without expression.

The front door bell rang again.

.   .   .   .   .

Julia closed the door without speaking, and Mannering stood quite still, watching his wife. She didn't move; they were like two statues. This wasn't really Lorna; she was steeling herself to show no reaction, to go on with what she had planned. He felt tongue-tied—with Lorna! He coughed as he forced himself to move forward and offer her a cigarette. She took one. His hand shook slightly as he gave her a light.

The caller outside was a man and he talked in a loud voice. Mannering wished him anywhere but at the flat.

"You talk about making me back out of the case, and then come and plunge yourself into it," Mannering said. "If this is dangerous for me it's ten times more dangerous for you."

"Now you know what it feels like," Lorna said.

He had known a dozen times before. The agony of suspense, when something might have happened to her—perhaps when she had been late home while he was working on such an affair as this; even times when she had fallen foul of bad men who had tried to get at him through her. She knew that, and yet could talk so; it made her a stranger.

"Why did you come?"

"I thought I might get some sense out of her—and I came to find out whether she can take a message to Fiori. I meant what I said. You'll give the *Tear* to either Fiori or Bristow—and I think I'm a fool not to insist that it's Bristow. But if Fiori gets the *Tear* he'll have nothing against you."

Mannering said: "No. I'd be high and dry, safe as houses. But Fiori will never get his hands on the *Tear* while I can keep it from him. I'd rather throw it in the river. Now there's no doubt where we stand, is there? Tell Bristow I have it—at least you can't tell him where it is. And think how happy you'll be afterwards."

Lorna said: "I just can't stand it any more. You've got to understand that."

There was nothing he could say, he had already said too much. . . . It was fantastic that they should talk to each other as if they had nothing in common. It wasn't natural and it wouldn't last, but before it ended something precious in the bonds between them might have broken. Should he let her have her way? Quickly, completely, promising to feel no bitterness? He couldn't promise that so he couldn't let her have her way.

Throughout all this there had been the sound of voices outside. Julia's and a man's. The man's grew louder. Twice he mentioned "Fay," and after the second time there came a tap at the door. Lorna turned her back on it.

"Come in," Mannering said heavily.

Julia opened the door. Kenneth Yule strode past her, then drew back, as if astounded.

CHAPTER XVI

ACCUSATION

AFTER the moment of astonishment Yule raised clenched fists and approached Mannering, anger in his eyes. They were tired eyes, glassy from lack of sleep. He was pale and haggard, his curly fair hair was tousled. He was taller than Mannering—and seemed to be spoiling for a fight.

Julia stood in the doorway. Lorna turned from the window and caught her breath.

Yule growled : "Where is she? Come on, out with it—where's Fay? If you don't tell me I'll break your neck."

Mannering said : "It's a tough neck."

"Tell me where she is!" Yule's voice was pitched so low it seemed to hurt him to speak.

"If I knew I don't think I'd tell you."

Yule rasped : "You'll tell me!" He leapt forward, driving a straight left that would have floored Mannering had it connected. Mannering moved swiftly, rammed home a stopping punch to Yule's stomach. But it didn't stop Yule, just made him grunt before he came on again; this time he was more careful. Left to the head, right to the body—powerful blows with fourteen stone behind them, and they drove Mannering back.

Lorna cried : "Stop it !"

Mannering caught his foot on a stool and stumbled backwards; another swinging left just brushed his chin. He drove for the nose, landed, saw tears of pain flood Yule's eyes. He went in, both fists working like piston rods, forced the man back, crowded him into a corner and floored him.

"Don't!" Lorna cried, and rushed towards them. Mannering heard her, saw Julia step forward swiftly, guessed that Julia was stopping her. He drew back. A trickle of blood showed on Yule's lips, his eyes glittered with rage. He got on all fours, then to his feet; he sprang at Mannering again, swung a wild left, took a body punch which drove the wind gustily out of his stomach. He stood swaying, arms down, chin forward—an easy

victim. Mannering dropped his arms and turned away. Lorna stood trembling, with Julia's arm round her shoulders.

"The answer is no, I don't know where Fay is," Mannering said.

Yule muttered: "That's a lie."

"Look out!" cried Lorna. "John! Mind!"

Mannering took his cigarette-case from his pocket, heard Yule coming, did nothing to stop him, put a cigarette to his lips and lit it. Yule was only a yard behind, had him at his mercy—but drew back and let his arms fall by his side. Mannering turned and offered him a cigarette.

Julia said: "Ken doesn't smoke."

"So you know him well." Mannering put his case away and said: "Who told you I know where to find her?"

Yule said: "I know you do."

Mannering went to a chair and sat on the arm, glad of the respite. He was tired; too tired. There was something in what Lorna had said—he was getting past this kind of activity. Yule had defeated himself. Now he stood, big and towering yet somehow weak and helpless. "Enrico Fiori knows where Fay is, no one else does."

"He doesn't!"

"What makes you so sure?"

"He told me." Yule flung the words out. Mannering drew deeply on the cigarette and waited. Yule's heavy breathing soughed about the room. Julia released Lorna, who didn't move.

"And when did you see Fiori?" asked Mannering.

"I didn't see him. He telephoned me."

"When?"

"Before I came here. I've been hunting for Fay all night. I hadn't been home an hour before he called me. He said it was no use looking for her; if I wanted to find her I should have to come to you. I went to your flat, you weren't there, and—" He broke off.

"You came to see Julia. Why?"

Julia said sweetly: "Young people in trouble always come to see me."

"I could tell them where else to go," Mannering said. "I don't know where Fay is, Yule. Fiori didn't mean that I did. He meant that he thinks I've got the *Diamond of Tears* and that he'll deliver Fay if I deliver the stone. It would be a help if I had it."

Lorna started.

The new Lorna—would she give him away now?

She didn't speak.

"I don't believe that's what he meant." Yule's voice was clipped. "He said he didn't know where she was."

"Is that true?" Julia asked sharply.

"Why the devil do you think I'd lie about it?"

Julia said: "No, you're not a liar. Nor is Enrico. He doesn't think that lying helps anyone, he either tells the truth or says nothing at all."

"The Devil reformed," suggested Mannering.

Julia said: "You don't know Enrico or you wouldn't talk like that. He is corrupt and evil but he's not a liar. He isn't being honest, just practical. He's too rich, too powerful, to worry about mean things. Kenneth, are you sure that he actually said that he didn't know where Fay is?"

"Of course I'm sure."

"Then he doesn't know," said Julia. "You'll have to start afresh from there, Mannering. And now it really is a puzzle, because if he didn't take her away, who did?"

Mannering said: "So he's not a liar." He took the letter out of his pocket, read it again and then handed it to her. "*Your good fortune will not last. It is easy for you to give me what I want. You can make it easy for others, too. Fay is a charming girl, I do not wish to hurt her.*"

Julia handed it back, Lorna took it, and Mannering let her have it.

"There's nothing in that that makes him a liar," said Julia. "He doesn't say that he knows where Fay is. He implies that he can do her harm. You ought to know by now. If it comes to lying, you do pretty well. You could get the *Tear* now, if you wanted it. Once Enrico has that no one need worry."

Mannering said: "Everyone thinks I keep the *Tear* in my pocket and can produce it by a wave of the hand." He stubbed out his cigarette, watched Lorna as she read, wondered if she would confirm what they thought; but she handed him back the letter without comment.

"If you've got the *Tear*—" Yule began.

"If I had the *Tear* I'd let Fiori break me to pieces before I'd hand it over."

Yule said in a low-pitched voice: "You do know where it is."
He turned away and went to Julia. He took her hand, was meek,
humble, and his voice was so low-pitched that the words hardly
carried to Mannering. "Julia, make him give it up. I—I didn't
know what was happening, I've been a blind fool. I knew Fay
was nervous but I didn't know that she had such a good reason.
Have you—seen these?"

He took out a large envelope and handed it to her. Mannering
had seen just such an envelope and knew what was in it; coldly
detailed police reports of the finding of four bodies; and a
photograph. Julia said: "Yes." Yule raised her hand, held it
between his, as if he would crush it—and Mannering thought
there were tears of entreaty in his eyes.

"That mustn't happen to Fay. You *must* give it up." Yule
turned, his eyes bloodshot, and there was fear in them—the fear
which was the keynote of this foul business. "Mannering, I—I'm
beside myself. I hardly know what I'm doing, I'm so frightened
for Fay. You must surrender the *Tear*. I—"

He broke off, raised his hands—and all of them watched him,
caught by his sudden tension, the hope that sprang into his eyes.
He touched Mannering's arm, and his fingers were cold and
quivering.

"Mannering, you know all about jewels! You know how
much that diamond is worth—fifty thousand pounds. I'll pay
you a *hundred* thousand if you'll let Fiori have that *Tear*. You
must do it, nothing else can save her." He tightened his grip. "A
hundred thousand pounds!"

.   .   .   .   .

If he were prepared to pay such a fortune then Fay meant
almost as much to Yule as life itself. Julia came forward, only
Lorna was behind them. Her gaze met Mannering's. Lorna's
didn't fall, but there was no answering glow in her eyes, no
encouragement.

Julia said: "Let him have it, Mannering, you'll never make
money so easily again."

Mannering said: "If I had the *Tear* money couldn't buy it for
Fiori." He freed himself, backed away, thrust his hands deep
into his pockets. "There are things you two forget. Fay is Jacob
Bernstein's heiress. The *Tear* belongs to her. If anyone has a right

to say what shall happen to it she has. You can't buy it, Yule—and Fiori can't have it as a gift. It isn't simply that, either—there have been five murders now. There's one way the *Tear* should be used, if we ever find it—by serving as bait to fix Fiori. You can try to bribe him, to buy him off—but you can't buy off that kind of savage and I wouldn't try."

Julia said softly: "Very high-minded. For the first time I doubt whether you have the *Tear*. Even the great Mannering couldn't refuse a profit of a hundred thousand pounds."

Lorna said: "Oh, you *fool!*" She looked into Mannering's eyes and at last he saw a glow of understanding. The rekindling of belief? It overshadowed everything else—Kenneth Yule's trembling anxiety, Julia's gibes. He felt an inner calmness which he had feared had gone for good. It remained, although Lorna looked away from him quickly, as if she regretted showing him what was in her mind. Mind? Or heart?

Julia said: "All this is most touching. Ken, I'm afraid you're wasting your time. Mannering doesn't know where Fay is, doesn't know where the *Tear* is. Enrico is going to be very disappointed."

"I must find her!" cried Yule. "Can't *someone* help?" It was like a cry in the wilderness. He went to a chair and dropped into it. Julia crossed to a cabinet, poured out whisky, splashed soda, and took it to him. "I don't want a drink," muttered Yule, but he took the glass and gulped the whisky down. "If only I had some idea where she is, I'd find her. I've got to find her."

"You won't find anyone until you've slept the clock round," Julia said. "Would you like to stay here?"

"I can't sleep!"

"I'll take him home," said Mannering, and expected an outburst from Yule, opposition from Julia. Yule didn't seem to notice what he said, and Julia smiled gently:

"I don't think you realise what you've done, or what you're facing, just yet," said Julia. "I've told you before and now I'll tell you again, so that your wife can hear. If anything happens to Fay Goulden it will be your fault. I've known Enrico for a long time. I knew when he first interested himself in Fay. I tried to help her, protected her against him. I think I'm the one human being he won't hurt, who can do anything with him. It was working until you came along. Whatever happens now will be on your conscience. I hope you haven't forgotten the photograph."

Mannering said : "Oh, you're as innocent as a lily."

"I've tried to help Fay."

"Why?"

"Because I'm fond of her." She paused, then asked abruptly : "*Do* you know where Fay is?"

"No. How long have you known her?"

Julia said slowly, gently : "For many years."

"Did you know her father?"

Julia turned away abruptly. The glint in her eyes startled Mannering, for it showed alarm—almost the fear which touched so many people and had touched Fay. She pretended to sneeze into her hand, but she hadn't turned away because of that, only to try to hide her expression. When she looked back she was smiling faintly, and yet there was something in her manner which told him he had touched a tender spot.

"Yes, I knew him."

"Here or in Germany?"

"In Germany."

"Were you married to Fiori then?"

"No, I hadn't met Fiori. I wish to God I'd never met him!" Passion rang in her voice. "But I did, and was crazy enough to marry him. I learned a lot about Enrico Fiori during those years. His heartlessness, his cruelty, his dispassionate, monstrous capacity for evil."

"And yet you help him."

"I've tried to save Fay," said Julia. "That's all I've done during the past two years. Longer. But if Fay didn't exist I should still help Fiori. Do you know why, Mannering? Because I know him well enough to be frightened of him."

Mannering said : "There are greater things to fear than your ex-husband."

"I don't think so."

Her eyes—bold, clear, challenging—met his, and he was impressed, felt something of the passion which still surged through her. He turned away, not wanting to meet her eyes. Lorna was looking at her with a horrified expression. Then the tension which had come into the room was broken by a new sound. Julia stifled a laugh and relaxed, crossed to the cabinet and said :

"Will you have a drink?"

In his armchair Kenneth Yule lay with his mouth wide open,

body relaxed, legs stretched out and wide apart, one arm hanging over the side of the chair. He was snoring !

Mannering said : "No thanks. How long have you known Yule?"

"Only a few months."

"How long has he been going with Fay?"

"For those few months."

"What do you know about him?"

"He had a wealthy American grandfather. He spent six years in the army and came out to find himself rich and useless. He started to collect jewels. He met Fay at the Hula Club. Fay was—" She hesitated, then went on quickly : "Fay was working as a hostess at the Club."

"Did Bernstein know that?"

"I've no idea."

"How well did Bernstein know Fay's father?" Mannering snapped that question, ready for alarm in her eyes, knowing that he had touched a sore spot again.

"I have no idea," she said.

"Bernstein left her a fortune, presumably out of gratitude. Do you know why?"

"I am not a thought reader."

"Did you know that she was going to inherit his money?"

In this flat were extracts from Jacob's will; she did know, and if she lied now then all his suspicions of her would be revived, re-doubled. She hesitated, weighing her words, and he felt sure that she was going to lie.

Then she said :

"Yes. Fiori discovered it. Don't ask me how. From that moment he was very interested in Fay and became her self-appointed guardian. I discovered why that was. Whatever else, he isn't a woman chaser and there was nothing in Fay that would interest him, he likes his women to be sophisticated. Like me !" She laughed, and there was bitterness in her voice. "Then he heard it rumoured that Bernstein had the *Diamond of Tears*, and I understood."

"Understood what?"

"Why he was so interested in Fay. She would inherit the *Tear*. It was the one thing he wanted above all else. Something has happened recently to make him desperate. I don't know what. He's always wanted the *Tear*. He's dreamed about it, fought for it, killed and mutilated for it—and it's always evaded him. This time he thought that he was safe, until Bernstein spread the rumour that he was going to sell. When Jacob did that he virtually killed himself."

"Why does Fiori want the *Tear*?"

"I don't know. There were questions which you didn't ask Enrico. If you—"

The telephone bell broke across her words. She seemed glad, crossed to the telephone, and said:

"Yes. . . . Yes, he's here."

But she didn't look at Mannering, only at Kenneth Yule, and went on slowly: "He's not free at the moment. Can he call you back? . . . Well, if it's that urgent." She put the telephone on the table, looked at Yule and shrugged. "I don't know whether we can wake him."

Yule's faint snoring was rhythmic and deep.

Mannering said softly: "All you care about is helping Fay. Is that it?"

"Yes."

"Give me the telephone," said Mannering, and stretched out his hand. Julia hesitated, then let him have it. Lorna moved restlessly, took a cigarette from a small box, lit it and said: "What are you going to do?"

Mannering covered the mouthpiece with his hand, looked at her with his head on one side, smiled faintly at Julia, and said carefully: "How does this sound?"

Julia started.

Mannering went on: "I'm out of practice, but it ought to serve."

It wasn't his voice; it was Kenneth Yule's. Julia backed away, as if before something uncanny.

"And speaking on the telephone will help to make it convincing," Mannering said. He framed his words carefully, sounded boyish, eager and intent—just like Yule. He took his hand away from the telephone and said: "Yes, what is it?"

A man said: "They've tumbled to it. That ruddy newshound. You'd better come quick."

Mannering said: "Where are you?"

"At the house, where the hell do you think I am?" and rang off.

CHAPTER XVII

'THE HOUSE'

MANNERING asked: "Where does Yule live?" He went across to Yule, stared down at him, made sure that his eye-lids were quite still, he wasn't foxing but was in a really heavy sleep. Mannering lowered his voice, as if afraid of waking him. "In London?" Larraby had told him but Yule might have two addresses.

"He has a house in St. John's Wood," Julia said.

"The address?"

"Five, Wrenn Street."

"Thanks." Mannering leaned forward, touched Yule's coat. "Do you know which pocket he keeps his keys in?"

"I—no," said Julia. "No."

Mannering said: "If he wakes I'm going to send him to sleep again. If he doesn't, keep him here until you hear from me." He moved his hand towards Yule's right trouser pocket and slid it in slowly, groping. He touched some coins. Yule didn't stir. He felt every coin; there was nothing else in the pocket. As he withdrew his hand the two women watched him breathlessly. To get at the other trouser pocket he would have to shift Yule. He felt first in his coat and waistcoat; there were no keys. He put an arm beneath Yule's left leg, raised it, crossed it gently over the other, then went to the side of the chair; the pocket gaped a little. His fingers crept in; he touched something soft; leather. He drew it out. When he saw it his eyes lit up; this was a key case.

"What is it all about?" Julia's voice was hushed, as if she were as anxious as Mannering not to wake Yule.

"I don't know yet. How far do you trust Yule?"

"I've no reason to distrust him."

"Just a good-time Charlie," Mannering said. But Kenneth Yule had been interested in the *Tear* and Larraby was checking on him, so was Chittering. The telephone call had brought things to a head but introduced nothing really new—except possibly suspicions of Yule. "Lorna, I'm not sure what Julia will try to do when I've gone. Watch her." He went across the room, picked up Julia's handbag and looked through it. "No gun, anyhow."

Julia said : "All I want to do is to help Fay. If I think you can do that I'll help you."

Could anyone speak with such apparent sincerity and be lying?

Mannering said : "That's fine, but still watch her, Lorna. The police are outside, they'll come at a shout. Don't let Yule leave for at least an hour."

"He'll lie like a log for hours," Julia said.

Lorna followed Mannering to the door, they paused, their hands touched. She said, "I'm not sorry. I know I'm right, and the awful thing is, you are, too. Be careful."

He smiled, and went out.

The C.I.D. man outside Fay's flat nodded. Downstairs there was another, whom Mannering had seen earlier that day at Chelsea : the man detailed to follow Lorna. Mannering said : "She's all right, and she isn't coming out for an hour. If she does there's something wrong."

"I understand, sir."

Mannering hurried towards Park Lane, and soon found a taxi. "Wrenn Street, St. John's Wood, please." He sat back, still fingering the leather key case, trying not to let his thoughts race too far ahead. But the significance in that call couldn't be exaggerated. *'They've tumbled to it. That ruddy newshound.'* He might have meant Chittering or the reporter whom Chittering had sent to follow Yule.

London was sprawling and too big, much too big, and there was too much traffic; it took an age to move along Park Lane, then the Edgware Road. But when the driver turned right into the side streets they went faster, reached the Marylebone Road, bowled along towards St. John's Wood. Mannering didn't know Wrenn Street but knew the district. He looked out at the big, tall houses, drab and grey, some of them surrounded by high brick walls. The driver knew just where he was going. He swung round a corner and said :

"What number?"

"Five."

"Other end."

Mannering looked out of the window, and saw nothing

behind them. He changed his mind, and said: "Sorry, it's fifteen." The man grunted, and stopped by a big yellow brick wall. Mannering paid him off, waited in the gateway of Number 15 for several minutes; no one turned into the street. He walked past Number 5, which stood well back from the road. The garden was well kept, he caught a glimpse of a trim lawn behind an iron gate. No one was in sight. He went into the next door garden, stood on a handy wheelbarrow and looked over the wall. No one was in the back garden of Number 5, and there was no rear garden gate. He peered up at the windows. No curtains moved, no one appeared to be looking.

He climbed the wall, jumped down on to a flower bed, and turned his ankle enough to hurt.

Here was tidiness and colour. On a clothes line at the end of the garden some socks and stockings blew gently in the slight wind. He heard no sound in the house, went to the nearest window and peered into the kitchen; it was much more modern than he had expected. He walked quickly to the front of the house, peering in at every window, and saw no one.

There was a wide porch and two round cement-faced pillars. The huge door was freshly painted green, the brass glittered. He tried two of the four Yale keys in the case before the lock turned. The door squeaked as it opened, but when he stepped into the spacious hall there was silence. He closed the door gently, risking another squeak, tiptoed to the foot of a carpeted staircase and listened intently.

He heard voices.

There were five rooms downstairs, including the kitchen. He looked in each one, locked the kitchen door to make sure no one could get in that way, bolted the front door and then went upstairs, keeping close to the wall to prevent the treads squeaking. The voices had stopped. There was a wide landing and a narrow passage; five doors altogether, and only one was ajar. Another flight of stairs, much narrower than this, led to the next floor. He couldn't spend too much time covering his retreat. He crept to the door which was ajar and a man said:

"He's taking his time."

"He'll be along."

"What are we going to do with that guy?"

"He'll keep."

"I'm not so sure. If we've croaked him—"

'Forget it !"

"You don't seem to realise the danger. We've got the girl away, we don't have to wait for the big boy, he can follow us."

"We wait."

Mannering could just see into the room between the door and the wall. He saw one man, sitting sideways to him a stocky dark-haired, tough-looking man—and a pair of feet that didn't belong to him. The feet, in highly polished brown shoes, belonged to someone on the floor, in a corner.

Chittering?

Mannering drew back from the door, opened another and entered a large bedroom. He took an ashtray from the side of the bed, a large brass candlestick from the mantelpiece, went back to the door and tossed the ash tray down the stairs. At the first sound a chair scraped and a man exclaimed :

"What's that?"

"He's come," said the harsh-voiced man; and the chair creaked, a footfall sounded, the door opened, a head appeared. Mannering brought the candlestick down on the head, pitching the man forward, turned and drove his fist into the other's face. Instantly, he struck the second man on the back of the head with the candlestick; the man grunted and lay still. The other had recovered, and was swinging round with his right hand at his pocket. Mannering jumped back into the room and slammed the door. A shot rang out, a bullet struck the wood. He rammed home the bolts as another shot came, aimed at the lock— Benoni's trick.

He stepped over the unconscious man's body and saw Chittering in the corner. Chittering's fluffy hair was matted with congealed blood.

.   .   .   .   .

Mannering searched the pockets of the man he had knocked out, felt an automatic pistol and drew it out. The shooting had stopped. He heard no sound outside, nothing to suggest that the man was creeping down the stairs. He looked round for a telephone; it was by the fireplace. This was a living-room, small, newly painted and papered. He dialled the police emergency number, 999, and was answered promptly. "Send to Five, Wrenn Street, St. John's Wood—attempted murder, and there's a man loose with a gun." He dropped the receiver back on its cradle, and went to Chittering. He knelt down, felt for the pulse, looking tight-lipped into the cherubic face.

His pulse beat faintly.

Mannering touched his head gently, seeing that he had been bashed several times. The skull was probably cracked—minutes mattered, but the police would send an ambulance and a doctor. He heard a car coming along the road and stop, then heard a shout. He went to the small window, but it overlooked the back of the house. He flung it up, looked right, saw nothing of the road but heard another shout.

A shot rang out in the street.

Mannering turned away, went to the man he had knocked out, sat him up against the wall and began to slap his face—not hard, just enough to bring him round. He heard more shouting, but no further shooting. The man's eyes flickered and Mannering said:

"That's it, wake up." He slapped again, and the man cringed away. "Where's the girl?" Dazed eyes blinked at him. Except that he didn't like the slapping, the man was hardly conscious. Mannering slapped: "The girl—where is she?"

"I—I—I dunno—"

Mannering said: "I'll break your fingers one by one if you don't tell me." He took the man's little finger between his, bent it back. Another car pulled up outside, men ran along the path, a door banged back—so the police were already in the house. "Don't move, or the bone will snap. Where's the girl?"

Terrified eyes peered into his; little ugly eyes in a small ugly face.

"She's at the cottage, at the cottage!"

"Where's the cottage?" Mannering pressed on the little finger, not caring in that moment whether it snapped or not. Men thudded up the stairs, flung open doors, reached this one and banged on it. A man called: "Open—open in the name of the law!" The law could be so stupid. "Where's the cottage?" Mannering demanded, and saw little balls of sweat break out on the other's forehead and lip.

"At Woking. Fell Cottage, Woking. I never—"

"Who owns it?"

"The Big Boy. Yule! You're hurting!" The man gasped and cried out.

The police challenge came again and a man said: "Tell

them to watch the window, and bring an axe. We'll have to smash this down."

"What part of Woking?"

"Near the golf course. I—I didn't bash him. Mellor did that, I didn't bash him. I tried to stop him. I didn't bash him."

Mannering said: "I hope they give you life." He stood up, went to the door and hesitated, then heard another, familiar voice outside. He laughed shortly, pulled back a bolt, and heard a man say:

"He's opening it!"

"Stand aside! Be careful, he may be armed."

Mannering pulled back the other bolt, unlocked the door and pulled it open. A policeman in uniform, a plain-clothes man and Inspector Gordon stood there, crouching, ready to pounce; one man had a truncheon in his hand. Mannering said: "Well, you get full marks for that, you didn't lose much time. Did you catch Mellor?"

"Mellor?" barked Gordon; he looked savage.

"The man with the gun."

"Yes, we did," said the constable. "We got him all right, *and* he didn't do any damage."

"Not a bad job, then, is it?" Mannering asked Gordon. "But it's not quite over. Fay Goulden's at a cottage near Woking Golf Course—Fell Cottage. And if friends of Mellor are looking after her we'd better not lose much time. Will you call the Woking police?"

Gordon said: "We could hear what was happening in here. You were hurting that man, and—"

"I would gladly break his neck." Mannering heard a bell ringing out in the street, the clear familiar clang of an ambulance. He turned and pointed to Chittering. "He got hurt, too. Argue about it afterwards, but warn the local police at Woking, and then let's get moving." Gordon stood and glowered but was shaken by sight of Chittering's battered head. The sergeant pushed forward and bent down on one knee beside Chittering. Mannering swung round, picked up the telephone, dialled and spoke savagely as the disk clattered round. "W—H—I—1—2—1—2. In case you don't know it, that's Scotland Yard." Gordon tried to take the telephone away. Mannering resisted, and the operator answered.

"Scotland Yard, can I help you?"

"Superintendent Bristow, please."

It wasn't long before Bristow was speaking.

Mannering said: "Bill, I'm with a half-cocked lunatic you call an inspector. Gordon. I've asked him to call the Woking police and warn them that Fay Goulden is at Fell Cottage, near the links. He doesn't seem to know how to use the telephone. Speak to him, will you?"

Gordon hissed: "I'll make you pay for this."

Mannering pushed the receiver into his hand and backed away. The C.I.D. man stood up from Chittering and said: "It's a bad job." Why speak at all, if one couldn't find anything better to say than that? Mannering heard the ambulance men coming up the stairs. He felt unsteady from reaction, the fact that chance had saved Chittering, if he were to be saved; in another hour it would have been too late. He saw Gordon's pale, angry face as Gordon listened, and had little doubt what Bristow was saying. The ambulance men and a police surgeon came in.

Gordon turned round.

"He's coming," he growled. "You're to stay here until he arrives."

Mannering said: "Thanks, I can do with a breather." He sat down in an easy chair, the chair that Mellor had been using a quarter of an hour ago. Suddenly he remembered Kenneth Yule sprawled back in the chair at Julia's flat, sleeping like a log. He spluttered; laughed. The surgeon glowered at him. Gordon swore beneath his breath, but no one took much notice until Mannering said:

"There's a man named Yule at 23 Clay Court. He owns this house. You might do something about him, too."

·   ·   ·   ·   ·

Bristow had a green Rover 2-litre. He had always had a green Rover, it always looked a little shabby, and it was always capable of surprising bursts of speed on account of its super-charged engine. Like Bristow, it was deceptive. It hummed along the Kingston by-pass an hour after Gordon had spoken to the Superintendent. Two other cars followed, but Gordon wasn't in this convoy, he had gone to Yule. The other cars had five men in each, but only Mannering and Bristow were in this one. Bristow wasn't in a talkative mood. He had concentrated on getting through the thick suburban traffic, and was now concentrating on speed. Houses and green fields flashed by. Mannering watched the speedometer creep up towards the seventy-five mark, and suddenly laughed again.

Bristow said : "What's funny?"

"It's all funny. Especially how quickly things can move. Thanks, Bill. If Gordon had his way he would be questioning me still, and probably deciding that it was time to telephone Woking."

"Sure the girl's there?"

There was no need to keep anything back, so he talked freely and easily—of the way Yule had come in, of what had followed, of the telephone call and all he had heard at 5 Wrenn Street. Bristow kept his eye on the road and the needle which was hovering between seventy and seventy five. They were now near the end of the by-pass; in ten minutes they would be at Woking.

"And that's all?"

"Isn't it plenty? I thought Fiori had the girl. Julia Fiori was sure he hadn't, and this has about clinched it."

"Yes. I'm glad about that girl." Bristow swerved to pass a lorry and Mannering snorted. "What's got into you? What's funny?"

"The things people say." Mannering took out a cigarette and gave it to Bristow, lit it for him, and went on slowly : "It's almost time to start thinking. Yule and Fiori were rival bidders for the *Tear*, that's pretty evident. I don't think they're working together—I'll have a big surprise if we find they are. The *Tear* is responsible for a lot. Fay was going to inherit it, so Fiori made himself her guardian, and Yule got engaged to her. And she was scared all the time."

"So Fiori made himself her guardian?"

"That's the story. She was a hostess at the Hula club, but she didn't use the name of Fay Goulden. She was Ella Carruthers. She started there at the tail-end of the war years, when she wasn't long out of school, if my information's correct. Did you know she also called herself Carruthers?"

Mannering said : "Bull's eye, Bill."

"Yes, we get some. We've been digging into old Goulden's past, too. You know he was at Bonn University. We know that he managed to pass himself off as a German for the first few years of the Nazi terror and helped a lot of refugees out of the country.

Then he had to fly himself, but didn't make it. He was caught, interned and died at Dachau. Jacob Bernstein was at Dachau—remember?"

Mannering said: "If Goulden helped refugees out of Nazi Germany this is beginning to make sense. I mean the legacy. I can imagine old Jacob would think that well worth repayment. There was nothing wrong with Jacob."

"It's a matter of opinion and depends on how you look at it. Jacob was clever and I wouldn't class him with Harry Green and other crooked dealers, but he smuggled a lot of stones into and out of the country. I'm not worried about that just now, I'm thinking more about Jacob and the *Tear*. Do you know how he got hold of it?"

"No."

Bristow said: "I wish I did. I can tell you this, if you haven't already discovered it, and I don't think you have. These four people who owned the *Tear* and were murdered didn't have the real McCoy."

Mannering exclaimed: "*What?* If this is a joke—"

"It's fact. They each had a paste diamond that looked like the *Tear*. I wouldn't like to take my oath on it yet, but it's pretty certain that Fiori knew they were supposed to have the *Tear*, and thought they had. Fiori went after them, dealt with them, and got a paste diamond each time. It didn't please the gentleman. The real *Tear* was under cover. Whether Jacob had it, or whether he came across it when he reached England, I don't know. He was expert at smuggling jewels out of Germany during the persecution days before the war—odd that a man does a thing one way and is a hero, does it another and becomes a criminal. But I don't make the law, I just see that it's carried out. One obvious question crops up now, and I'd like to know the answer. Did Jacob have the real *Diamond of Tears*, or was it another paste stone?"

Mannering said: "It was—" and stopped abruptly.

Bristow looked quickly away from him, Mannering ran his hand across his forehead, and began to sweat. The trick was clear, but he had nearly seen it too late. Bristow had talked freely, lulled him into a sense of security, then dropped out the casual question—and he'd nearly answered, nearly admitted that he had seen the *Tear*.

"It was what?" asked Bristow.

"It was pretty crazy that four different people should think they had the *Tear*, and actually had a dab of paste," said Mannering. But the fact that he had stalled Bristow wasn't so important as another fact—that there were five paste diamonds, all like the *Tear* in Julia Fiori's jewel drawer.

Bristow didn't force his question; he didn't even show any sign of disappointment.

"A lot of people are fooled by paste; you ought to know that. It's still a question—was Jacob's *Tear* real or a fake? If real, where did he get it, where has it been all these years? I don't get it, do you?"

"Not yet."

They passed under the railway bridge and were at the edge of Woking Common when a police patrol car, parked just ahead of them, stuck out its indicator and moved off. As they slowed down a policeman put his head out of the window and shouted something. They couldn't hear the words, but guessed what he meant—they were to follow the patrol car. It swung left, then turned across the open commonland. Here and there were small cottages, but no one was near them. Mannering saw the golf course in the distance and, at one side of it, several cars and little knots of men near some pine trees and a cottage. He forgot the paste diamonds and all that Bristow had told him. He watched the cottage closely, looking among the crowd of men for Fay.

The front door of the cottage was ajar. A burly man stood in front of it, and hurried forward as Bristow's car drew near. Mannering felt an intense excitement, an anxiety which numbed him.

Had they found her? Was she all right?

Bristow opened the window and called: "Did you get her?"

The man didn't answer, probably didn't hear. Bristow pulled up outside a small wooden gate and switched off the engine. The burly man opened the gate as Bristow asked again: "Did you get her? Is she all right?"

The Woking man said: "Someone's been pulling your leg." He laughed, looked as if it delighted him that the great ones of Scotland Yard could nod. "Fay Goulden isn't here and has never been here. And this is Fell Cottage."

Bristow looked round at Mannering, and said: "So you're good!"

He opened the car door and got out, while Mannering stared

at the name of the gate of the cottage, there for all to see. It was an old place, with a red tiled roof and mullioned windows. It stood back from the road with its back towards the golf course. Smoke curled up from one of the two large chimneys. This was Fell Cottage, but Fay wasn't here, had never been here.

Bristow looked back into the car.

"When you've recovered you might come and join us." He walked with the Woking man towards the open front door.

CHAPTER XVIII

ORDER FROM FIORI

THE group of policemen seemed to be watching and laughing at Mannering as he got out of the car and walked in Bristow's wake. Bristow, deep in conversation, didn't look round. A plainclothes man came to the door and saluted. Bristow had to duck beneath the lintel as he went inside. Mannering lit a cigarette, glanced over his shoulder, and saw the dozen men staring. And ten more were coming—eighteen men, in all—on a wasted journey because a little man had lied to him!

But he felt sure that man hadn't lied.

He had been too frightened, sure that his finger would snap if he held out. A simple fact dawned on Mannering: Fay hadn't been mentioned by name—the two crooks had talked of "the girl," not of Fay. That meant a girl who had been at Wrenn Street; one man had said "she's gone."

There was no hall or passage at the cottage. He stepped over the threshold into a small, low-ceilinged room, charmingly and expensively furnished. The policemen looked huge as they stood in front of a wide open fireplace, questioning a girl who sat in an armchair, looking scared but no more than scared—not terrified and laden with fear, like Fay.

She was a pretty little thing.

Bristow said : "Now let's hear what you have to say."

"I've told these men once," she protested, and moistened her lips. "I've never seen the Goulden girl. Until I read the newspaper I'd never heard of her !"

"Let's have it all again," Bristow said.

"Well, I hardly know where to start." She had a pleasant voice, good, clear blue eyes. She wore a plain grey top coat, stout brown shoes, and was neat and tidy. "I work for Mr. Yule."

"And he owns this place?"

"Yes, he owns the cottage *and* a house in London—5 Wrenn Street. Sometimes I work here, sometimes at Wrenn Street. I had a message this morning, asking me to come here. So I came and opened up the cottage because no one has been here for a week."

"Who was at Wrenn Street when you left?"

"Mellor and Brownie. Brownie does odd jobs in the garden, doesn't work regularly. Mellor is Mr. Yule's chauffeur. I can't understand why you thought that Miss Goulden might be here."

Bristow glanced at Mannering.

"Any idea?" he asked dryly.

Mannering said: "My man was Brownie, and apparently Brownie lied." But Brownie had told the simple truth—this was the girl he had talked of.

"And you'd never heard of Miss Goulden until you saw her name in the newspapers," Bristow said sceptically. "Didn't you know that she was a friend of Mr. Yule's?"

"I only work for him," said the girl. "Miss Goulden has never been here or at the house while I've been present. I'm *quite* sure."

She sounded transparently honest—but was she? She'd been sent here, and—

There were various possibilities. That Mellor and Brownie had known there was danger, that Chittering had got onto them, so they had been afraid that there would be a raid at the house. Therefore they had sent the girl away, where they could do what they liked without fear of being overheard. Chittering had walked into the trap—and Chittering was now lying on an operating table, where the surgeons might save his life.

Bristow said: "Go into another room for a few minutes, will you?"

The girl jumped up. "I don't know what Mr. Yule will say." She went out, tossing her head—but from the door she shot a swift look at Bristow and the Woking man. Mannering caught the look, the weariness of it, the doubt and anxiety. Bristow missed it, because Bristow was looking at him.

"You want to take a holiday, John," he said sadly.

"Yes," Mannering agreed ruefully. "I can see how it happened, but—"

"The time to see what's happening is while it's going on, not after the damage is done," said Bristow. "Well, I won't rub it in. What's the girl's name?" he asked the Woking man.

"Elizabeth Warren."

"Is she known?"

"The constables who cover the golf course say she's worked for Yule for a couple of years." He shrugged. "The story is that she's both housekeeper and mistress. She's often here at night, alone with him. She's friendly, plays a good round of golf, has a lot of spare time. There are two daily women who do the heavy work, and she gives them their orders. Yule's not well known, but has a reputation of being a nice young chap. You know how it is—a love nest, and no one's poked their nose in too far."

"I hope they've kept their eyes open, we want to know who visits Yule here," said Bristow. "Get the girl's statement ready and have her sign it, won't you? I'll check in London." It wasn't surprising that Bristow thought it likely that the girl had told the whole truth, and was thinking of a routine check.

*   *   *   *   *

No evidence that Yule was implicated in any form of crime was found at the cottage or at Wrenn Street.

*   *   *   *   *

On the way back Bristow said: "We can hold Yule if either Mellor and Brownie implicate him, but not if they don't. I believe that you took a call intended for Yule, but it wouldn't stand up in court and you know it wouldn't. Better let him go, and keep tabs on him, rather than put him on a charge. Taken on its face value your statement isn't much good."

Mannering, in a subdued mood, had to agree.

Bristow dropped him at Oxford Street and Mannering took a taxi to St. George's Hospital, spent twenty futile minutes trying to get a precise report on Chittering, and left with the assurance that the operation had been successful but the patient's condition was dangerous; his wife had already been summoned.

Outside the hospital Mannering bought a *Daily Record*. Chittering's last job had been well and truly done. A mysterious foreigner was believed to have visited Jacob Bernstein shortly before his death; there was reason to believe that the *Tear* had been smuggled out of the country, and much more. Mannering stood reading it and felt someone bump into him. He started round; a little man stood at his side, squinting at the paper.

"Wonder who thought that one up," he said. "Shouldn't think it would convince anyone with any sense, would you? These newspapers. And the police—bah!" He looked up at Mannering with a twisted grin, then suddenly stepped into the road in front of a stream of traffic. He reached the opposite pavement while Mannering stood stranded on the kerb—actually waved and grinned before he jumped into a taxi and was driven off.

Just like Fiori—

A quick jab of a needle; a sharp jolt to his mind; a cryptic letter—each with its evidence that Mannering was watched and followed wherever he went. Had he been followed to Woking and back, or picked up in London by accident? How could he have been picked up in London? One way was obvious; if Fiori knew about Chittering he would expect Mannering to visit the hospital and send a man to watch. How many men worked for him? Where was he? Where was Fay?

Mannering walked along crowded Piccadilly keeping a sharp look-out, seeing no sign that he was followed. He took another taxi and went to Quinn's. On jobs like this he almost forgot that he owned Quinn's and had work to do. His manager, portly, courtly, dressed in morning clothes and with a grey cravat, reported that all was well. He went into detail about some inquiries for Dutch miniatures and an exquisite Genoese silver table which stood in the discreet gloom of the back of the shop, then asked whether Larraby was likely to be off shop-duty for any length of time.

"Probably, yes. Can you manage?"

"Oh, quite well, Mr. Mannering, but I shall have to hire a porter for several odd jobs."

"Make sure it's a man you know," said Mannering. He went to the small office at the back of the shop, saw a pile of correspondence awaiting attention, glanced through it impatiently, made notes, and was nearly through when the telephone bell rang.

"This is Quinn's."

"And I believe that is Mr. Mannering," said Fiori.

.   .   .   .   .

Mannering pressed a bell-push which rang a bell gently in the shop, pulled a notepad forward, started to scribble, and said: "Yes, this is Mannering, and I want to talk to you." He wrote: "*Try to trace this call, it's Fiori, say you're police*," and pushed the note across to the manager who had come in response to the bell. He read it without raising an eyebrow and went off.

Fiori said: "I am not vengeful, Mannering, and you know what I want. Take it to my brother's restaurant, and leave it tucked behind the cushion of your chair between eight and nine o'clock to-night."

He rang off.

* * * * *

Mannering inserted his key into the lock of the front door of his flat and the door opened. Lorna looked up and said: "Why didn't you call me?" but there was no reproof in her voice. She didn't smile, but her heavy frown was gone. Mannering slammed the door behind him, took her in his arms, kissed her fiercely and passionately.

"I'm forgiven!"

"You're not forgiven but I suppose you aren't to blame for what's born in you. Why I had to marry a man who always keeps me on a knife edge I don't know, but I did it and I've got to put up with it. Do you think you'll get Fiori with the *Tear*?"

"Yes."

"When?"

"When a lot of little things are cleared up." Mannering led the way into the study. "Do Fiori and Kenneth Yule work together or are they rivals for the *Tear*? If they're rivals, do they want it for the same reason? What did Chittering discover that put him on the murder list?"

"Chittering! Is he hurt?"

"Didn't you know?" He told her, and needed no telling how dreadfully upset she was.

He told her everything else, omitting only the jab from the needle and the other reminder of Fiori outside the hospital. She had won this new battle with herself, for she said:

"Will you go to the café?"

"Probably, but not with the diamond. I don't think I should be allowed to get as far as the café. Enrico may not have any love for brother Toni, but he would hardly embroil Toni and take the chance that I'll tell Bristow and have the café raided. I wouldn't even say that I think Fiori hopes I'll go, it's just part of the unnerving process. What happened at Julia's flat?"

"Gordon came and took Kenneth Yule away. I don't think Yule realised what was happening, he was still asleep when Gordon arrived."

"Clever Julia," murmured Mannering.

"Where does she come into that?"

Mannering laughed. "That drink was drugged. Remember how Julia once put Fay to sleep, to prevent her from talking to me? Yule put up a pretty act, Julia went one better. What did you make of her?"

"I like her."

"Attractive, almost gay, quite a personality. But how much of her talk about Fiori's corruption was bluff? Does she hate him as much as she says she does? Is she really concerned for Fay? Bristow told me that the earlier victims in the *Tear* hunt owned paste gems—and they were stolen. Julia has a nice little collection of paste *Tears*. That reminds me!" He went to his desk, took out an illustrated catalogue, ran through the pages and stopped at a black and white illustration of the *Diamond of Tears*. Beneath this was printed the weight and measurements of the gem. He checked these with the measurements he had taken from the paste replicas; they were identical. "These fakes were not only made for the *Tear*, my sweet, they were almost certainly made by someone who had the *Tear* as a working model. I'd like to know more about the first four of Fiori's victims—how they came to have the *Tear* or to think they had, why they thought it worth suffering hell before they would tell him where to find their copy of the pretty thing. Care to do some research for me?"

"I'll see what I can find out."

"The *Record* office will help as much as anywhere," Mannering said. "While you're there you might try to find out what happened to the reporter who watched Kenneth Yule last night."

"Are you *sure* Yule was putting on an act? I've never seen a man who made me feel more sorry for him."

"Young man in love? It wouldn't surprise me if he is in love with Fay, but he's also deep in the hunt for the *Tear*. Don't trust your feelings. Feelings ask us to trust Julia, but we can't; or trust

Yule, and we daren't. I hope the police hold him, but they won't unless they get a squeal out of Mellor and Brownie. Of course, you don't know Mellor and Brownie. . . ."

*   *   *   *   *

At half-past six that evening Bristow telephoned. Neither of the men caught at 5, Wrenn Street had implicated Yule, neither had talked at all—except that Brownie had accused Mellor of attacking Chittering, and said he had tried to stop him.

"So you're letting Yule go," Mannering said heavily.

"We'll watch him."

"Before the night's out you'll have lost him."

"Still think you can do better?"

"No, Bill," said Mannering humbly.

"I had a message from your shop about Fiori's telephone call. You can never trace anything on the automatic system, but at least you had the sense to tell me that Fiori had called. What did he say?"

"He still clings to the odd notion that I can find the *Tear*. He also threatened what he'll do if I don't hand it over."

Bristow said : "He'll probably carry out his threat. What are you going to do tonight?"

"Have a good dinner and ruminate on the sins of the world," said Mannering.

"So you're going to the café," Lorna said, when he rang off.

"Yes. But I've other things to do first. Will you try the *Record* for that dope about the early Fiori victims, and come straight back here? The police will watch you. Make sure you don't get mixed up in crowds and can always be seen by the Yard man. Better tell Susan that I'll be at Toni Fiori's until ten o'clock; anyone who calls can find me there. After that—"

"Home."

"Woking," said Mannering.

CHAPTER XIX

VISITOR AT WOKING

Julia's maid answered his ring. Julia came out of the drawing-room to greet him, superb in a black evening gown with a rare orchid at her breast, shoulders and arms like alabaster. "You ought to have a key," she said. "What will you drink?"

"Gin and something, please. I'm sorry you're going out."

"I'm not, so we can have a delightful evening together. Or is your wife coming?" As Julia went to the cocktail cabinet, Mannering watched the smooth grace of her movements and tried to picture Enrico Fiori by her side.

"How well do you know Toni's restaurant?"

"I haven't been there for months."

"Come to-night?"

Julia brought him a pink gin. "You like asking for trouble, don't you?"

"Thrive on it. Will you come?"

"Yes." She sipped, eyed him smilingly, but wariness lurked in her lovely eyes. "What's the reason?"

"I want you to bring something with you."

"What?"

"One of the imitation *Tears*."

Julia turned away, took a book from beneath a table, opened it revealing photographs; it was a thin album covered in wine-red leather. She flipped over the pages, came to a photograph which occupied a whole page, studied it but didn't speak. Mannering joined her and saw Enrico Fiori. The photograph was so lifelike that it might have been taken yesterday. The lowered lids, the solemnity of expression, the heavy jowl—everything was there. Sinister?

Julia closed the book.

"Enrico, I'm beginning to think you've met your match," she said slowly. "So you discovered the paste *Tears* yesterday? Why did you leave them?"

"Everything is useful at the proper time and place. To-night I want a fake because Enrico asked me to go to Toni's and leave the *Tear* there. He's so used to finding imitations that I shouldn't like to disappoint him. Why five, by the way? Only four have been stolen, as far as I can trace."

"He bought one, years ago."

"So you've a right to it!"

"When he discovered that the others were not what he wanted he passed them on to me. I seldom saw him in a temper, but several times he lost his self-control completely. I didn't feel safe—and I usually felt safe with him. After he'd cooled down he gave a *Tear* to me."

"And you didn't feel blood on your fingers?"

"I didn't know how he'd got them then. I knew he only wanted the *Diamond of Tears*. We were in America at the time. I knew that he'd visited an old man about the *Tear,* that the old man wouldn't sell. Two days afterwards the old man was murdered—you know how. The following day Enrico gave me the imitation, after blowing off as he had before." She spoke very softly and coldly. "The fact that the old man had the *Tear* was splashed all over the American newspapers, that was the first I really knew about the diamond's history. I walked out on Enrico then, and we've never lived together since."

"And Fay?" asked Mannering.

"When Enrico began to show an interest in Fay I made it my business to find out why. When I learned that she was going to inherit the *Tear,* I was worried about what might happen to her. I asked him how he knew. He gave me those extracts from Jacob Bernstein's Will; I suppose you saw them in the deed box."

"Yes. How did he get at the Will?"

"He heard a rumour that Jacob had the *Tear* and sent a burglar to search for it. The man brought back those extracts and other information."

"You've an answer for everything."

"I haven't. I don't know why Enrico wants the *Tear.*"

"Does anyone else want it?"

She didn't answer, and Mannering said: "Why did you stop Fay from talking to me the other day?"

Julia said. "Come with me." She led the way to her bedroom and went straight to the dressing-table, unlocked the drawer and took out the narrow jewel case. The five tear-shaped artificial diamonds glowed and winked up at them. The platinum settings were lovely. She held the open case out to him.

"Take which one you like."

He took the box, closed it and slipped it into his inside coat pocket. "Thanks." He turned to leave the room, but she caught his hand, making him turn round. They were very close. She was nearly as tall as he, and again she looked like the painting of a Madonna. Her lips parted slightly, she held her head back and gazed at him between her lashes; and she didn't let go of his hand.

"John, don't go on, please don't go on."

"So you've something in common with my wife."

"She's very lovely, and so deeply in love with you. I can understand any woman being in love with you." Julia smiled, her lips curving and making her more enticing, more desirable. "Don't go on. You think that you've the measure of Enrico, but no one has. I sometimes think that he has the special dispensation of the Devil." She drew nearer, her soft encompassing warmth soothed and yet excited him. "Tell Enrico where to find the *Tear*, and be done with it all."

"It would be easy, if I knew where to find the thing."

She said : "Oh, you fool !" and let him go, moving towards the door. He thought it was because she didn't want him to see her expression. "You know where it is, but it's useless trying to make you see reason. Do you still want me to come to Toni's?"

"Yes."

"Why?"

"I'll try to be as truthful as Enrico. He has eyes everywhere— you know that." Mannering was behind her as he talked. She led the way into the drawing-room and took up her glass but avoided looking at him. "He knows I've been here several times. If he sees us together at Toni's he might get the wrong idea. If he gets the wrong idea he might get angry, and angry men make mistakes. But you don't have to come."

•   •   •   •   •

Toni himself welcomed them warmly. If he were surprised at seeing Julia he made no comment. It was good to see her again, very good to see Mannering, he hoped Mannering's head was better. He had been reading—this in a whisper—about the case in the newspapers. He was distressed that his brother was involved —why, the police had actually been here to question him, Toni !

But he had satisfied them that he knew nothing about Enrico's affairs. Now! For dinner. . . .

They left at half-past ten. A single fake diamond, wrapped in cotton wool, was hidden between the cushion and the back of Mannering's chair.

*   *   *   *   *

Julia said: "Don't come up. I should hate you to go away, and I know you wouldn't stay. Thank you, John." The pressure of her hand on his was cool, firm. "Good-bye."

"I'll report progress to-morrow," Mannering said.

"Will you?" She drew her hand away, turned and hurried into Clay Court, where another commissionaire in resplendent uniform, just visible in the light of the hall, saluted her smartly. Mannering sat at the wheel, watching a C.I.D. man opposite who lit a cigarette. No other car was in the street, no one approached, he did not think he had been followed to or from Toni's. But he had that feeling of being watched. Of course the C.I.D. man was watching. He let in the clutch, and jerked his head up when he heard a thump; more crash than thump, as if two cars had collided.

He drove round the block, and saw nothing; drove off, and was not followed.

He parked the car in a side street off Edgware Road, walked several blocks and came to a small shop. A light glowed at the back, although the shop itself wasn't lighted. He rang the bell. A little old man opened the door, a man who was well-known in London theatrical circles, for he was a supreme artist in make-up.

He peered up, frowning, for he had not switched on the shop light. Then: "Why, Mr. Mannering!"

"Hallo, Solly! Am I a nuisance?"

"It is always a pleasure to see you. Come in, please come in." Solly stood aside; Mannering went to the room at the end of the shop. This was a familiar workshop. Solly was obviously in the middle of preparing grease paint; there was a strong odour of grease in the warm room. An electric fire glowed beneath a little oven in one corner, pigments in small jars stood on a long bench.

"What's going to happen to your secrets when you retire?" asked Mannering.

"When I retire I shall be dead," said the old man, and smiled as if that were a pleasure to anticipate. "My two sons will carry on, I hope. They show promise, especially Matthew. You have time for a cup of coffee with me, upstairs?"

"I wish I had."

"I thought it unlikely, with so much going on. I also read newspapers! Now, how can I help you?"

"I want to pay a visit without being recognized."

"So. Well, you know the difficulties, it is never easy, but"— the old man chuckled—"if you wanted it to be really safe then you would not come to me, you would do it yourself. You wish to pass unnoticed, yes, not under close scrutiny. Sit down, please sit down, and I will see what I can do." Solly touched a chair of the kind usually found in a barber's shop, unfolded a case-mirror on the wall, switched on a light above Mannering's head, and spread a towel round his shoulders.

He hardly spoke while he worked. When he had finished the mirror showed Mannering a round-faced man with a sallow complexion and a broad, close-clipped moustache, heavy eyebrows, an expression of sour discontent.

"It will do?"

"You're still a genius," said Mannering. "Now I want to go out the back way."

.   .   .   .   .

He walked quickly along the narrow alley at the back of the shop, along side streets until he came out near the sprawling area near Paddington Station. The chug-chug of trains sounded clearly on the still night air. He approached a large garage and stood in the shadows near it. By hunching his shoulders he took inches off his height; no one would recognise him here.

A lanky, laconic garage attendant said: "Self-drive car? Sure. Twenty quid deposit."

"That's all right."

He chose a Hillman Minx, modern and fast enough. He drove through the crowded north-west of London and across country to Richmond, then along the main road to Woking Common. He parked the car a mile from the cottage and walked the rest of the way. As he drew near he saw lights shining from two windows, one upstairs, one down. There were no lights nearby, but he could pick out the figures of two men, one at the back, one at the front; Woking policemen. One of them came forward as he approached, and shone a torch into his face. Mannering blinked, protested :

"What's all this?"

"Sorry, sir." The torch went out, the man satisfied that he could describe this visitor. Mannering opened the garden gate; the hinges creaked but he doubted whether the sound reached anyone at the cottage. He walked softly, quickly. He paused at the tiny porch, looked round, could not see the police and knew that he could not be seen. He would rather break in than be admitted, but—the temptation to force entry and shock whoever was there came sharply; he forced it back. He groped for the bell and heard it ring inside. Movements followed at once, and a light showed through a small glass panel in the door.

Elizabeth Warren opened it and the hall light fell on Mannering's face. Being behind her, it showed her head and shoulders in silhouette, revealed her for a really pretty woman. Her brown hair was fluffy, she wore a scarf round her shoulders. She stifled a yawn.

"Good evening."

"Is Mr. Yule in?"

"No, I'm afraid not," she said, and smiled. "I haven't any idea when he'll be back. I'll give him a message if you like."

"I'll stay," said Mannering.

He took her arm, thrust her back into the hall, stepped in and closed the door. She had no chance to stop him, and his bulk hid her from the watching police. As the door closed he let her go. Anger, surprise and fear chased each other across her face.

"This is—"

"I know, outrageous," said Mannering. "Don't waste time and don't waste words. I want to see Yule."

"He's not here !"

"Then who's upstairs?"

"No one else is in the house, but there are—"

"Police outside. You ought to feel happy with police protection. I'm sure Yule is." He took her arm again, pressed hard enough to make her silent. "Who's upstairs?"

"No one !"

Mannering said : "We'll see." He turned her round, forcing her towards the stairs. The stairs were narrow and crooked. She stumbled half-way up and he saved her from falling. The light shone on to the landing from a bedroom; it was empty.

"I told you no one was here!"

"And I don't believe you." But as they stood looking at each other the house seemed silent. She was probably telling the truth. He went with her into the other rooms and now she led the way without being forced, and recovered from the shock of fear and was defiant. But she hadn't called out for the police.

There were three bedrooms and a tiny bathroom, all well furnished. One was obviously Yule's, another as obviously hers. He went along a narrow passage near the landing, seeing the loft hole with the cover in position. By it was a ladder.

"How often do you go up there?"

"Seldom."

"Did the police go up to-day?"

"I don't know where the police went. You've no right to do this."

"We'll go up now." Mannering put the ladder in position and motioned to her to go up. She drew back, tight-lipped, pale, attractive in the poor light from the landing.

"No!"

"Don't let's argue," Mannering said. "Up." He took her arm again. This time she mounted the ladder, slowly; was she nervous of slipping or of what would be found in the attic? She reached halfway, put up her hands and shifted the hatch cover; the attic was dark. She put her hand inside and switched on a light, then clambered into the attic. He joined her.

There was hardly room to stand upright. Big suitcases, two trunks, a dressing-table, dozens of parcels and bundles, stood or lay about the dusty floor. He sneezed.

"*Now* perhaps you're satisfied. Who are you?"

"A friend of Fay Goulden."

She started. "Who—"

"Let's get down," Mannering said. He went first and helped her down. As he stood with his back to the landing he wondered whether there had been anyone downstairs, whether he would have been wise to make sure of that first. There was no alarm. Downstairs the kitchen and dining-room were empty. The only light was in the living-room, where he had been with Bristow.

"Now will you tell me what you want?" Her voice was shrill. Her grey eyes looked enormous. She had lovely smooth skin, was prettier under this light than by day. She wore a skyblue dress and a fluffy skyblue scarf. By the side of an easy chair was a tray with the remains of her supper, a coffee pot, an evening paper and a book lying open and face downwards. It made a simple picture and she looked a simple creature.

"I want to see Kenneth Yule."

"He's gone away."

"Where?"

"I don't know. He was detained by the police, the fools, and he hasn't come back here. He telephoned to say that he would be away for a few days."

"Where does he usually go when he's away for a few days?"

"It might be anywhere."

"And he doesn't leave an address?"

"No!"

Mannering said abruptly: "How long have you been living with him?"

"I've worked for him for two years. I do *not* live with him. You're as bad as the police. *Are* you a policeman?" She stared at him and he knew that something puzzled her, some indication that he was disguised, perhaps; even a hint of familiarity.

"No, I'm not a policeman. Why does Yule want the *Tear*— the *Diamond of Tears?*"

He expected her to say that she didn't know what he was talking about, to protest, to threaten to call the watching police. Instead, she backed to her chair and sat down heavily, and all her colour fading from her cheeks. She moistened her lips and looked at once old and young—old with a weight of care and anxiety which had suddenly descended upon her.

She said: "I don't know."

"Did the police ask you about the *Tear?*"

"No. Who—who *are* you?"

"Still a friend of Fay Goulden. Do you know where she is?"

"No. But—" She caught her breath, as if she had been on the point of blurting out something else and had stopped herself only just in time. She groped for a cigarette. He lit it for her, wondering how he could find out what she knew.

"But you think you might know?" he said sharply.

"I've no idea."

Mannering pulled up a stool, sat down, and looked up at her. She drew at the cigarette until it glowed red for a quarter of its length. Her pallor wasn't assumed, she was scared now—and she had been scared from the moment he had mentioned the *Tear*.

He said: "Let's have the truth. Yule works for Fiori."

She gasped: "No!" The cigarette dropped from her lips into her lap. She let it stay there, gripped the arms of her chair and glared—and her fear had turned to terror because of the name Fiori. He took the cigarette away and tossed it into the hearth.

"He works for Fiori. Why lie about it?"

"He doesn't. He *couldn't*."

"They both want the *Tear*, and—"

The telephone bell rang, sharp, loud. She closed her eyes. Her bosom was heaving. The telephone was near the fireplace and he had to stretch across to reach it. He touched it, but didn't lift the receiver, and the bell kept ringing. She made no move to answer it, seemed eaten up with the terror which a man's name had caused.

Was the caller Fiori?

Had Mannering been followed here?

He lifted the receiver, hesitated, then touched her arm; she opened her eyes. He handed her the receiver. She looked as if she didn't want to take it, so he put it into her hand, was ready to snatch it away if there seemed any cause. He heard her say unsteadily: "Hallo? Who is that?"

She paused, then gave him back the receiver and said: "It's for a—a Mr. Mannering. So you're Mannering." But there was no feeling in her voice, she didn't care who he was.

And the caller? Fiori, of course it was Fiori.

.   .   .   .   .

He felt as if a door had opened and an icy blast had swept into the room. He didn't take the telephone at once, but tried to think how Fiori could have known or even guessed where he was. Guessed? The man *knew*. In spite of all his precautions he had been followed here. It was as if Fiori had a secret host watching in the darkness of the night. Mannering took the telephone, and put it slowly to his ear. Above all things Fiori wanted to unnerve him.

"Well, what is it?"

"John, you'd better come back," said Lorna.

CHAPTER XX

NEWS FROM LORNA

MANNERING said: "Why?" Lorna, of course; he had told her where he was coming, he was a victim of his own foolish fears. "What's it all about?" he asked.

"I think you'd better come back. Julia Fiori has been hurt."

"*Hurt?*"

"That's all I know. One of Chittering's friends rang up just now, and Bristow called me. I was going to call you, anyhow, I've a lot you ought to know."

"Such as?"

"Chiefly about Kenneth Yule and the early victims," said Lorna. Her matter-of-fact voice told him that she was on edge, trying hard to school herself not to show emotion. "One of them was an old man, an American—remember?"

"Yes."

"He was Kenneth Yule's grandfather," Lorna said. "There isn't any doubt, John. The *Record* people discovered it. They've checked with the Yard and it's quite true. It's only just been realised. Yule inherited all his money from that old man."

"What about the others?"

"I haven't learned much about any of them, but all three were Jewish—and the two men escaped from Germany before the war. The woman was the wife of an American collector of precious stones. The *Record* people say they haven't been able to trace any relationship or connection between the woman and any of the men. The only significant thing is that Yule was the old man's grandson."

"Have you discovered anything more about Kenneth Yule himself?"

Elizabeth Warren leaned forward. Her hand moved and touched his, as if she wanted to wrench the receiver away from him; her fingers were cold on the back of his hand.

"A little," Lorna said. "Larraby came in half an hour ago and has a report. Yule was orphaned when he was quite young, and went to Repton and Oxford. He joined the *R.A.F.* and did well—he won the *D.F.C.* in Cyprus. His grandfather was killed a few months before Yule left the Service. Yule went to America and was there for six months, clearing up the estate."

"That's his history—what's his reputation?"

"A gay dog. One girl after another, until he met Fay Goulden."

"Still think he's in love with Fay?"

"The evidence—" began Lorna, but Mannering didn't hear the rest. Elizabeth Warren struck at his hand, knocked the receiver away from his ear. She leaned forward, eyes blazing, mouth open.

He put the receiver close to his ear again.

"Sorry, I missed that."

"We mustn't stay talking. Can you come back at once? Bristow said it was urgent. He asked me not to tell you more over the telephone, but—it's Julia. She's asking for you. She's at St. George's Hospital."

.   .   .   .   .

Elizabeth Warren sat beside Mannering, huddled in a mus-quash coat, shivering now and again although it couldn't be with cold. The police car followed, and although Mannering drove fast he made no attempt at evasion. He didn't talk until he was away from the common and driving towards the by-pass. Passing lights shone on the girl's pale face and glistening eyes.

He said suddenly : "In love with Kenneth?"

She didn't answer.

"So you are. And he's in love with Fay. It's how things happen, and it won't hurt for long."

She said : "He *can't* be in love with her !"

"You think he's gone to her now, don't you?"

She didn't answer, and he needed no answer. Her story, or part of it, was as clear as the white streaks on the road which showed starkly in the headlights. The speedometer touched seventy. The warm fur was close to his arm, but a keen wind cut through the driving window. He wound it up slowly, swerved past a rumbling lorry, saw the twin orbs of the car behind him in the driving mirror.

"It's really a good thing," Mannering said gently. "He's bad, I'm afraid—as bad as they come."

She turned her head abruptly: "That's not true!"

"He's nearly as bad as Fiori."

"Don't say that!"

"What do you know about Fiori?" Mannering asked.

She said: "I hate the sound of his name, I hate everything about him." She shivered again. "I'm not going to talk, I've nothing to say! I'd kill myself rather than let Fiori get me."

"Why?"

"Because I know—what he's done."

"Are you sure that Kenneth doesn't work for him?"

"You must be crazy! Of course he doesn't, he hates Fiori. He's afraid of him, anyone who knows Fiori must be afraid of him, but—Fiori killed a—a close friend of his, killed—"

"His grandfather."

"So you know that?" She was startled, and turned to look at him. Lights flashed by, the car was in darkness one moment, brightly lit the next. "Yes. The *Tear* belongs to Kenneth. It belonged to the old man, so Kenneth has every right to it. He's been looking for it for years."

"Why?"

"It's his!"

"He's wealthy. One diamond more or less would make little difference to him. He doesn't know much about jewels, does he?"

"He's learned a lot since he started to look for the *Tear*," Elizabeth said. She talked of the diamond as if it were a familiar thing and she knew it well. "He was even going to buy it. I've helped him look for it. We know what happened to the others who were supposed to have it, we know what Fiori did. And in spite of having to fight against Fiori, Ken's kept on. He wouldn't let anything stop him."

"Oh, he's a fighter."

She didn't respond to that.

"Why did he start going round with Fay Goulden? Because he knew she would inherit the *Tear*?"

Elizabeth cried: *What?*" and started so violently that she knocked his arm. He lost control of the car and it swerved towards an oncoming lorry. The lorry passed within a few inches, a vague shout came from the driver. Elizabeth took Mannering's hand, pulled at it, dug her fingers into his knuckles until it hurt. "That's not true! It can't be true!"

"Take it easy or we'll crash."

Her grip slackened, but she didn't let him go.

"It's quite true, Elizabeth. Jacob Bernstein left everything to Fay Goulden. As he owned the *Tear* before he died it belongs to her, not Ken. It's no use talking about it belonging to Kenneth; Jacob had a legal right to it."

"It can't be true," she whispered. "He wouldn't do that. Not Ken, he wouldn't do *that*."

Mannering tried to sound casual. "Do what?"

She didn't answer. Her hand fell from his, between them, he could feel it limp against his leg. "Do what, Elizabeth?" he asked again, but she was silent. When they passed beneath a lamp he looked at her. She lay back, chin thrust forward, her eyes closed, her pallor dreadful. He pulled into the side of the road. The police car passed and drew up in front. He felt the girl's cold hand and knew that she had fainted, this wasn't just an act. He stretched to the back of the car, pulled up a rug, folded it behind her head, so that her neck was supported. He had no whisky flask. Her handbag lay on her lap. He opened it, but there was nothing of use there.

A policeman got out of the car in front and looked back, as if wondering whether to come and find out what had happened.

Elizabeth's pulse was beating faintly and her lips moved as she breathed. There was nothing to worry about, no reason why Mannering shouldn't drive on. He opened both the front windows wide, let in the clutch and started off, driving slowly at first and giving the police car plenty of time to catch up. It was very cold, now. They were at the end of the by-pass and he turned towards Roehampton and Putney. At the top of Putney Hill she stirred, whimpered a little as if she were dreaming. At the foot of the hill, as they drove on to Putney Bridge and across the Thames, her eyelids flickered.

He gave her a few minutes respite, then said:

"Better?"

"I—I'm all right."

He didn't ask more questions; she wouldn't answer, because she was completely numbed by what he had told her. Why?

.   .   .   .   .

Lorna opened the door at the flat, Larraby hovered about the kitchen door and Susan's shadow showed on the floor. Mannering said: "Hallo," and led Elizabeth Warren in. Lorna took charge of the girl and helped her into the drawing-room. Elizabeth seemed unable to move her legs freely. Lorna helped her to sit down in an easy chair, pushed a pouffe beneath her legs, and said to Mannering:

"Who is she? What's happened?"

"Yule's house-keeper, and she's had a shock," Elizabeth took no notice of them. She stared blankly ahead of her. He drew Lorna aside and lowered his voice. "Don't force her but encourage her to talk. She's in love with Yule, is afraid he's deserted for Fay. The shock came when I told her that Fay was old Jacob's heiress. Direct questions won't—"

"I'll manage."

"And you also want to know where she thinks Yule might be. Any news of Julia?"

"Bristow telephoned again a quarter of an hour ago and I said you'd called up and were on your way. I didn't tell him where you were." Lorna brushed the hair out of her eyes. "You can't see Julia like that, she won't recognise you."

"That's one reason why I came here first."

Ten minutes with cleansing cream and a rough towel brought back the normal Mannering. Ready to leave, he glanced into the drawing-room where Lorna was looking through a magazine and Elizabeth sat with a cup of tea at her side; she didn't seem to have tasted the tea. "I'm off." Lorna nodded, Mannering went out and Larraby hurried out from the kitchen. Was there anything he could do?

"Stay here and entertain Susan, and make sure that you shout 'police!' if any strangers look in."

Mannering drove fast through the deserted streets to the hospital. A detective-sergeant in the hall came forward: "We've been waiting for you, Mr. Mannering." He led the way along wide corridors which smelt of disinfectant, and rubber flooring muffled their footsteps. The man had no time for talking, made no comment when Mannering asked how Julia Fiori was.

They went up one flight of stairs, along another passage and round a corner. A policeman in uniform stood outside a door. He opened the door as they approached, and subdued light came from the room beyond. Mannering stepped in and saw Bristow sitting by the side of a single bed, a doctor in a white coat standing near him.

All he could see of Julia was her eyes and mouth.

Her head and face were heavily bandaged; so were her shoulders. The room was warm, a sheet and blanket were spread over her as high as the breast. He could see the outline of her body as far as the knees, below that the bedclothes were *flat*. He felt a surge of horror that went through him like a knife. Julia's legs had been amputated. *Julia's*. He drew back, knowing that those great eyes were turned towards him. She was conscious in spite of what had happened.

This didn't make sense; none of it made sense. How could such horror have come upon Julia in the short time since he had seen her? Why wasn't she still unconscious, under the anaesthetic? He moistened his dry lips, stepped forward and saw her right arm move; her right arm wasn't bandaged. She drew it gently from beneath the blanket. There was an angry red scratch on the white skin, and two dark bruises. The fingers moved weakly; she was beckoning him to go nearer. The bandage over her face covered her chin and her nose; the smell of the anaesthetic was very strong.

She moved her lips. "John." He lip-read rather than heard the word.

The doctor drew back, Bristow stood up. Neither spoke to Mannering. Bristow turned away from Mannering's single, searing glance. Mannering knelt down on one knee and took Julia's hand gently. He remembered her as she had been when they had examined the paste *Tears*; as she had been at Toni's. Tall and lovely, superb body, superbly gowned. Now she was a wreck.

"What can I do, Julia?" He spoke softly, close to her, wondering if she could hear. The doctor said: "I doubt whether she can hear you." Mannering bent closer. "What can I do?" She didn't move now. Her fingers rested in his, there was no strength in them. He knew that she was dying; it wouldn't be long before she had gone.

She whispered: "Look after—my child. Ella, look after Ella. Please. Don't let him hurt her."

Ella?

"I won't," Mannering said. It was useless to speak, because she couldn't hear him. She was looking into his eyes, not at his lips.

He forced a smile, drew back a little so that she could see the whole of his face.

"I'll look after her—I'll look after Ella."

Ella? He'd heard the name in this case before, but where? Who was Ella?

The whisper came again. "Look after Ella. Don't let him hurt her. Please don't let him hurt her." He had to put his ear close to her lips to hear the words. Bristow crouched low over the other side of the bed; Mannering could hear his heavy breathing.

"I'll look after her." He smiled again with his eyes.

And Julia also smiled.

CHAPTER XXI

YULE OR FIORI?

MANNERING said savagely: "If that's your idea of being clever I don't like it. Why the devil didn't you tell me how she was?"

Bristow didn't answer as they walked briskly along the passage, away from the ward where Julia lay dead. Two nurses passed them. They reached the hall and went outside; Bristow's green Morris and Mannering's hired Austin were parked round the corner in Grosvenor Crescent. Bristow spoke for the first time.

"We'll use my car."

"You can use what car you like. I'm going home, in mine."

"Taking it hard, aren't you?"

"That was a piece of senseless brutality and I don't like it. What did you think I'd give away if I knew how bad she was?"

"You've worked your own way in this job, I'll work mine," Bristow said. "It did her no harm and it shook you. I'm all for shaking you because I don't like the way you're behaving. Where have you been to-night?"

"Doing a job you should have done. Looking for Kenneth Yule."

"We'll find Yule."

Mannering snapped: "So he's missing." A cold wind blew up Grosvenor Place, traffic hummed towards the Park. Two or three men hung about in the shadows of the building. Police, or Fiori's men? Mannering looked bleakly round him and knew that it was futile to behave like this with Bristow, but he couldn't keep back anger when feeling like this. It was partly shock.

"If you're going to Chelsea I'll come with you," Bristow said grudgingly, as they reached the car park.

That would mean that Bristow would see Elizabeth, and she was in no state to be questioned by the police. Mannering said: "Oh, I'd better come your way, I might get some sense out of you." They got into Bristow's car and Bristow drove off. They didn't speak until they got to the Yard and were on the way to his office. It wasn't unlike the hospital, except that there was no smell of antiseptics.

Ella Carruthers! The name Fay Goulden had used at the Hula Club.

Mannering missed a step. Bristow looked at him and said: "Now what?"

"I've placed Ella. Did you hear what Julia asked?"

"You're to look after Ella—her child."

"Or Fay Goulden."

"That's right. Formed a high opinion of you in the short time you'd known her, hadn't she?"

Mannering said: "Now I get it. You thought Julia and I were old friends, thought you'd prove that if you sprung it on me. This time you're wrong, I'd never met her until yesterday."

"And she chooses you for her last request!"

"She could have chosen you." They reached Bristow's office. Bristow pushed open the door and switched on the light, offered cigarettes, then pressed a bellpush in the desk. A uniformed constable appeared at the door.

"Yes, sir?"

"Get me some tea and sandwiches. Want anything, Mannering?"

"No, thanks."

"Tea for two, sandwiches for me," Bristow ordered. He dropped into his chair, staring up at Mannering bleak-faced, hard-eyed. "Yes, she could have asked the police to look after her daughter, but she didn't. She chose you, and the only possible reason she could have had for choosing you was that you know something which we don't—something she didn't want us to know."

Mannering said: *"Daughter?"*

"That's it. Daughter. She was married twice, and Ella was a child of the first marriage. Didn't you know that?"

"No, I didn't. And I don't know why she chose me instead of you, except that she can't be impressed by the job you've done, after what happened to her. What did happen?"

"The lift at Clay Court crashed when she was getting out of it, just after you'd left the place. Didn't you hear the crash?"

Mannering remembered.

"Yes, I heard it. I thought there'd been a car smash." He felt hot; two minutes after she had left him she had been injured as horribly as Fiori had injured any of his victims. At least she hadn't known what was coming, hadn't suffered the same torture. Her voice and her face were clear in his mind. He had said that he would report to-morrow, and she had asked: "Will you?" and turned away. She had not expected to see him again. He felt heavy of heart; vengeful.

"Who did it?"

The lift had been tampered with, someone fixed it while she was in it. A simple job by anyone who knows the lift mechanism, almost impossible for anyone who doesn't. It had been planned beforehand, they were waiting for the right moment."

"Catch anyone?"

"No."

Mannering said: "I've stopped being happy about Lorna. I'll look after her myself."

"Talk is easy. The job was done from the basement. There's a side entry to the basement, it was watched but no one we know to be associated with the case went in that way. There was plenty of time for the killer to get out before we knew what had happened. The question is, who wanted to kill her? Yule or Fiori?"

Mannering said: "Possibly both."

He didn't think that it was Yule. He felt suddenly convinced that Julia had died because he had visited her so often, because she had gone out with him that night. He had told her that he was inviting her to danger, and that hadn't stopped her from accepting. Enrico Fiori knew that she had known too much about him, was afraid that she would talk, and had silenced her. This was Fiori's job, and Bristow asked: "Yule or Fiori?" He was in no mood to wrangle with Bristow. He felt suddenly tired and flat because he had no idea where to find either man, and Bristow was obviously in the dark.

"Anything else?" he asked.

"Where have you been to-night?"

"To Yule's cottage."

"He's not there."

"I know he's not there," said Mannering. The feeling of depression began to lift. Bristow hadn't yet had a report from Woking, or else hadn't had time to read it. By now Lorna might have learned much more from Elizabeth Warren, too.

The constable came in with a tray, put it on Bristow's desk, saluted and went out. There were two large cups of tea and a pile of thick sandwiches, a small bowl of granulated sugar. The tea was black and much too strong. Mannering drank a little and put the cup down.

"It's time I went home, I'm worried about Lorna."

"I've two men watching her. John, if you've a clue about where to find Yule or Fiori, and you don't tell me, I'll get you somehow. If you hold out on us—"

"I haven't a notion where they are."

"You've said that about the *Tear*."

"And I'm saying it about Fiori and Yule. I warned you to hold Yule, you thought it would be clever to let him go. Now that he's run out on you I hope you're satisfied that there's something on his conscience. What about Mellor and Brownie? Anything from them yet?"

"No. Have you the *Diamond of Tears*?"

"What would you do if I said I had?"

"I'd send you a wreath. Holding that jewel is an invitation to murder."

"And what would you do, if you had it? Send Fiori a postcard and ask him to come and collect?" Mannering stood up. "I'm glad you haven't got it. If that diamond ever comes in useful it will be as bait for Fiori. I suppose you would have told me had there been any word from Fay."

Bristow touched the box file which was crammed full of letters. "They're the reports we've had saying she's been seen. There are three hundred and five so far. The *Record* says that they've had nearly as many. It will take days to get them all answered, sorted and checked—we shan't find Fay Goulden that way. Have you any idea where she is?"

"We keep asking questions, don't we? No."

Bristow said unexpectedly: "All right, John. We're both on edge. You've done a lot and I appreciate it. I think you're crazy to stick out your neck like this but I suppose nothing will stop you. I know you've got the *Tear*. I know you went to Solly's to-night and had yourself decked up, so you probably went to get the *Tear*. I can't prove it, and there's nothing I can do about it, but if you're thinking of using the diamond as bait for Fiori you're crazier than I thought you were."

Mannering said: "All right, I'm crazy." He leaned across the desk, stubbed out his cigarette, and added: "Do you know why Fiori wants the *Tear* so badly?"

"No. There isn't much I do know, is there?—now I've said it for you."

He smiled faintly; Mannering smiled back. Understanding between them was always there, even though events weakened it.

"Good night."

"I'll be seeing you."

Mannering went briskly along the corridors, wondering how long it would be before he got a taxi. He was stopped by the sergeant on duty in the hall.

"Your car's ready, Mr. Mannering."

"Eh? Car?"

"Mr. Bristow has put one at your disposal."

Mannering laughed.

.   .   .   .   .

Lorna and Elizabeth were still in the drawing-room. Mannering heard them talking as he went in. Larraby came out of the kitchen, taking off a pair of pince-nez. His hair was frizzy and soft, he looked rather like Chittering. How was Chittering? Mannering had been to the hospital and hadn't thought to inquire!

"Susan has gone to bed, sir. I promised I would get you anything you might require." Larraby smiled.

"Thanks. Nothing here, but I've a job for you."

"Anything, Mr. Mannering."

"There's a Hillman Minx parked in Grosvenor Crescent at the side of St. George's Hospital. Here's the key. Drive it to Mayner's Garage, in the Edgware Road, and get what change there is to come out of a twenty pound deposit. In Elkin Street, nearby, you'll find my car. Bring it back here, will you?"

"And after that?"

Mannering laughed. "You'd better stay here the night."

"I'd *much* rather go to the shop," said Larraby. "I'm a little uneasy about leaving it without anybody there by night. Will it be satisfactory if I go back there when I've brought the car?"

"Please yourself," Mannering said.

Larraby went off, Mannering went into the study and watched the street, seeing a C.I.D. man follow Larraby. They would follow him because they knew there was a chance that he was going to get the *Tear*. There was no need to worry about Larraby.

Mannering telephoned the hospital. Chittering was "as well as could be expected," the old formula. At least the reporter was still alive, and his chances were improving hourly; he was better off than Julia. Mannering felt on edge, wanting to see Lorna yet not wanting to break in when they were talking; he might choose just the wrong moment and dry Elizabeth up. Better not chance it. The church clock nearby stuck one, he was surprised that it was so late. He sat at his desk and scribbled notes, trying to fit more pieces into the puzzle. Was there one or were there two puzzles? Fiori's, with his mysterious lust for the *Diamond of Tears*, and Kenneth Yule's, with an equal lust? Or were they working together? The one thing that seemed certain was that they wanted it for the same reason. On the whole he thought they were antagonists, and that probably didn't augur well for Yule. There wasn't really much of a puzzle about Fiori, that man who was too contemptuous to lie. He wanted the *Tear*, went all out to get it, had persecuted Fay Goulden because she was to inherit it—no, it wasn't as simple as that. Fiori must have known that Fay—or Ella—was his own stepdaughter. Or would he? There just weren't any answers, it was a waste of time posing the questions afresh. But he went on probing : old Jacob had left his fortune to Fay Godden, alias Ella Carruthers, Julia's daughter, and—

But Jacob had done nothing of the kind !

He'd left everything to Fay Goulden, daughter of Professor Goulden. Ella Carruthers and Fay Goulden were not one and the same person, they couldn't be. Mannering jumped up, light flashing through his mind with a dazzling brilliance. The girl he knew as Fay was Ella Carruthers, Julia's daughter—yes. *But he didn't know Fay Goulden*. At least, he hadn't met her at old Jacob's shop because she hadn't been there. Ella, pretending to be Fay, had been.

He hurried to the drawing-room and saw Lorna and Elizabeth together on the sofa. Elizabeth was talking in a low-pitched, earnest voice. She looked as if she were prepared to go on talking for a long time, as if the repressions of years were lifting.

She looked up. She was much less haggard and there was some colour in her cheeks.

Words burst out of Mannering. "Well, *Fay*. Have you told my wife all about it?"

CHAPTER XXII

THE TRUTH ABOUT FAY

THE GIRL half rose from the sofa. Lorna held her hand, made her sink back. The girl's eyes were bright and startled, she stretched out a hand, and Mannering smiled down at her, took her hand and squeezed. "It'll work out." She turned to Lorna and said wonderingly:

"How did he *know*?"

"He must be good at guessing."

"He couldn't have guessed." The girl turned to Mannering. "How did you find out? Who told you? Have you found Ken? *Have* you?" She was tense again, hands clenched, fear back in her eyes. "He was the only one who knew."

"I haven't found him," Mannering said quietly. "I discovered that the other girl isn't Fay and jumped to this conclusion. Why did you drop your real name, Fay?"

"I wish you wouldn't call me Fay, it's years since anyone did." She said that to gain time to think, but it was clear that she meant it. "There were—there were two reasons. I was frightened of Fiori, and—well, I just wanted to forget. Ken helped me so much. I've been telling your wife—"

"Everything?"

"Yes."

"Do you want to go into it all again?" Lorna asked. "If you'd rather go to bed—"

"No, I'm too wideawake, I'd never sleep. In a way it's a relief to talk.

"It started long ago, when I was a child living in Germany with my father. He was working against the Nazis. When Jacob Bernstein escaped from Dachau my father hid him. The Gestapo found out and were coming to search the flat. A friend told me and I was just in time to warn father. He moved the old man to other friends nearby, but they took my father away and I never saw him again.

"Jacob was terribly shocked that father suffered through helping him. He couldn't do enough for me. Although he was in hiding he seemed to have plenty of money. I had none, and he gave me everything I needed. He managed to send me back to England. I had no relations there, but Jacob gave me some jewels to smuggle out, so that I could live. He also gave me the *Diamond of Tears* to bring over. He told me it was to be sold to help refugees who were escaping from Germany—it had been given to him for that purpose by a man who had been in Dachau with him—the man had died. Jacob made me promise to tell no one, but to take it to Toni Fiori who would deal with it."

"Toni? Not Enrico?"

"No, Toni. He wouldn't take it. He said it was dangerous. He'd been doing some work for old Jacob, but couldn't go on doing it. He said I must get rid of the diamond some other way. There was no one I could trust, and I thought of putting it in the bank. Then Toni Fiori sent a woman to see me to tell me he'd changed his mind."

"And the woman?" But he felt that he knew the answer.

"Julia Fiori," said Elizabeth.

* * * * *

Somewhere buried in the past was the whole truth. The truth, as Mannering knew it now, was that Julia had once possessed the *Diamond of Tears*. When he came to England Jacob Bernstein had it again. She must have given it to him, after holding it in trust, while knowing that Enrico Fiori was seeking it with ruthlessness and savagery.

Julia had done that.

* * * * *

The girl went on slowly:

"After I'd given it to her the other Fiori came to see me. He said that he knew I had it, threatened terrible things unless I gave it to him. I was terrified. If only you knew Fiori you would understand. But Julia had told me that I must tell no one where it was. I lied to Fiori, and he went away, still threatening me. Two days afterwards I was attacked in the street. I shall never forget that night, what two men nearly did. There were other attacks, too. I began to feel desperate. Fiori kept telephoning me and threatening. He sent pictures of what he'd done to people who had defied him.

"Then the house where I lived was bombed, several people were killed, and I—I ran away. I think they thought that I was dead. I wasn't hurt much, but I was dazed. I couldn't remember everything. I'd lost my clothes, my papers, everything. I was cared for by a family named Warren, and—well, I became one of the family. I was free from fear. I didn't want to go back because there was nothing to return to, except fear.

"Then I met Kenneth.

"I've told your wife. I fell in love with him, and he was so very kind. Oh, I know everything about him, that he was always going with different women, but he was very kind to me, and I told him who I was. I hadn't told the truth to anyone for years, it was a good thing to have off my mind. He gave me work at the cottage and Wrenn Street, and—"

Mannering said: "How did you meet him, Elizabeth?"

"We met at a café. I often had lunch there. He came two or three times, and once we sat at the same table. It wasn't difficult to become friends."

It wasn't difficult, either, to guess that Ken Yule had by then discovered who she was; knew that she had the *Tear;* had forced his acquaintance on her and employed her so that he would always know where she was.

"And then?"

"He told me one night that he had seen Fiori. I'd told him all about Fiori. He said that there was another girl posing as Fay Goulden, and said he was going to get at the truth somehow. I begged him not to try, but he laughed at me, and—well, nothing happened to him. I was telling myself that nothing would when I read about Jacob's murder. I knew Ken had been going out with a girl; I guessed it was this Fay Goulden. I didn't want to think that he'd fallen in love with her, but when he realised she was in danger it was hateful. I'd never seen him so wild before, so desperately afraid. He had learned all about Fiori then, I suppose, realised that she might be suffering what I'd suffered.

"That's nearly all," said Elizabeth. "Yesterday he telephoned and told me to go to the cottage. The next thing that matters is that you and the police came. That's all." But she went on in soft but urgent voice: "I don't want to be Fay Goulden, I want to stay as I am. I want—Ken."

"Have you no idea where he might be?"

"There's one place you might find him," Elizabeth said.

. . . . .

Mannering said to Lorna: "Give me half an hour's start, then telephone the Yard and give them that address—10, Mayberry Hill, Hampstead."

. . . . .

It was a tall, narrow house, one of a terrace in the oldest residential part of Hampstead. Larraby had brought back the Sunbeam-Talbot, and Mannering pulled up a few doors away from Number 10. The police had followed him from Chelsea, but it wasn't hard to shake them off.

No one arrived.

Number 10 was in darkness. He walked boldly up to the front door and examined the lock in the light of a street lamp. It wasn't new and would be easy to open. He took out his knife, a replica of the one which Fiori had taken from him. No one passed, no one approached. In five minutes the door swung open. He stepped in swiftly, closed the door and went straight upwards to the top floor.

Elizabeth knew that Yule's flat was in two parts, up there. She did not know why Yule kept this third establishment. Of the two doors on the top floor Mannering didn't know which was the bedroom. The house was old; the doors and the locks were simple. He spent five minutes forcing the first; that left him a twenty minutes start of Bristow. He shone his torch. The room, a living-room, was empty.

He should have told Lorna to give him an hour, he had cut it much too fine.

He turned to cross the passage, then noticed a door in the corner of this room; he went to it quickly, and found that it wasn't locked.

He crossed a tiny bathroom and entered a third room, the door of which was ajar. Before he opened it he heard a faint sound of snoring.

He put on the bathroom light; it was enough for him to see clearly about the bedroom. He stepped inside softly, his footsteps muffled by the carpet. The bed was against the far wall—a double bed, with two people sleeping in it. Yule was on the outside, a woman on the other side, with her face turned to the wall. He saw that she had fair hair. Mannering crept across the room. Yule's faint snoring went on and on, deep and rhythmic. On the bedside table there was a clock, cigarettes, a lighter—and an automatic pistol. Mannering was near enough to take the gun but was not able to see the woman's face. He backed to the door, gun in hand, and switched on the light.

Yule started up at once.

The woman turned.

Mannering said: "Brave Yule and False Fay. Don't shout, don't get out of bed!"

His gun covered Yule, who glared wildly at him, hair tousled, pyjama coat wide open at the neck. Fay said: "What is it?" sleepily, and then, seeming to sense that there was trouble, sat up sharply and saw Mannering.

"Brave Yule, False Fay," repeated Mannering. "Now I'm going to know all about it. I shouldn't trust Ken too much, Ella. He's a man with a nasty reputation as a Don Juan, and isn't likely to make an honest woman of you."

Yule said: "You interfering fool!"

Julia's daughter cried: "We're married! Don't talk about Ken like that, we're married!"

Poor "Elizabeth."

.   .   .   .   .

Mannering watched Yule, who pushed the bedclothes back slowly and climbed out of bed, looking at the gun. He sat on the edge of the bed, buttoning up his pyjama jacket. He poked his fingers through his unruly hair, while Julia's daughter pulled the sheet up to her neck. She wasn't looking at her best but she was lovely.

Mannering said: "I should think fast, Yule. The police will be here in a quarter of an hour."

"That's bad for you, they're not fond of burglars." The retort came out easily but there was an undercurrent of strain. "How did you find me?"

"I had a talk with a friend of yours."

"No one knows about the place."

"You forget too easily," said Mannering.

Yule stood up, ran his fingers through his hair again—but didn't look as if he were going to launch an attack, there was nothing of the wild youth about him. Why? A romantic might think that it was because he had found his "Fay"—that he had been frantic because he couldn't find her, because he feared that Fiori had got her. How long had they been married?

"So Elizabeth told you. I didn't think she'd ever talk."

"You thought she was too scared, that you could do what you liked with her because of her excessive gratitude. I don't think she's any reason to be grateful to you. She won't like the idea that you're married, either."

Yule said: "I can't help that. I did all I could for her. I knew she was fond of me, but—" He shrugged his shoulders. The fact that the police were coming, the fact that Elizabeth had talked, didn't seem to worry him. What was the explanation for his confidence? Instead of being ready to crack, as a guilty man might be when woken like that, he behaved as if he had no serious worries. "Never mind what Elizabeth thinks. Do you know who she really is?"

"Yes, and also who your wife really is."

"That's not news to me," Yule said. "She hasn't kept anything from me." He turned to Fay and gave her the kind of smile one would expect from a young man in love. "I shouldn't worry, pet, there's nothing the police can do, we've not committed any crime. And Mannering can't throw his weight about, either." He looked back at Mannering. "When you forgot to tell the police that my wife had gone to see Bernstein that night you put yourself in a jam. Don't forget it."

"Did you know she'd been at the shop?"

"I did afterwards."

"Why did she go?"

Julia's daughter said in a taut voice: "I knew that they were going to try and get the *Tear* from Bernstein and that he was in terrible danger. I went to warn him—to beg him to give up the diamond, but I was too late." She shuddered.

"Take it easy," Yule said. He stretched a hand out behind him and held her arm. "Take it easy, sweetheart, Fiori can't do anything to you here. You can believe it or not, Mannering, but it's the truth. She was dead scared but she made herself go. You didn't help."

"You may change your mind about that. When did you find her?"

"This evening, here. When she came to meet me at the Hula Club she saw Brownie and Mellor talking to Benoni; she realised suddenly that they must be in Fiori's pay and was so frightened that she ran away and came here. I'd brought her here once, on the day that we were married; we kept this place a secret."

"Why didn't she let you know where she was?"

"I—I thought Ken's telephone might be tapped," Fay said.

"It probably was," said Yule. "Fiori's up to every sort of trick. We hoped we could lie low until it was all over but—" He shrugged. "You're so clever, you showed the way here. If anything happens to my wife now you'll know who's to blame."

Mannering said slowly: "So Mellor and Brownie work for Fiori?"

"They do!" cried the girl. "They're Fiori's men and they've been spying on Ken."

"Why?"

Yule said: "A clever man like you ought to guess. He knew I was after the *Tear* and thought I might get it. He didn't mind whom he took it from provided he got it eventually. I've been doing some hard thinking since I came here. You picked up a call from Mellor, didn't you? You went to Wrenn Street in my place, and nearly walked into trouble. If I'd gone there I would have walked into plenty. They attacked that newspaper man and would have framed me for it. I think they would have tried blackmail, to find out whether I had the *Tear*. You did me a good turn there."

It was plausible; it might even have happened.

Mannering said: "Do you know where Fiori is?"

"No."

"Do you know why he wants the *Tear*?"

Yule laughed. "I can guess!" He stood up, yawned and stretched his hands above his head. Was he foxing, was he going to spring? Mannering held the gun casually, made no attempt to cover him now, gave the man a chance to leap forward. If Yule leapt and tried to disarm him, then Yule's story wasn't worth a sniff.

Yule sat down again.

"Yes, he wants the *Tear* for the same reason that I do, Mannering. I don't know how much you've picked up about this business, but I believe that I own that Tear because it belonged to my grandfather. Or it should have done. The *Tear* itself doesn't mean a thing, it's just a key."

"To what?"

Yule laughed again. "A treasure house of precious stones! Hundreds of them, some of the finest jewels that ever came out of the earth. They were smuggled out of Germany and Nazi Europe before and during the war. There's a platinum setting for that diamond." So he knew that. "Unscrew the setting and you'll find a tiny hole. Dig out what's in the hole and you'll find the secret of the treasure house. Oh, you may as well know now! Bernstein got most of the stuff out of Europe. He worked with my grandfather; they were partners. My grandfather sold some of the stuff for refugee work, but not all of it, there's plenty left. Fiori discovered that. There were several in the plot, the leaders being in Germany, one in the States, one in England. The one in England was Toni Fiori—fat Fiori's brother. He must have blabbed, that's the only way Enrico Fiori could have discovered it. Whoever finds the *Tear* finds a fabulous fortune! You could argue that it belongs to the real Fay Goulden. I could argue it belongs to me—I think it does, if there's a legal title to it. But the *Tear* and everything it leads to doesn't belong to any individual, it belongs to the refugees it was meant for in the first place. Get me?"

Mannering said: "I'm beginning to."

A car turned the corner of the road. All three glanced towards the window, which was open a few inches at the top. Yule's wife said: "It's the police," but neither of the men spoke. Yule shrugged his shoulders, as if it didn't matter who was coming.

"If you think I was going to cheat the real Fay, you're all wrong. I discovered who she was. It was a hell of a job tracing her, but I managed it. I didn't believe that Fiori's Fay was the right one. When I first met her I wanted to use her because I thought she could help, and then—we fell in love. You can't do anything about it when a thing like that happens. We just fell in love. It didn't take me long to discover that Fiori was keeping his claws on her. He got tired of waiting for the old boy to die. He knew Jacob was worth a fortune apart from the *Tear*, and planned to sit pretty with both fortunes in his lap. That's the trouble with Fiori. He worships money. He can't have too much. And he's dangerous, he'll get you before he's finished."

A door banged, downstairs; footsteps sounded.

"Your friends," Yule sneered. "Will they stay friendly for long?"

"Long enough," Mannering said. "It's a pretty story. Are you prepared to tell the police?"

"Now that you've made Elizabeth talk, why not? I've done nothing they can get me for. I kept quiet because it paid me to, but it won't pay me now. I was looking for the *Tear* but I didn't kill Jacob. I've never committed a crime in my life, unless you call fighting Fiori a crime. Some people would call it suicide. Yes, I'll tell them now. I've even stopped caring who finds the *Tear*."

Footsteps sounded on the landing, there was a mutter of voices, and then a heavy thump on the door and a deep summons.

"*Open in the name of the law.*"

"How they love their formula," Yule sneered.

Mannering slipped the gun into his pocket. Yule had another chance to spring at him and didn't take it. Mannering turned, unbolted the door and stood aside, expecting to see Bristow.

It wasn't Bristow; wasn't Gordon; wasn't a policeman. It was a man whom Mannering recognised vaguely without being able to place him—a man with a gun.

CHAPTER XXIII

BRISTOW REGRETS

MANNERING dropped his right hand to his pocket. The man with the gun swept forward. Three others behind him poured into the room. The first man gripped Mannering's arm, pulled his hand from his pocket and Mannering's gun dropped.

The girl screamed.

The man whom Mannering vaguely recognised growled: "Shut her mouth!" One of the others crossed the room. Yule jumped up, eyes glaring, fists clenched—but the man kicked him on the shins, sent him staggering back on to the bed, kicked him again and then said: "Keep quiet, sweetheart, or you'll kiss the world good-bye." The girl shrank against the wall—while Mannering's mind clicked, and recollection came swiftly. The man who had knocked his gun from his hand should be dressed in resplendent uniform; it was the commissionaire from Clay Court.

The man said: "We're in a hurry, and we're going places. Bring the others." He pushed Mannering round and jabbed the gun into his back. "Don't try any tricks. I was told to rub you out if you were awkward."

Mannering said: "That's one way of rubbing out your chances of getting the *Tear*."

Bristow ought to be here at any moment, ought to be here now, he was overdue. Lorna would have been watching the clock, so as to warn him the moment the half hour was up.

"No lip." The off-duty commissionaire poked the gun in the small of his back and pushed him towards the landing. He glanced over his shoulder. Another man was pushing Yule, a third pulling the girl from the bed. This was like Fiori; bold, ruthless, aiming direct to get exactly what he wanted. It was a waste of time wondering how Fiori had traced this address. Would it be a waste of time saying that the police were on the way? He strained his ears to catch the sound of more cars approaching, and thought he heard an engine not far off. The man pushed him again. He gripped the banister rail to save himself from falling. On the next landing a door opened and a man waiting there said: "Shut the door—police." There was a guard at each landing. The door closed tightly. Another door on the ground floor was opened and closed as quickly. Mannering reached the front passage with the gunman a couple of yards behind him—and a car turned into the road.

A man shouted: "Jim! Someone coming."

"They'll pass by."

"It's the busies!" The cry was shrill. "They're coming here, get a move on!"

Mannering said: "What's the hurry, they—"

A heavy blow on the back of his head knocked him forward. He felt someone grab his arm and hustle him ahead. But it had been a mistake to hit him, for he was a dead weight. The blow on his tender head caused him agony, he hardly knew what he was doing, couldn't think. Vague noises filled his head—the roar of the blood in his ears, voices, sharper sounds—shots. He felt himself fall, hit his forehead on the pavement and rolled over twice. Someone tripped over him and went sprawling. He heard two more sharp reports, a scream—no mistake about that, it was a scream. Then someone trod on him; his back seemed to break in two. He tried to cover his head with his arms but he was lying awkwardly and couldn't do it. Another foot stamped on him, the wind was driven out of his body, he was swallowed up by pain. There was a new sound—not the roar of the blood in his ears but the roaring of a car engine. The voices were all raised, men were shouting wildly. He didn't hear another scream—

He lay between consciousness and stupor, back and head aching, but free from new pains. He didn't know how long he had lain there when someone touched him and a man said:

"Who is it?"

"It looks like— It is! Mannering!"

"Tell the super."

"You bet."

Someone eased Mannering up, helped him to sit against the wall and kept saying: "Take it easy, you're all right." But his back was breaking and they didn't seem to realise it. Sitting up was fresh agony. The pain dulled. He heard footsteps, saw a vague figure approach, and recognised Bristow.

Bristow knelt beside him.

"Was he shot?"

The other policeman said : "I can't see any sign of a wound."

"John, did they get you?"

Mannering licked his lips. "I'm all right. Back's a bit—troublesome. Elephants about." He didn't feel like being funny, and his back was excruciatingly painful when they helped him to his feet. "How's Yule?"

"Not badly hurt. The girl's all right."

"Get the others?"

"Some of them. Don't worry, we'll get them before the night's out."

Bristow was always sure of himself, but Mannering stopped thinking about it, was led into the house and then into a downstairs room where an excited woman was fluttering about, saying that it was outrageous—*thieves*. Mannering lay on a sofa, half dazed, until a police surgeon came. He was undressed, poked and prodded, winced when the cold fingers pressed into the small of his back.

"Could just be a bruise, might be serious," the surgeon said. "We'll get him to the hospital."

* * * * *

Would the police find Fiori's other men? Would they find Fiori? That was the only thought in Mannering's mind as he was driven along in the ambulance; it seemed a long drive.

* * * * *

He remembered the stinging prick of a hypodermic needle, and little else, until he came round. It was daylight—and he was at home, in his own bedroom. Recollection of the raid and all that had followed it flooded his mind; next relief—for there was nothing much the matter if he had been brought home already. He heard movements about the flat, felt too dazed to call out, dozed off for a while. When he came round again he felt much clearer in the head and hardly conscious of pain. He moved gingerly; his back hurt, but it wasn't agonising. He lay looking at the door. The hands of the bedside clock pointed to half-past twelve, so he'd been unconscious for ten hours or so. Quite long enough.

Footsteps drew near and the door opened.

He grinned : "'Morning, my sweet !"

Lorna flew across the room, took his hands, seemed to want to pour her life into his. Her eyes glowed, her cheeks were radiant. He wanted her to stay like that for a long time, but at last she drew back, brushed her hair out of her eyes, and said huskily :

"How do you feel?"

"For an invalid, all right. How am I?"

"You've a badly bruised back, but nothing serious. What happened?"

"Hasn't Bristow been here this morning?"

"He's called up twice and wants to see you as soon as you're awake."

"Isn't that now?"

"He can wait for an hour," Lorna said.

"I won't argue about that." Mannering sat up cautiously, then put the question he was longing to ask : "Did he get Fiori?"

"No."

"His men?"

"Some of them."

"Tell him that one of them is the commissionaire at Clay Court, the day duty—"

"He caught that one. And it was he who made the lift crash," Lorna said. "Bristow hasn't told me much, but I've been to see Ella Carruthers—"

"*Alias* Fay, married name Yule—yes?"

"She's told me what she told you, or what Yule told you," said Lorna. She wasn't very coherent, seemed as if she were recovering from a great strain. I think everything's over, except—"

"They haven't got Fiori. Quite a job."

Lorna pleaded : "John, give it up now. You know the secret of the *Tear*. The rest is up to Bristow."

"But can Bristow bait Fiori with it?" asked Mannering.

*   *   *   *   *

He wasn't so badly bruised that he couldn't move about, although he took every step gingerly. The pain was like acute lumbago. When Bristow arrived Mannering was sitting back in an easy chair, eating a cold lunch that Susan had prepared without any foolish preoccupation with an invalid's diet. Only a hint of tiredness showed in Bristow's eyes. At first glance he seemed brisk and alert and he had a fresh gardenia in his button-hole. Mannering needed that glance to tell him that Bristow was not in an aggressive or sour mood.

"Well, John! It's a good job I wasn't five minutes later at the love nest. Next time, don't keep me waiting."

"Sorry, Bill," murmured Mannering.

Bristow laughed. "Yes, you're sorry! I can see it in the look in your eyes. Lorna tells me that you're not so bad as you ought to be. Pity."

"Thanks. What's the bedside manner in aid of?"

"I'm just trying to be friendly because I think you've had a rough time. I'm satisfied with the way things have gone, too. We lost only one of Fiori's men. We're pretty sure that Fiori's on his own now, and it won't be long before we get him. You haven't lost your memory, have you?"

"Nor you your optimism."

"I don't see how he can get away. We're watching airports and ships, we've tabs on all private airfields, all aircraft leaving the country are being watched and we get news from abroad about them. Not that Fiori is likely to go without having another stab to get the *Tear*. Yule told us something when he told us about that, didn't he?"

"You believe him?"

Bristow said: "Yes. Brownie has cracked. He and Mellor did work for Fiori, and were watching Yule. After the trouble with Chittering they were going to frame Yule. Fiori wanted him out of the way so that he could concentrate on the girl, Julia's daughter. Not much doubt about what happened—it's pretty well as Yule said. A clever move on Fiori's part. It might have worked if he'd been patient and waited for the *Tear*. He stepped up the pressure because he knew that Yule was after it and that Yule knew old Jacob had it."

Mannering said: "Is Chittering coming through?"

"Yes. He's talked, too. He discovered what was in the *Tear*, dug it out of papers at Wrenn Street. We also dug it out, we've known about the setting and what's inside it since then. In fact we know something more." Bristow leaned back in his chair and gave an almost cherubic smile. "There aren't many who know this John; it'll shake you. There were six parts of this message or plan about the *cache*. A piece in each of five paste stones, and the final piece in the real diamond. Funny thing, but you had four of the paste gems in your pocket. Why not laugh? We found the fifth at Toni Fiori's. We've heard about your trip there. We also know that one of Enrico Fiori's men was a waiter at his brother's place. The waiter found a paste gem where you'd been sitting, recognised it for a fake, and left it there. So now we have all five and all we want is the *Tear*." Bristow chuckled. "Fiori seems to have made one of his major mistakes by not examining the fakes after realising they were paste. We've the other pieces of the message safely lodged at the Yard. Even if Fiori were to get the *Tear* now he wouldn't have all he was after."

Mannering said: "For the first time I feel almost sorry for Enrico. He didn't know that the fakes are part of the secret! These people who had the paste gems were all in the secret, weren't they?"

"Trustees for Yule's grandfather, yes. That's why they held out so long before telling Fiori where the stone was, why they pretended to believe that they had the real McCoy. Now it's all sorted itself out, and Fiori just can't win. We're keeping Yule and his wife in custody—for their own protection. I'm making quite sure nothing can happen to Lorna, Larraby or Elizabeth— there's no knowing what Fiori might try. He's still sure that you have the *Tear*."

"Is he?"

Bristow said with elaborate unconcern: "Yes. He telephoned Lorna to say so. He takes a lot of convincing, doesn't he? I almost wish you had it!"

Mannering said: "Getting frisky in your old age, aren't you? Wouldn't possession be a crime!"

"Oh, I don't know. You're a trustee of the estate. Even if you had it you couldn't get at the *cache* because we have the rest of the message at the Yard. I can't see you trying to sell that *Tear*. Yes, it's a pity you haven't got it," Bristow mused. "If you had you'd be able to lure Fiori to have his last shot, wouldn't you? You know, I've been wondering what I'd do if I really thought you had it. I've decided that I'd let you go your own sweet way—look after everyone else who might come to any harm, but let you stick your neck out." The bantering tone faded from Bristow's voice. "It would be worth risking a lot to catch Fiori. We can make sure he doesn't profit by anything, but we want more than that—we would like to see him hanged. Yes, it's a pity you haven't got the *Tear*."

"I'll try to find it as soon as I'm able to get about," said Mannering sardonically.

* * * * *

It was three days before he could move without hurt to his back. During those three days he saw a great deal of Elizabeth Warren, who stayed at the flat. He was glad, because in trying to help the girl Lorna dwelt less on the danger from Fiori. He hadn't told her what he was going to do; she needed no telling.

On the fourth day he left the flat and drove to the Strand Post Office to get the *Tear*. None of Bristow's men followed him; he saw no sign of Fiori's men, but he didn't think that was because Fiori was now on his own.

He put the little package in his inside coat pocket and it lodged there and seemed to burn him.

Fiori wanted him to hand over the stone and there was only one place he knew where he might contact Fiori.

He telephoned Bristow from the post office.

"Listen, Bill, and don't argue. Have you two good men, not well known, who could visit a certain restaurant and look as if they're talking business?"

"Yes. Toni Fiori's?"

"Yes. To-day. Say one o'clock."

CHAPTER XXIV

BAIT FOR FIORI

THE DIAMOND was like fire against Mannering's breast; fire which parched his mouth, made him sweat, seared his mind. It was no use pretending that Fiori had not seen him and did not know that he now had possession of it. He could not be logical where Fiori was concerned. Mannering drove slowly along the Strand and hardly noticed where he was going. In his mind's eye was a picture of a mutilated woman; in his ears Green's tortured cries seemed to ring. Fiori had done those things because he wanted the *Tear*, and the *Tear* was in Mannering's pocket.

He drove to Toni Fiori's café.

Toni was upstairs, but hurried to welcome him, was delighted to see him looking so well. Then—in a whisper—what a tragedy about Julia. Such a beautiful woman, so good and kind, she had always been too good for his brother. That brother of his! He was a devil. He, Toni, confessed that there had been times when he had been frightened almost to death by his brother. It wasn't any use denying it, Enrico had a quality which frightened everyone who knew him except—Toni laughed, but uneasily—Mr. Mannering. *Nothing* frightened Mr. Mannering.

He, Toni, had a message for Mr. Mannering—

Mannering sat back on his seat and looked up into the plump, earnest face.

"From Enrico?"

"Who else, *signor*? He is *my* brother, who am I to refuse to pass on a message?"

"Especially as you might get hurt."

"I confess I would not like to cross Enrico," said Toni softly. He leaned forward, his breath brushing Mannering's cheek. "Two or three times each day he telephones me, and asks if you have come. For some reason he expects you here. Each time he says the same thing. You are to leave the *Tear* where you left the imitation diamond—he knows everything, you see, everything. That is one of the terrifying things about Enrico. You hide, you run away, you try to lose him, but he always knows where you

178

are. Sometimes he seems to know where you are going to be, even before you have decided yourself. Do you not agree?"

"Oh, he's good."

"I tell him you have not the diamond, such a man as John Mannering would give it up at once to the police, but he will not believe me. I do not ask if you have it—please don't tell me, I do not wish to know, Mr. Mannering, it would not be safe for me to know! But this I say to you—if you have it, leave it where you are sitting. It will be well for you and for everyone you love. Please!" The brown eyes were close to Mannering's, the likeness between the brothers was much more evident. "*Please,* Mr. Mannering! Remember what has happened to Julia because Enrico thought that she was helping you against him. You did not know? That is one of the things he tells me, yes. And he will find a way to do great harm to you and to your loved ones. I say that if I had the *Diamond of Tears* I would leave it where Enrico tells me."

"And how would Enrico get it then?"

Toni shrugged. "I do not know his methods—why, it would not surprise me to know that some of my waiters, perhaps my kitchen hands, work for him! I wash my hands of it. I only give you the message."

Mannering said: "Yes. Now what about luncheon?"

"The very finest there is in London, *signor*! Guisseppe!" He clapped his hands for a waiter. "Guisseppe! You will attend the *signor*. I will go to the cellar and find the wine." He rubbed his hands and hurried off, moving with surprising speed and smoothness on his little well-shod feet—moving very much as Enrico would move. But he wasn't Enrico. The trite thought flashed into Mannering's mind, flashed out again. He glanced round the restaurant. There were a dozen well-dressed couples, most of them eyeing this favourite of Toni's with veiled curiosity. Two well-dressed men in one corner looked at him intently. One gave a slight nod.

Guisseppe recommended this, recommended that—but he was on edge. There was little doubt that everyone at the restaurant was, too. The hatch leading to the kitchen, usually firmly closed, was open. The chef peered at Mannering, darted out of sight when Mannering caught his eye.

Toni was gone a long time.

When he returned Mannering was eating a superb grilled sole

with a delicious mushroom sauce. The tension had passed itself on to Toni, he brought the wine but he let it swing carelessly, although it was a wine to be reverenced. He put it down heavily, and Mannering could hear his harsh breathing.

"*Signor!*"

"So he's telephoned again?"

"It is so—always he is on the telephone. *Signor*, I beg you to believe me, he is angry, he is prepared to do anything, and he will not wait. I am to tell you that unless the diamond is left, *to-day*, then he will not be patient any longer. You—you *have* the diamond, *signor?*"

"I thought you didn't want to know."

"Forgive me, I am not myself." Toni brushed his hands over his forehead; he was sweating. "He will telephone again, I am to give him your message."

"Blood is so much thicker than water," said Mannering. He slid his hand to his pocket, drew out the package, and held it in his hand. Toni's pink hand came forward, drew back again sharply. Mannering broke the seal and began to unfasten the brown paper; Toni watched with baited breath. Two of the waiters hovered near, as if to hide Mannering from everyone else in the restaurant. Inside the paper was a box; inside the box, cotton wool. Mannering plucked at the cotton wool. Toni gave a strangled sound, half cry, half gasp.

"Signor—"

The *Diamond of Tears* shimmered like fire in front of their eyes. Toni closed his and raised his hands as if in supplication.

Mannering held the stone in cotton wool, appeared to brood over it, then placed it carefully in Toni's moist palm. Fat fingers closed about it, and Toni drew in a shuddering breath.

"Tell him you have it," said Mannering.

"Signor, how—how wise you are!" Toni clutched the *Tear*, seemed to sway, steadied himself and then hurried off; as a drunk might hurry. He went into the kitchen—and as the door closed behind him Mannering stood up and beckoned Bristow's men. One hurried outside, the other came to Mannering. Mannering pushed open the kitchen door. The staff inside was staring at Toni, who reached a hole in the floor and started down a flight of wooden stairs—the stairs to the wine cellar. Mannering led the way across the kitchen. No one spoke, no one cried out, the tension had touched them all.

Toni reached the foot of the stairs and didn't turn round.

Mannering and Bristow's man went stealthily after him. The cellar was dry and smelt dusty, cobwebs hung low. There was a dim light from naked lamps. They walked along, footsteps echoing faintly. Had Toni not been drunk with the *Tear* he must have heard them. He stopped in front of a large wine cask and turned the tap. The cask moved slowly to one side and brought part of the wall away with it. Toni stepped aside—and caught a glimpse of Mannering.

He threw his arms upwards and his mouth opened to shout. Mannering reached him and struck him in the stomach. He felt his fist sink in and heard the wind gush out. Toni dropped the *Diamond of Tears*. The Yard man picked it up. Mannering thrust a handkerchief into Toni's gaping mouth to silence him, then he turned to the hole in the wall. He had to bend double while getting through and his back hurt. Inside the passage beyond it was dark and fusty, but he could stand upright. He saw a glow of light not far away. He tiptoed along, came upon an open door, and beyond was a small room. A pair of slippered feet were in front of an electric fire.

He stepped inside, and Fiori looked round at him.

Fiori drew his legs up but made no attempt to rise. He blinked, looking like a man roused out of a heavy sleep. His pale, plump hands rested on the arms of his chair, he held his head back to look at Mannering. The heavy lids drooped over his eyes. His mouth was open; he closed it slowly.

The room was small and windowless. In one corner was a divan covered by a gaily coloured eiderdown. Nearby, a radiogram stood next to a bookcase. An untidy pile of newspapers were on the floor near Fiori.

A man moved outside.

"All over," Mannering said.

"You say so." Fiori sat upright but did not try to get up. "I don't agree with you. Have you brought me the *Tear*?"

"You won't need it now."

"I shall always need it." Fiori's eyes shifted, he looked past Mannering, who moved so that Bristow's man could come in. Muffled sounds further away came from more policemen summoned by Bristow's second man at Toni's.

In the detective's hand was the *Tear*.

Fiori's eyes glistened. He stood up with a swift, easy movement and stretched out his hand.

"Give that to me."

"This is as close as you'll get. Keep back."

"Give that diamond to me." Fiori moved slowly forward, ignoring Mannering, oblivious of everything but the *Tear*. In his eyes there was a glow which turned them a reddy colour—lust and desire lit up his face. The look was of terrible intensity, as if sight of the stone caused him physical agony. His outstretched hand trembled, his whole body quivered.

Mannering said: "Let him have it."

"But—"

"What harm can it do?"

"Harm!" sighed Fiori.

His gaze seemed to hypnotise the detective who let him take the *Tear*. Mannering, only a yard away from Fiori, heard the sharp, almost sobbing intake of his breath. Fiori lifted the *Tear* close to his eyes, peered at it as if at a sacred thing; and smiled. The smile was at once grotesque and beautiful. He stood like that for a long time, scarcely breathing.

Then he raised his head.

"Did you have it all the time, Mannering?"

"Does it matter?"

"The truth, please."

"I knew where to find it."

"Ah! I was right. Julia was right, too. She told me that you would defeat me. Is this man a policeman?"

"Yes."

"It was worth everything—everything," said Fiori. "It is a lovely thing, and more than lovely. It is the key to great riches, the key to great power. Money *is* power. I saw myself as a great and powerful man, richer perhaps than any other in the world. You say this man is a policeman?"

"Yes."

Fiori said: "And you say it is all over. No, Mannering, it has only just begun. Oh, I am helpless now, there is no hope for me, but the *Diamond of Tears* will live on. It *is* alive. All the riches it can bequeath will create hatred and greed and bitterness, will cause bloodshed and pain and suffering. You blame me for what I have done. What have *you* done, Mannering? You have unleashed great, unbridled passions and you cannot tell who will suffer, how it will all end. Had I found the *Tear* in time I would have prevented much that will now happen, the power would have been in my hands."

He looked at the *Tear* again, then handed it to Mannering. As Mannering took it Bristow came into the room.

Mannering stood back, Bristow cleared his throat, motioned to men who were standing outside the room. He said in a formal voice which failed to hide his excitement:

"You are Enrico Fiori?"

"I am."

"It is my duty to charge you with the wilful murder of Julia Fiori, and to take you into custody. Other charges may be preferred against you. I have to warn you that anything you say may be used in evidence."

"I have nothing to say," said Fiori.

He stood motionless.

Then his hand flashed to his pocket. He struck at Bristow and pushed him aside. A knife glinted. He swept round, slashing at Mannering's throat. Mannering felt the sharp edge on his chin and struck at Fiori's hand. The knife fell. Fiori drew back, making no attempt to get the knife; he did not struggle or fight again.

"It's almost a pity you can't hang a man these days" said Bristow. "I wish his brother were for life, too, instead of getting ten years for complicity."

Mannering said: "Toni was forced to help."

"Toni got cold feet and tried to back out, but couldn't," Chittering said.

He was one of the group of three who stood outside the Old Bailey, one afternoon two months after the arrests. Judge and jury had made their decisions. The trials of the lesser men were also over. The commissionaire who had crashed the lift was sentenced to life imprisonment, like Fiori and Harry Green. Nearby, a crowd of sightseers raised a cry when Yule and his wife came out. A way was cleared for them by the police. As they were driven off they caught sight of Mannering and smiled and waved.

"They look happy," Chittering remarked.

"They are. Julia would be happy about it."

"The sentimental John! Well, I don't want another job like that. I now know what is meant by lying at death's door. Must rush off and get my story written. I—oh! What's the news about Elizabeth?"

"She's all right," Mannering said. "I don't think she'll forget Yule in a hurry, but it doesn't hurt so much now. She's taking Elizabeth Warren as her legal name."

"Any idea who legally owns the *Tear*?" asked Chittering.

"Read your newspapers and you'll find out one of these days," Bristow said.

Chittering grinned and hurried off. Bristow and Mannering strolled along the narrow road and were soon lost among the crowds near St. Paul's.

"Is Elizabeth going to fight for the *Tear*?" asked Bristow. "As an executor you ought to know."

"She isn't. Her identity's been proved, and she has more money than she knows what to do with. She doesn't want the *Tear* or any fabulous hoard. It's worth millions! The jewels were all given to Jacob to help refugee Jews out of Germany. Elizabeth Warren, the only claimant, has agreed to hand them over to a Trust Fund."

"In trust for what?"

"Europe. The jewels came out of Europe, and their value is going back. To help rebuild Germany and to help the displaced poor. So to dry some tears!" Mannering laughed. "There's sentiment for you!"

"What about the *Tear*?"

"It will become a museum piece."

"That's about right for it," said Bristow heavily. "John, I've often wondered why old Jacob Bernstein saw Harry Green alone, why he left the secret in the *Tear*. He must have known the risk."

Mannering shrugged.

"We can only guess. I would say that he thought Green could be trusted. He was pretty sure no one would be able to find the *Tear* unless they knew the secret hiding-place."

"As you did."

Mannering laughed.

At Chelsea, Elizabeth Warren, wearing a sky-blue dress with a fluffy sky-blue scarf to match, was waiting with Lorna when Mannering entered. She looked both young and contented.

The One and Only

JOHN
CREASEY

 THE INSPECTOR WEST SERIES

 THE HALLIDAY BOOKS

 THE BARON SERIES

 THE TOFF SERIES

 THE DR. PALFREY SERIES

 THE DEPARTMENT Z SERIES

More BARON Books published by
Hodder Paperbacks

BOOKS FOR THE BARON

The Earl of Lithom, a skilled rider, was thrown by his horse and broke his neck. An accident or a murder? Gloria, his beautiful daughter and heiress, claimed to have seen a corpse in the library with its throat slit. A hallucination or a murder? In his search for the answer to these questions the Baron meets danger, temptation, espionage and death—everything, in fact, that make books worth reading.

A SWORD FOR THE BARON

There were just two Mogul Victory Swords; a pair of the finest jewelled swords John Mannering had ever seen. So when Lord Gentian, who owned them both, came to him with one and asked him to find the other, the Baron was ready for action, however unprepared he might have been for the flood of fraud, blackmail and fear that emerged.

THE BARON AT BAY

The five jewels of Castille once formed the inheritance of a noble family. But they were stolen, separated and their identity was lost. Few men could recognise them for what they were. But the Baron could, and he was after them — and among his competitors were three of the ugliest criminals he had ever met, men to whom robbery and violence were merely a game.